THE SWEETEST KISS

"I tried to keep my distance, Jenine," Nat said softly. "you ought to kick me out right now. I'm probably more trouble than I'm worth. Definitely more than you deserve."

Raising herself on her toes, her hands slipped up his arms, bringing him closer. Her mouth moved over his in a series of slow, shivery kisses that elicited a small sound of wonder from his throat. Then the pressure of her hungry warm lips increased, and she demanded entry into his mouth with her tongue. He let her possess his mouth in a thorough and tender kiss, and all thoughts of leaving left his mind.

Taking control of the kiss, Nat smothered her mouth in a wild kiss that performed magic with her senses, and her hunger burst forth in a heated gush. His lips traipsed leisurely along her neck, up to her ear where his tongue dipped into the center. Like a thief, it stole her breath away.

"Jenine, Jenine," he murmured, drawing her against him. "Tell me it's true. Tell me you're mine."

"Yes," she said in a tone as pure and natural as truth.

QUOTES FOR MARGIE WALKER

A Sweet Refrain
Margie Walker

PINNACLE BOOKS
WINDSOR PUBLISHING CORP.

PINNACLE BOOKS are published by

Windsor Publishing Corp.
475 Park Avenue South
New York, NY 10016

First Printing: August, 1994

Printed in the United States of America

Chapter One

The night was cold and etched in darkness. Splashes of yellow haze glowed from tall lamp posts that intermittently lined the deserted road. The chubby poles rose from the ground like giant sentinels in the dark, standing watch over the sloping, endless stretch of public highway.

The luxury car roared along, heading northwest of Highway 27. The speedometer teetered crazily past ninety miles per hour—as the car gobbled up the distance that separated the driver from his destination.

He had turned off the radio because static interfered with the broadcast signal. Now, only the monotonous hum of the car's engine and heater harmonized with the eerie silence of the wintry night.

It had been a long, lonely drive. Nearly seven hundred miles separated Houston, his last major stop, from Highland Heights, which was of equal distance between Amarillo and Lubbock, Texas. The town was so small that he practically needed a magnifying glass to find it on the travel atlas. But he was adjusting to it—the driving—for it seemed he'd done little else since leaving New York on Wednesday.

Nat arched his shoulders, then massaged his thighs, numbed with inertia. Shifting his long frame in the plush seat, he began bearing down on the gas pedal with his rested left foot, undaunted by the awkwardness it posed in driving.

He was exhausted. Not just from driving, but from having to stay awake and alert. And now—no music. He absently fell into his old habit of humming and thumping beats on the wheel. It was a little after two in the morning. He estimated they were roughly fifteen miles outside the city limits.

He allowed his mind to drift to a time long past, and the face of a cute, brown-skinned girl floated to the surface. She was short and kind of chubby, with long, thick hair framing her small round face. The sensitive, inspired expression of an artist shone in her watchful brown eyes, and when she spoke, her voice was wonderfully low, soft and clear. Although she didn't do it often enough, he recalled, she had the prettiest smile when she did.

That low-key, unassuming nature of hers seemed at odds with her talent, he mused memorably. When she sat at the piano, even the heavens quieted to listen. He smiled to himself, remembering that her playing had called her to his attention in the first place; he had no motives whatsoever of making a move on her. Rather, sensing her loneliness and insecurity, he had wanted merely to draw her out.

That was how it always started, Nat thought with a chuckle, remembering how his intentions of friendship started to blossom into something more. It was another reason for his abrupt departure.

God, he missed her when he went off to New York all those years ago. He surprised himself over the years with how many times he thought about her, wanted to call her, wanted to see her. He often wondered if she felt the same. Maybe he really was a coward, he thought with a sigh, contenting himself with second-hand messages from home about her, having his best wishes added to Christmas cards sent by his mother.

When he first left, he hoped to break off their relationship completely and start over in the big city. But he missed Jenine and a year later he attempted to get in contact again by writing her letters. He never got a response. Then, his career started to take off and he had no time to follow up. He continued to write short notes to let her know what was happening in his life. He first wrote her every three months, then every six, then sent only cards on holidays and still received no response from Jenine Jones. His mother would tell him that she's doing well, that she became a fine music instructor and was very busy, but to Nat that was no excuse. He'd traveled the world, was stuck in a recording studio for months and still had time to drop a note.

His last letter was returned to him. Jenine had moved and had left no forwarding address.

He hoped that she wouldn't hold his self-imposed exile against him now and turn him away. Not now, when he needed her more than ever, he thought solemnly.

The voice of Goldie Hawn, coming from the television set on a shelf on the built-in wall cabinet, intruded on the quiet of the combination kitchen-family-and-dining room at two o'clock on a Sunday morning. Wearing baggy gray sweats, Jenine ambled barefoot around the cozy three-room setting, the living room separated from the kitchen by an island and the dining room off the kitchen. She felt emotionally displaced, unable to hold a complete thought.

Rubbing her hands together, she paced the narrow space between the coffee table and couch before dropping onto the beige, brown and blue flower print upholstered couch. Hugging her knees tightly to her chest, she gazed at the television, hoping to become hooked by the make-believe on the screen.

She laughed at some of the hilarious antics in the movie, then sighed enviously at the adventurous life of the woman on the screen. The next commercial break found her staring blankly at the TV—the picture there replaced by images of a full and exciting life, starring herself in the lead role.

The late-night movie returned, snapping Jenine from her fascination. Sighing restively, she got up to turn off the television. With her hand poised inches from the power button on the set, she changed her mind. Indecision lined her forehead and she grasped a hand full of soft dark hair, pivoting to scan the contents of the area.

Sitting tall on the floor next to the wall cabinet was the evidence of accomplishment from a recent trip—a silver and blue trophy with a musical emblem at the top. As she circled the steel-plated note with a slender brown finger, a proud smile came slowly to her full lips.

With her eyes closed, Jenine hummed a tune of staccato tempo. Her body sashayed to the beat as her hands danced in the air, conducting an invisible band. The song in her throat was the number that merited the Academy's Jazz Band the second of three huge trophies.

Struck by a poignant yearning for something infinitely more precious than a pretty prize, Jenine abandoned the solitaire performance. She longed for someone with whom to share the victory.

The trophy wasn't hers anyway, she reminded herself. It belonged to the students. Come Monday, it would take up residence in a glass cabinet at Highland Heights Senior Academy.

Spinning sharply on her heels, Jenine strode to the kitchen. Looking for nothing in particular, she jerked open one cabinet door after another, slamming each shut before taking her frustrations out on the refrigerator similarly. She eyed the gift basket of fruit on the edge of the island counter, reached for an orange, then dropped it just as quickly as she picked it up.

She had everything she needed—job, home and health, she thought. What more could be possibly want? What more was there to be had?

Burying her face in her hands, she silently blamed her inner dilemma on the trip. Even though there had been many, this one seemed to have infused her with ingratitude, dredging up discontent with her life.

Straightening to her full height, Jenine inhaled deeply. Once the excitement from the trip wore off, she would return to being the steady, secure, independent adult, whom parents trusted with their children, she told herself confidently. She would.

Deciding to call it a night, she switched off the television and headed for her bedroom, darkening the area on her way out.

Nat's index finger was suspended less than a centimeter from the doorbell. There was an heaviness in the pit of his stomach and he noticed his hand was shaking. He couldn't believe his hesitancy, standing at Jenine's front door, beads of sweat dotting his forehead in spite of the brisk wind blowing its cold breeze around him. The baby in his arms was still cranky from the long drive and squirming restlessly.

He shook his head from side to side in disbelief, then paced back and forth, trying to calm the baby. Second thoughts plagued him. It was almost three o'clock in the morning, he silently argued with himself, what kind of fool would show up with no warning on the doorstep of a woman he hadn't talked directly to in over a decade? He must be delirious with exhaustion.

Then, Nat remembered his logic for choosing this small Texas town. It would be easy to assume that he would run to his brother or his mother or any of the number of friends and fellow musicians that he's known over the years. No one would guess that he would run to the town of the woman who, for all intents and purposes, wanted nothing to do with him.

Nat sighed heavily, rocking the baby, so as to not wake Jenine or her neighbors. He was on the edge of total exhaustion and knew he'd have to get some sleep soon. He'd have to find a hotel tonight.

But he needed to talk to Jenine. He needed her help. Nat hated to admit that he needed someone's help, but, he thought as he looked at the baby in his arms, he couldn't keep running. "You've got to give it up for Natasha," he whispered to himself.

When Natasha heard her name, she began to wail. Suddenly, Nat heard movement behind Jenine's door.

With her pulse skipping a beat, Jenine stiffened in the dark hallway. Wondering who would be on her doorstep at this hour, she took a cautious step forward. Flipping the light switch, she asked, "Who is it?"

Instead of an answer, she heard a baby's cry. Opening the heavy wooden door, she blinked, then focused her gaze on the figure on her step.

"Jenine? It's me. Nat. Nathaniel Padell."

"Nat," Jenine whispered in disbelief. His voice was bass deep, rich and faintly Southern, a tone peculiar to Texans who had been living on the East coast. But behind it, she noted hints of strain.

"Jenine," Nat pleaded as he stepped closer to her.

Jenine looked into his eyes and noted that his were as extraordinary for their versatility of expression as the rare, duo-toned olive-brown hue were peering down at her. But they were tired and bloodshot, and she noticed a thin sheen of sweat across his brow.

"Nat?" she said slightly louder. He smiled awkwardly, still rocking the crying baby. Jenine stood motionless before she opened the door a little wider. "Come in here with that baby. It's cold outside."

Once inside, Nat waited while she secured the locks on the door. "I'm sorry, Jenine, for the hour and everything," Nat began. "It's just that I didn't have anywhere else to go. I mean, I'm going to find a hotel, but Highland Heights was the only place and I need you and . . ." He caught her staring at the bundle in his arms. Turning the baby toward Jenine, he said, "This is Natasha."

Jenine moved her gaze from the baby up to his face. Despite the slight smile on his face, she thought she detected a strange gleam lurking in the depths of his eyes. Slowly her gaze left his to peer down at the cuddly, fidgety baby in his arms. She reached out to touch the little girl's cheek.

Lifting a confused gaze to Nat, she wondered what other surprises were in store for her tonight.

"She's my daughter." He gave her a crooked smile. "We need a place to hang our booties."

Jenine offered Nat a seat as she went to her kitchen with the baby's bottle to find milk for Natasha. She knew her movements were awkward and stiff as her mind raced. Why had Nathaniel Padell decided to grace her with his presence at three o'clock in the morning? As she opened the almost empty refrigerator to grab the carton of milk, a slow burning rage began inside of her chest. She unintentionally slammed the refrigerator door shut, as she contemplated the gall of him popping up as though he had come for Sunday afternoon tea. She banged the pot on the stove and poured the milk. And with a baby, of all things, she raged to herself as she waited for the milk to heat. She looked to the figure sitting on her couch, bouncing the baby on his knee. He has a lot of explaining to do, she thought as she poured the milk into the bottle, tested it, then left the kitchen.

She returned to the living room to find Nat slumped on the couch in an exhausted sleep and Natasha's face contorted as she prepared for another wail. Nat's head was hanging down yet his hands held tightly to the baby on his lap. Jenine stood motionless as she watched the sleeping man tightly embracing the little girl. "God, Nat, why are you here?" Jenine said out loud, which only served to irritate Natasha. Jenine eased the baby from his grip. Jenine placed the baby in the crook of her arm as she placed the bottle nipple in her hungry mouth.

"Natasha is it?" Jenine whispered to her. Her resemblance to her father was remarkable: her soft brown face, the same sloe-shaped eyes except hers were dark brown. She found herself becoming charmed by the baby girl. "What a pretty baby," she continued. "What are you doing here in the middle of the night? Why did your daddy decide to visit me without even a phone call or postcard to let me know he was coming? Why on earth did he say that he needs me?" She walked the now calm baby around the living room. "Why is your daddy so exhausted? What made him come back to Texas?" She asked her next question so softly she barely could hear herself. "Why did he come back to me?"

An unexpected wave of grief flooded Jenine as memories filled her mind. She had loved him madly years ago and continued to for years after he left for New York. She would have done anything for him then, anything he would have asked she would have done without question, but he never took advantage of her feelings or of her desire for him. She did think that he loved her then, if just a little bit.

But she was too young. Her mother, his mother, even Nat himself had told her, too young to fall in love so strongly. So, she tried to put Nat out of her mind and out of her heart but when she least expected it, memories returned full force particularly when she would get word from his mother about how he was doing. His mother had failed to mention a baby.

Natasha stopped feeding and Jenine looked down to see the little girl's wide eyes begin to close slowly. Jenine walked to the kitchen to grab a towel to throw over her shoulder before she would burp the baby. She had always wanted children but so far, teaching was as close to having a family of her own as she could get. Jenine had once thought that she and Nat would get married, have a family together and that they would live happily ever after. But those things only happened in the movies.

Stroking the soft, fine hairs on Natasha's head, she stared wistfully at the baby girl who was quickly succumbing to sleep.

As the baby's gentle breathing blended into the early-morning quiet, Jenine sat in a chair opposite Nat and slipped into memories of her childhood muse. She had no recollections of affectionate displays or fun outings or even friendly mother-daughter chats. Instead, her mother's nagging discourse on the perils of dependency on a man was always the first to surface, followed by the example she set proving it after Jenine's father left them.

Elise Jones worked two jobs to make ends meet, and to ensure that her daughter was afforded an education that would make her self-sufficient. That's what her mother lived and died for. She literally worked herself to death for Jenine's comfortable independence.

She gave a glance to Nat and wished he had not pushed her away all those years ago.

She wondered where such an irrational notion had come from. The lack of sleep was making her crazy with matriarchal memories and wanton dreams, she thought. Gently, she clasped the baby's tiny hand, wondering whether Nat and his daughter would prove to be a god-send or a curse.

Soon the baby was as in deep a sleep as her father, but Jenine was wide awake. How could she sleep? How could she when the man she thought she'd never see again was laying on her living room couch? She sighed as she walked the baby to her own bedroom. She put Natasha down on her back in the middle of the bed and left the door open. She returned to the couch and stared at her father.

As it happened fifteen years ago when she'd been caught staring at Nat Padell, she was speechless. She felt a strange giddy sensation come over her, as if she were eighteen all over again. For a flutter of a moment, her eyes left his face to take in the full presence of Nathaniel Padell—all 6'3" of him. He looked better than she remembered him and much better than his photos on his albums or the photos his mother showed him every so often. He had a beautifully proportioned body, sculpted with muscles from his wide shouldered back down to his slim waistline, a fact not hidden by his shirt.

Jenine ran her hand through her hair in frustration. She must be losing her mind to let visions of lust take control of her thoughts now. "Wake up, Nat," she said loudly. "Wake up and tell me why you're here and what you need from me." Nat's head simply lolled back onto the couch's headrest as a snore escaped his throat.

Jenine sat back in her chair and suspected the rest of the night would be the longest she'd known so far.

Abruptly, Nat sat up, his daughter's name on his lips. He adjusted his vision to the bright light of the room and realized he was looking right into Jenine's lovely brown eyes.

"Would you like coffee, Nat?" she asked coolly.

Nat rubbed his eyes with the balls of his hands. "Where's Natasha?"

"In my bedroom, sleeping. Coffee's all ready." Jenine stood up from the chair she'd occupied all night and walked to the kitchen.

"She's safe?"

Jenine turned quickly at that remark. "Absolutely," she responded.

Nat watched Jenine's shapely form move about her kitchen. Dipped in a caramel complexion, her slender body reminded him of island women and insouciant tropical evenings. Her facial bones were delicately carved in smallness, with dimples and a full mouth. Her eyebrows were long and thick, yet of a fine grade like her hair, the curls short and close cut on her perfectly oval head. "Thank you for watching her while I slept. I was exhausted." To her silence, he continued. "It's been a long couple of days."

"Um-um." Jenine responded as she offered him the steaming cup of coffee. "You've got some explaining to do, mister. I'm going to go check on the baby now, then we've got some talking to do."

Nat was sitting on a stool at the island in the kitchen. His hands were wrapped around a mug of steaming coffee as he pondered his next move.

There had been only one thing on his mind when they

had set out on the Northeast to Southwest expedition they had journeyed on—finding a secure place for his baby. One objective had been met—Natasha was safe. But what was to follow? he wondered.

Recalling the wasted effort of involving the police, he entertained leaving Natasha with Jenine to return to the East Coast and challenge David Cissoko face-to-face. *But to what end?* the cynic in his head demanded to know. Grandstanding was no guarantee David would back down from his pursuit of Natasha.

He drew a deep breath, then released the hot air quickly, weary of his fruitless thoughts.

Jenine, unnoticed, watched Nat from the doorway. A bleak, tight-lipped expression masked his handsome profile.

Before he awoke Jenine got up from the couch to shower and change. Usually, Sundays were spent preparing for school, selecting clothes and reviewing lessons for the week. But this was not a normal Sunday, she thought, wondering at the troubles eating away at Nat.

"Nat," she said tentatively.

He shifted to face her, then stepped off the stool. The muscles in his face relaxed into a leisurely smile, and her left brow rose a fraction at the abrupt and complete change.

He was the epitome of power, from his handsome, ebony suntanned face with sharp features, to the way he towered over her, exuding a cocky determination. He wore his trademark clothing: black. The thin-knitted pullover stretched across his expansive chest and was tucked in at his narrow waist; jeans were worn low on his hips, molding powerful thighs and endlessly long legs.

Jenine forgot what she wanted to say. Or was it a

question she meant to ask? She studied his face with an enigmatic gaze for an extra beat. "Nat, what's troubling you?"

Flashing pearly white teeth in a lazy grin, he replied, "Nothing right now."

Returning his intriguing look, Jenine trembled involuntarily. In a matter of seconds, she took inventory of his features. His eyes were indeed magnificent, deep-set with long lashes and smooth, thin brows. An enchanting color, translucent brown or barely perceptible green, depending on the light. His mouth was not to be ignored either; wide, firm and kissable. Aw, but that voice. No tenor ever came out of his mouth, and he exploited every nuance of the deep register—commanding without raising pitch, enticingly low. In other words, just plain old sexy.

And he purposefully conjured up a seductive tone for her, she thought, disgusted with herself for reacting to the powerful combination. She was not the shy girl he used to know and would not be put off by evasive answers, she reminded herself. Her annoyance increased when she saw that her hands were shaking as she poured coffee in the extra cup on the counter.

"Excuse me, Nat, but I'm a little curious as to why you've appeared on my doorstep years after you stopped writing," Jenine said, trying to keep the anger out of her voice.

"I sent letters. You never wrote back."

She still had every letter and card he'd ever sent her. She kept them in a box which she pulled out every so often. She shook her head to rid herself of the romantic memories. "Nat, answer me. Why are you here? Why now?"

"It's a long story, Jenine," Nat said. "Natasha and I will go to a hotel, don't worry."

"That's not what I'm worried about," Jenine shot back. "Tell me why you're here?"

Nat looked away. "You always made the best coffee I'd ever tasted. Can't even find coffee this good in New York. I never knew how you did it."

"Stop it, Nat," Jenine shouted. "Answer me."

"Well now, you've gotten mighty sassy in your old age, Miss Jones," Nat replied.

"Remember that," she said, although she didn't know whether the reminder was self-directed or not. She sipped her coffee to keep her from losing control of her anger then walked to the refrigerator. She felt his laughing eyes at her back as she poured a liberal dose of cream in her coffee. He had always teased her about how much cream she put in her coffee.

"Why do you even bother to drink coffee if you're going to drown out the flavor with cream?" he asked as if reading her mind.

Jenine looked at him from the corner of her eyes, a secret smile on her lips. "I'll give you three guesses." It was her pat answer to the coffee question.

Her eyes never left his as she raised her cup to her mouth to drink. She felt comfort seep into her body as she stared at Nat. How could he do this to her when she hadn't seen him for years?

Nat shook his head with pondering and laughter, thinking about the reply and the woman. Several guesses ran through his mind. He voiced none.

He felt his insides relax, realizing for the first time how anxious he had been about being in the company of Jenine, now a new woman. She was definitely different; gentle, but direct.

With his laughter subsiding, Nat sighed, wondering if

history repeated itself. He stared at Jenine, entranced by the chocolate of her eyes, bright in playfulness and her dimples appearing as if loving fingers had pinched her cheek. His gaze went lower with approval of her chic dress in a gold, button-down front sweater over baggy khaki slacks. The ensemble was capped by small gold earrings piercing her ears, and the exotic scent of jasmine. He felt the ruffle of a forbidden attraction.

Growing uncomfortable under his rapt stare, Jenine opened her mouth to speak, the same time he did. Laughing with him, she said, "You first."

"Remember the late rehearsals we used to have?" he reminisced. "Sometimes when we walked out of the music building, the sun would be up to greet us."

Nodding with melancholy on her face, Jenine recalled they never seemed to tire of creating music. As long as she was near Nat, things like sleep and food had not been required as life-sustaining substances.

"Yeah, it was nice," she said dreamily.

"Too bad things can't remain so simple," Nat said, a frown replacing his smile. He raised the cup to his lips to take a sip, then set the cup down, coffee untouched, on the counter.

Jenine eyed his somber profile furtively from the rim of the cup she was holding to her mouth with both hands. She wondered to what he referred, guessing it had to do with his presence. Her questions continued to mount inside her. Her lips parted to pry, but for no reason she could discern, she swallowed the first one with a sip of coffee.

Three years older than she was in physical years—even more in maturity because of her closeted life with a domineering mother—Nat had always looked younger than his age. However, with the peppering of gray strains in his coarse hair, he no longer looked like the classic all-American male. The better to impress high-school principals, he used to say when teased about it.

"I want to know why are you here, Nat." she said, the cup steady in a two-handed grip. She noticed his jaw tense the instant the question was out.

"I'd rather not talk about that now," he replied, taking a leisurely sip of coffee. He turned away from her.

Setting the cup on the counter to lace her fingers together, Jenine asked, "Don't you think I deserve to know why a man I haven't seen in over a decade lands on my doorstep?" She gazed at his back as if imploring him to look at her.

"What is it?" he asked, turning to look at her crossly. "Do you think I kidnapped my own daughter?"

With her mouth hanging open, Jenine stared at him. Her eyes flared up, but she cooled it. "I didn't, but maybe I should have," she replied.

"No, Jenine," he said tiredly. "I didn't kidnap Natasha from her mother."

The timbre of his voice was like a refrain in her ear, striking a chord of familiarity. Feeling a sense of foreboding, Jenine swallowed hard and masked her intense curiosity.

"Okay, Nat," she said with calm dignity, scanning her memory to place that tone of voice.

"Aw, Jenine," he drawled dishearteningly, running his fingers through his hair.

Her gaze followed him to the family room. His long-legged strides didn't seem to have enough room to carry out the indecisive steps he took in one direction before changing to another. His fidgety manner, she now knew, was a prelude to bad news. He'd acted the same way when he'd told her he was going to New York.

She remembered the flesh on her face seemed to fall off like wax, tears flooded her eyes, and she felt as if the world had collapsed around her. She had been crushed by what she considered his betrayal. It had taken her a while to realize it was a young woman's pain she suffered at the time, and nothing permanent.

"I came because I didn't have anywhere else to go," Nat blurted into the empty room.

Jenine sensed it was the hardest thing he ever had to admit. And he wasn't pleased by it, either. She sat at attention on the stool.

"I guess," he said, running a hand through his hair, "I might as well start at the beginning," with grudging resignation. Following a short pause and a deep breath, he said, "I met Natasha's mother at my birthday party year before last. We had just finished a show in D.C. September 5th," he added, his gaze and voice distant. "I was feeling pretty old since most of the guys in the band were in their early to mid-twenties, and there I was," he chuckled a bittersweet sound, "celebrating my thirty-third birthday."

Nat paused to look at her, assessing her reaction to his vanity. He started to sit on the couch, changed his mind, and instead slid into the armchair and propped his feet on the matching ottoman.

"It was cold and raining that night. We were packed in that house. You could barely move around without bumping into somebody."

He hadn't felt like celebrating because it signaled another year gone by and he still had yet to achieve all he wanted. Since the guys had gone to all the trouble, he felt he couldn't just walk out.

"Everybody was gathered around this gigantic, conga-shaped cake to sing 'Happy Birthday,' " he said with a fond look.

He was glad he hadn't left, particularly after seeing Annette, or Netta as he came to call her. She was standing on the other side of the table, staring straight at him with those big, beautiful seductive eyes that critics and photographers alike had loved. And he had been no different, believing he discovered the meaning of love at first sight.

"Her name was Annette Cissoko. One thing led to another and I was convinced I'd found everlasting love." Summarily, he said, "She got pregnant and we got married. She died last July right after giving birth to Natasha."

Nat swung his feet to the floor and rested his chin on his hand in a pensive posture.

Attuned to his agony, Jenine grieved quiescently as one would for any loss of human life. Yet, the tears stinging her eyes were not for him, or for the woman who was his wife, but for the child who would never know the mother who had given her life.

Though she knew regrets were futile, she harbored a few regarding her own mother. By the time she was old enough to reverse their roles and give her mother a vacation from the stresses of surviving, it was too late. But poor Natasha would never know her mother, she thought somberly. There would be no memories of her mother at all.

And maybe one or two tears were for her, she realized by the dull ache in her chest. By the tone in Nat's voice, she could tell that he had loved Natasha's mother and that he missed her, which meant that there was no room in his heart for anyone else. Jenine chastised herself silently. What did she expect, that the boy she fell madly in love with years ago would still have any feelings for her now?

Nat had gone on with his life; he'd become a successful musician in his own right, experienced the love of a woman and was the father of a wonderful little girl. Dabbing at her watery eyes with her fingers, she respired unevenly.

"Don't cry for me, I don't deserve your tears," he said, treating her to a hard stare. "We got along all right," he said, standing, looking indecisively about the room. "Anyway, that's not the end of the story. None of that explains why I'm here, which is what you want to know. What you need," he said, in a parenthesis, "to know." He perched on the edge of the chair across from her. "Natasha's grandfather is very determined to have her."

Her mind refused to register the significance of his words. "What do you mean by determined?" she asked.

"Last week, a man whom I suspect was hired by David Cissoko, Natasha's grandfather, broke into my place. Natasha's nanny, Ms. Cramer was tied up when I got there, apparently just in time to prevent a kidnapping. I believe David was behind it."

"But . . . I, uh don't, . . . Why?" the monosyllabic words tumbled from her mouth.

"After I buried Annette, I took Natasha back to New York with me. Nearly five months passed before I heard from him," he said as he resumed pacing. "He claimed he was calling to find out how she was doing, if she needed anything. Like I couldn't provide for my own child," he said bitterly. "Anyway, I didn't think anything about him calling. Then he started hounding me about giving up Natasha. Only he calls her Candace," he said mockingly.

"Candace?" Jenine queried. She couldn't help her interruption.

Nat stopped pacing to explain. "It's not really a name the way he means it. You see, Candace was the title given a line of ancient Nubacush queens who ruled the country.

It's from a Latin word I can't pronounce that means queen mother."

"Oh," Jenine replied, not sure what to make of the information.

"Anyway," Nat continued, "he backed off after I told him what he could do to himself, so I figured I'd heard the last of him. I was mistaken."

Silently, Jenine watched Nat struggle with an invisible demon. She sensed there was more to his problem. Feeling she'd had all the inactivity she could take, she sprang from the couch to move around.

"Are you sure, Nat, that it was a kidnapping attempt, and that he was behind it?" she asked.

"You sound like the police," he snorted, angling his body away from her in disgust, crossing a long muscled thigh over the other.

Ignoring his outburst, she asked, "What did they say?"

"That I was victim number 999,000 in another one of the long list of crimes in the city, and I should consider myself lucky that no one was hurt. Case closed."

"But you didn't—don't believe them? Why?"

"Let's just say I found it a little too coincidental that the man who broke into my home was of African nationality, as is my former father-in-law. Regardless of what the police believe, I wasn't willing to take the chance that it might have been a simple burglary attempt. I had to get my baby out of David's reach until I could come up with a plan to prevent him from even being in the same breathing space."

"If you felt that strongly about it, you probably did the right thing," she said musingly as she paced. "Who is this guy anyway?" she asked aggressively. "I mean besides being Natasha's grandfather."

"He's Minister of Culture and Education for the nation of Nubacush," Nat replied with mocking.

"Hm," Jenine muttered with a slightly raised brow. A diplomat, she thought. That could account for the police department's lack of action. "Have you contacted an attorney?"

"No," he said, sitting with his elbows resting on his thighs. "I stopped in Houston first, hoping that my mother could recommend someone. But she was out of town, as she often is these days, since she retired."

"She does get out a lot now, doesn't she?" Jenine giggled. "I haven't heard much from her lately. How is she?"

"Fine, fine. I'm sure she doesn't know I'm in town since I didn't get a chance to talk to her before she left and I didn't leave a note before I headed here with your address in hand." He smiled to himself. "I'm sure she'd be happy to know that I turned to you for help. She always liked you, Jenine."

Jenine blushed as she lightly rubbed her hands together. "Well, I know just the person for you to talk to," Jenine said rearing for action.

"Robbie Franks. She's an attorney and a very dear friend of mine. I could probably get her over here now," she said, looking at the time on her wristwatch.

Nat smiled admiringly at her. "Thanks, but it'll keep until tomorrow. Today is Sunday, remember?" he replied, pulling her gently to sit next to him.

As they settled snugly in the chair, Jenine was overly conscious of his virile appeal. Staring hypnotically at his fine handsome face, as sleek as the rest of him, with his eyes closed and a satisfied smile pursed on his mouth, she felt unsanctioned desires awakening in her.

Nat opened his eyes to look at her and Jenine froze, appalled at being caught mooning at him.

Taking her hand in his, Nat traced an imaginary line down the center of her palm as he spoke. "I don't want you to think that I don't appreciate what you're doing for us, because I do. But, I do want you to think this thing through carefully."

Jerking her hand from his light possession, Jenine stared at him incredulously, bubbling with the irritation she felt over her own behavior compounded by his patronizing manner. There were too many emotions to contend with at once. She cautioned herself not to say anything now, not while her nerves were raw. But with one glance at his face, his ingenious eyes cloudy with brotherly concern—she snapped.

"Oh, come off it, Nat!" Squirming out of the chair, "I am not some kid who can't be held responsible for her own actions." He opened his mouth to explain himself, but she continued, shaking a finger at him. "If I didn't want you here, you wouldn't have gotten in the door! And it's a little late to play Monday-morning quarterback," she ended, her hands on her hips.

Her anger evaporated as quickly as it had erupted, leaving her shaken and embarrassed. Returning Nat's nonplused expression—eyes wide under the raised arch of his brows and mouth gaping open—an apology shone in her eyes. Deflated, her hands fell to her sides, but her chest was still moving laboriously from her exuberant release.

Comprehension crystallized in his head and on his face, prompting him to go to her and drape his hands across her shoulders. There was a tender-hearted expression in his eyes, looking down at her with their warm olive-brown centers before he enveloped her in his arms.

"I'm sorry," she murmured against his sweater where her head rested on his chest, wrapped her arms around his waist instinctively.

"It's understandable," he replied. "I knew I was dropping a bomb. I just didn't know how to protect you from it."

"I really don't need protection, you know?" Her tough words were belied by the whispery quality of her voice. His closeness was like a balm, stroking her body to life as fluidly as his hand along the small of her back.

"I know."

She heard the small laugh in his voice before he stepped back to look down at her, then saw the merry lights of humor in his eyes.

"You're a tough teacher," he teased gently, then became serious. "This time, you're not going up against a rebellious student or an irate parent."

Nodding gloomily, Jenine backed out of his embrace, thinking she did have to fight more than a student, or parent, or even an obsessed African diplomat. Nat had only been here several hours and already she felt herself becoming attached to him as if they had never parted.

Hugging her arms to her, she asked, "What are you going to do now?"

Nat shook his head, lines of contemplation deepening around his eyes. "I'm not sure," he replied.

"I'd like to punch that man's light out," she pouted.

Amused, he chuckled. "That about begins to describe what I'd like to do. I guess I'll give that lawyer you mentioned a call before I do anything. Then if the law fails," he finished with a shrug.

With her head tilted at an angle, Jenine searched his face with a wide, wary-eyed look. "If the law fails, then what?" she pressed.

"I'll have to take care of it myself."

Frightened by his thoughtless candor, she snapped, "Right. That makes a whole lot of sense."

"You don't have a child. You can't possibly know how I feel," he said, poking his chest. Shoving the words at her, "I'm going to do what I have to do."

With a steady gaze, Jenine replied in a soft voice,

"She's already lost her mother. Do you want her to grow up without her father, too?"

Seeing Nat flinch as if she'd struck him, Jenine wished she could take the words back. Reaching out to him, she said, "Nat." Her hand dropped to her side when he backed out of reach.

She watched helplessly as he wrestled with the truth of her distasteful rejoinder—his eyes sharp, the hairs of his mustache bunched together over his mouth, thin with displeasure. She didn't realize she'd been holding her breath, until air began to seep slowly from her mouth in a show of relief when he smiled at her, a boyish grin that caused a fluttering in the pit of her stomach.

"You're right, of course. Okay, okay," he sighed, shaking his head in agreement, "I promise," squeezing her next to him in an affectionate embrace.

Held next to his strong body, Jenine felt a warm kernel of contentment explode in the center of her being. With pulse-pounding certainty, she knew better than to enjoy his presence, or get used to him. He would be leaving just as abruptly as he'd arrived, she reminded herself. It didn't matter that it felt right.

Chapter Two

Monday morning and Jenine was running late. She was running late because she overslept; she overslept because half the night was spent reminiscing with Nat about the good old days and the other half spent trying to forget them.

In the parking lot of Highland Heights Academy, she pulled the collar of her wool coat up to her chin and hurried from her car, a nine-year-old, orange Volvo. She raced ahead of stragglers bundled in overcoats to the three-story, white stone building.

Reaching the warmth inside, she remembered she'd forgotten to bring the trophy. The presence of the Padells had short-circuited her regular schedule so that she couldn't seem to get organized.

Teachers were signing in and administration officials were going about their normal routine in the school's main office. Before reaching the sign-in sheet at the counter, Jenine was stopped to accept congratulations on the band's second-place win.

Finally able to break free, she spotted her friend Gloria Allen, standing at the counter filling out some forms. Gloria was the drama teacher at the Academy; acting was her specialty. A tall, raven-haired woman with expressive aquamarine eyes, Gloria was an excessive talker.

"Wait up, Jenine," Gloria called. Stuffing forms into her bag, she rushed to catch Jenine at the door. "I want to know what's going on with you."

"What?" Jenine replied innocently.

"I heard you were seen in the grocery store with a gorgeous man," Gloria replied.

The disadvantages of small-town living, Jenine thought, rolling her eyes skyward. "I'm running late, Gloria," she said, pleading an excuse, though she knew she was trapped.

Gloria pulled her out of the office, into the crowded hallways and to a quiet corner near the top of a stairway. "If I didn't know better, I'd think you were trying to keep something from me." And without stopping to take a breath, "I've been in suspense all night. Now, tell me. Who is he? Where did you find him? Is he from around here?"

Jenine pictured Gloria vigorously brushing her hands together like a child eagerly awaiting a signal to tear into a gift-wrapped package. She burst out laughing at the image, earning a sulky frown from her overly dramatic friend.

"His name is Nathaniel Padell," Jenine said, though she knew the name would mean nothing to Gloria. Her friend's knowledge of music and musicians was limited to show tunes in musical productions.

"And?" Gloria prodded.

"Gloria, I have a first-period class," she said, traces of laughter in her voice, "and I'm running late."

"I wonder why," Gloria retorted with a grin, wiggling her brows suggestively.

"I'll satisfy your inquiring mind during lunch."

"Oh, no, you won't," Gloria rebuked. Familiar with

Jenine's habits, she said, "You'll lock yourself in your office and practice. And I won't get anything out of you."

Gloria was going to get it out of her one way or the other, Jenine thought. Resignedly, she said in a matter-of-fact tone, "Nat's just an old friend. Someone I went to college with, that's all."

"What is he doing here?" Gloria demanded instantly.

"Gloria," Jenine exclaimed exasperated. "It's nothing. I extended a token invitation for him to visit so I could see his little girl and he took me up on it." Suppressing the smile within her, Jenine thought her friend would have been proud of her for the lie that rolled glibly off her tongue.

Gloria eyed Jenine speculatively. With a meaningful tone in her voice, she said, "You're holding something back. I can feel it!"

Jenine chuckled at Gloria's skepticism. But telling Gloria the reason for Nat's visit would have been like advertising on national television. She was grateful when a student interrupted with a message for Ms. Allen, effectively ending what would have been a grueling interrogation. Still, Gloria was not about to let her off the hook.

"Lunch, Jenine," Gloria said in a tone which threatened repercussions should Jenine fail to make good on the promise.

Nodding her head in resigned assent, Jenine knew it was useless to avoid Gloria when she wanted her curiosity satisfied. A somewhat appeased Gloria returned to the main office, and Jenine, to her class.

Bursts of laughter joined the low din of conversation in the cafe-style lunchroom for faculty, staff and administrators. Some were still in line, ordering lunch, while Gloria and Jenine were sitting at a window table, their salad lunches in front of them.

The morning classes had gone by so quickly that it was lunchtime before Jenine knew it. Having missed practice for a week because of the band trip, she was eager to feel the piano keys beneath her fingers. Plus, a tune had been forming in her head, and she wanted to test it out. It was not to be.

"You remember Denise, don't you?" Gloria asked—a tomato chunk perched on the end of fork she held. "She's the librarian at the elementary school."

Pretending interest, as if hanging onto Gloria's every word, Jenine nodded as she chewed. It was the extent of her participation in the largely one-sided conversation. Gloria had maintained a steady stream of chatter since snagging her from the practice room.

"Anyway, Denise saw you two in the grocery store, over in frozen foods section," Gloria was saying. "She said y'all remind her of that husband and wife singing team . . ."

What if Robbie couldn't help Nat? Jenine asked herself, her jaws suspended in chewing. Nat couldn't hide out in Highland Heights forever. Nor would he.

Snapping her fingers, Gloria asked, "Oh, what's their names? I know you know who I'm talking about."

"Ashford and Simpson," Jenine replied absently. She could just imagine what it cost Nat in self-esteem running from trouble in the first place, recalling that he had always been a proud and sometimes stupidly courageous man. The youngest in a family of overachievers, he had fought hard for his individuality and independence.

"Right," Gloria said. "Is he a musician or something? God, wouldn't it be something," pleased by her supposition, "if you and Nat became a popular duo like them?"

Maybe that was why he had sought her out rather than

going to any of his siblings. It said quite a bit about how he felt about her, Jenine thought before cautioning herself to not make too much of his impulsive decision.

"Have you showed him some of the songs you've written?" Gloria continued. "I think you ought to take advantage of this opportunity. It would be a sin not to. I know you haven't had much luck with them before, but it's time to blow the dust off that music now. Don't you think?"

Spearing a bite-size slice of tomato from the salad, Jenine wondered what Nat was doing right now, what he did in the normal course of a regular day? When Natasha was under the safe care of a nanny, he was no doubt free to come and go as he pleased. More importantly, free to write music.

"And I want you to know that I didn't buy that story you gave me," Gloria said. "No man would come all the way to nowhere Texas on such a flimsy excuse. I think he has something else in mind."

He wasn't free now, Jenine reminded herself. But at least he could write music, she thought with envy. And what had she done with her life? Discomfited by the nagging refrain, she squirmed in her chair.

"Jenine," Gloria said forcefully, "are you listening?"

"Oh yeah, right," Jenine replied enthusiastically as if she had been paying attention all along.

With a bright eager look alive on her face, Gloria asked, "So you think it's likely?"

Jenine paused, a puzzled expression lining her face. "What?" she asked.

"That Nat is just using your invitation as a ruse for something else," Gloria supplied.

Looking at Gloria dumbfounded, Jenine asked, "Something else like what?"

"You know," Gloria replied.

Interpreting that hopeful look, Jenine laughed.

"Gloria, what am I going to do with you? I keep telling you there's nothing between us except friendship." Setting her fork on the table, "And that's all it'll ever be between us." *He loves a dead woman.*

"Oh, shoot," Gloria said disappointed. "You really know how to destroy an illusion."

"I've had enough destroyed for me," Jenine replied cryptically; wiping her mouth with the napkin.

"Hey Jenine!"

Looking in the direction from which her name was called, Jenine spotted Bruce Richards, director of the marching band, and woodwind teacher, heading their way. Of medium height and compact build, Bruce was a nifty-dressing jokester with a durably boyish brown face and perpetual jovial disposition. He was also a pretty good trumpet player who shared her love of African-American classical music, also known as jazz.

"I need to talk to you," he said nearing the table. Grabbing a chair from another table, he pulled it up to theirs and sat down. "Hi, Gloria."

Peeved by his interruption, Gloria said, "Bruce, we're trying to have a private conversation if you don't mind."

"Oh yeah, I heard Jenine has a houseguest," Bruce replied undaunted. "I don't have many details but I suspect it could be Nat Padell, also known as Mister Drums, right?" To Jenine's shocked silence, Bruce continued. "He's one of the best in the business," he said to Gloria. "He's one of the few who remain close to the true essence of jazz. He's sat in the bands of some of the greatest musicians around. His own band is extraordinary, too. But he'll never be a millionaire, right, Jenine? You only play jazz because you love it, not necessarily for the money."

"You know him?" Gloria asked.

"Most jazz musicians aren't recognizable but I've been

a fan of his for years. What a group of friends, Jenine," Bruce finished with a smile.

"Bruce," Jenine finally found her voice. "Don't let it get out, okay? He wants to drop out of sight while on vacation." She looked to Gloria. "You too. Promise you won't say anything."

"It's a small town, Jenine," Gloria informed, then at Jenine's piercing stare she held her hands up in surrender. "Okay, okay, but you know this makes our next conversation much more interesting, Jenine."

"I won't confess," Bruce answered. "But I'm here to talk business, Jenine . . ."

Bruce was cut off by the long ring of the school bell, indicating the end of the lunch period.

Saved, Jenine thought. Getting to her feet, she smiled. "Sorry, Bruce. It will have to keep. I have a fourth-period class." She picked up her tray. "Gloria, I'll see you later."

"All right," Bruce said, rising. "But later, okay? We got to talk."

"Later," Jenine replied, walking off with her lunch tray.

Jenine didn't linger around after school as she was known to do. That too was bound to cause more tongues to wag, she thought laughingly as she walked into the study of her home. She laid her briefcase on the desk, then left the room to check the house, wondering where the Padells were.

Nat and Natasha were nowhere to be found, but traces of their presence were everywhere, especially in her bedroom. Before their invasion, it had been uncluttered. A description which aptly described her life.

Now, Natasha's baby bed was set up on the other side of the king-sized bed. A table of baby paraphernalia was placed next to it.

The room seemed to have come alive, she thought, thinking for the first time how drab and dull it used to be.

With the exception of the cream-colored walls and curtains on the twin, floor-length windows, everything was a shade of brown, from the carpet to the king-sized bed which lacked a headboard.

In the closet, Nat's clothes hung alongside hers. More of his personal things occupied three of the six drawers on the dresser. Evidence of him was also to be found in the adjoining bath; his shaving kit rested on the counter next to her bath oils and beads. Impulsively, she moved her toiletries to the guest bath.

Where were they? she asked herself while changing into comfy grey sweats. Maybe Nat got in touch with Robbie.

Taking comfort in that explanation, she headed to the kitchen with thoughts of preparing dinner. Tacked to the refrigerator door was a note: "Gone to the store. Be right back. N & N."

Her curiosity satisfied and corrected, she nodded as she opened the freezer side of the refrigerator. Seeing the frozen dinners stacked in the freezer, she shook her head, wondering what she was doing.

She didn't normally cook. The Padells were not to become an imposition. It was Nat's request.

Grabbing her briefcase off the couch, Jenine veered to her study to do what she normally did. She could tell Nat had been in the room, for a whiff of his tangy scented cologne lingered. How was she ever going to stop thinking about him if he were everywhere?

But it was only natural that she think of Nat, she rationalized. They had a history together and now he was in her life again. It was also natural for her to remember him leaving her behind to pursue his dreams.

Jenine unsnapped the briefcase. She had dreams, too. Or she used to have them, she thought, picking up the stack of student papers.

She was disinclined to grading papers. Her gaze did a

slow slide to the piano with longing in her big brown eyes. Indecision marred her expression. Where had her dedication to teaching gone? she asked herself.

Dropping the papers on the desk, she moved to the piano as if it were a magnet, and she, the object of its pull. Her fingers itched to touch the ivory and black keys, remembering the lilting tune that had haunted her all day. It seemed to come note by note, precipitated by each thought she had of Nat.

Hoping she could recapture the music into one piece, she sat before the regularly tuned Baldwin and began her practice with long-ago learned lessons from the Hanon's virtuoso pianist exercise books, displaying not only ability, but strength, suppleness and perfect hand positioning on the keys. Deep concentration wasn't required, allowing her thoughts to drift to yesteryear—to the first time she laid eyes on Nathaniel Wayne Padell.

Her high school band was participating in the annual Spring City-Wide Jazz Competition at Texas Southern University in Houston, where Nat was one of the judges. He was a graduate student, as well as the assistant director of the University Jazz Ensemble, an award-winning troupe in those days. Her school won first place, and as one of the graduating seniors, she received a music scholarship to the university. The award guaranteed her a position in the summer music workshop where Nat was also one the instructors.

Over the rejections of the other girls in the band, who thought he was too skinny, she secretly thought him the most handsome man alive. But he didn't notice her at all. Which was no fault of his. She was not only short, but slightly overweight, and shy. Her best friend for as long as she could remember had been the piano. He was the complete opposite—tall, slim and his popularity extended campuswide.

Jenine burst out laughing, recalling how she used to hide every time he would come into the band room. She just wanted to get an uninhibited view of him without having to endure the teasing she surely would have gotten had anybody known of her infatuation.

On more than one occasion, he teasingly accused her of trying to get out of rehearsing. She could never seem to find her tongue when she was around him during that initial period, so she never corrected his wrong assumption. He soon found out, however, that she was a far from lazy student.

She had been so eager to master her instrument that she spent more than the required four hours a day in solitary practice. At least, that's what she told herself at the time. The main reason, of course, was that the more time she spent on campus, the more opportunities she would have to see or be near Nat.

Her mother hadn't been fooled, however, and dared her to deny that her lengthy practice sessions had little to do with self-improvement, but rather, that she was chasing or being chased by some boy at the university.

Nevertheless, her dedication and more-than-competent performance soon brought her to the attention of the workshop leaders. Nat had been particularly impressed and began to take a greater interest in her than in any of the others.

His interest in her musical development evolved into a more personal one. He began to notice the slightest changes in her temperament, as well as her physical appearance: she started losing weight, wearing her hair differently and using makeup. On her eighteenth birthday, in July, he surprised her with a gift, an album by McCoy Tyner.

She still had that album, and it was still in mint condition.

* * *

The exercise gave way to the beginnings of another sound, an intense arpeggio several times up and down the keys. The unconscious tune she played was a mellow ballad that had been popular among young lovers in her undergraduate days. It was a light uncomplicated tune that mimicked the sweet innocence of youth.

By the end of the summer, she and Nat were considered an item. Only they knew that nothing more than holding hands transpired between them. The entire summer passed before he even kissed her.

The first time was on his twenty-first birthday, she recalled. They had gone out to celebrate, attending a performance by Yusef Lateef at La Bastille, then a popular jazz club. Afterwards, they sat in his purple VW parked outside her home. Over the stick shift protruding from the floor of the car, he kissed her. Though she had no comparisons, it was the best kiss she ever had. Moments later, so as not to miss her midnight curfew, she had raced inside the house believing she was in love. No one could have convinced her it wasn't forever. Three weeks later, Nat was gone.

Shaking her head at the ease in which her thoughts evolved around Nat, she laughed. There was a trace of melancholy in her laughter. Memory lane was not for you, she chastised herself. There was simply no future in memories.

Resuming play, she struck the keys with sure, conscious fingers. The notes bounced off the walls, piercing her heart with a bittersweet sound. The music told a tale of frustrations mingled with pain and wishes for what could be. A bluesy left hand fought for control over a lightning quick right hand, trying to elude capture of reality.

She had intimate knowledge of these feelings that were finding release through the keys her fingers played with confidence. Lately, they had been in continuous conflict within her—mental battles demanding that she reconcile with her reality, which insisted she leave the dreams for the young with time to fulfill them.

But she played on, her thoughts guiding her fingers, telling them which note to strike next. With her eyes closed, she read the music from a page visible only in her head. Loneliness and longing came out in flats and sharps, expressing a bittersweet refrain.

Then it stopped. With her fingers resting on a chord that died abruptly in the air, Jenine was shocked to look down at her hands to see them trembling on the keys.

"Thank God," she moaned out loud.

She hadn't been able to compose anything in a long time and was afraid that maybe her music had deserted her. It didn't matter that the song she heard was not a joyful one, only that the music had returned to her.

"You've missed your true calling, Jenine," came Nat's voice.

Emitting a shocked gasp, Jenine turned abruptly to look up at Nat. He was leaning casually against the door. "Nat," she said, sagging with relief, a hand over her heart.

"Sorry," Nat said, "I didn't mean to scare you."

With her curiosity piqued over his comment, Jenine shifted on the bench to face him fully. "What did you mean by that remark?" she asked.

She watched entranced as Nat pushed himself away from the door lazily, white teeth bared below the freshly trimmed mustache in a languid smile. It was a look that shortened her breath and quickened her pulse.

Returning from a quick trip to the grocery store for seasonings, he had heard the music coming from the study. After setting Natasha in her playpen, he had been drawn by the remarkable power in the playing, believing it was a recording. Stunned to discover it was Jenine romancing the keys with masterly control and intimacy, he had been listening quietly at the door.

Staring down into her slightly protruding, remarkable eyes, vivid and questioning, Nat replied, "Simply that I believe you could make it professionally."

Stunned more by the intensity of his vibes than by the declaration, Jenine stared open-mouthed, a comeback staggering in her head. He just stood there, on the side of the piano, gazing down at her with a sagacious look in his eyes, a barely perceptible smile on his firm mouth. His brows rose a fraction, cueing her to reply.

Summoning an affronted frown to her face, she said, "I have a profession, thank you." Good, she thought; she sounded duly insulted. "I'm a teacher. I teach music."

A cynical inner voice chided her proud assertion. Turning toward the piano, her brown eyes swiveled downward to the keyboard, hiding her shame. Middle C was a blur in her sight.

Nat eased onto the bench next to her. "I'm not putting down teaching," Nat replied, not confessing that he thought teaching music was for those of mediocre skills. "The world needs teachers," he said, spreading his fingers over the keys in the bass register. "It's just that you have so much more talent."

"And so much more to develop," Jenine replied in a rush of breath, springing up from the bench to go to her desk.

Turning her back to him to shuffle papers in the brief-case, Jenine felt as if he possessed a keenly insightful view of the dissonance in her soul. She wouldn't dare admit it, even if he pressed her. She was much too fragile to subject herself to the smirking gleam that would surely tarnish his eyes, accurately guessing what she only suspected was the cause of her waning interest for teaching.

In teaching music, she had found a mindless solidity that camouflaged an old wound. Besides, it afforded her financial security and independence. More importantly, she had been a success at it. Her students excelled, performing magnificently in competitions and winning scholarships to prestigious music schools and universities.

In writing music, she had been a failure. A box of rejected sheets of music was stacked in the study's closet.

Now, she felt as if the camouflage was shedding, and she was unable to shake the feeling that she should try again. After all, that had been many years ago. Certainly she'd matured enough at least to be willing to compete and handle the rejections. Hadn't she?

With his head cocked at an angle, Nat observed her prim and foreboding profile. Rather than being dissuaded, he was enthralled by her very grown-up personage. She was quiet and deep, but with an inbred force that signaled a strength and stamina at odds with the slenderness of her body, and his memory. Out of nowhere, he felt branded by an urge to protect her, a mark synchronized with an intense physical awareness of her. The emotion bore no relation to music, he told himself, switching his attention to the keyboard.

Nat began to play a lighthearted tune on the piano, snapping Jenine from her private thoughts. She watched and listened, lured by the melodic movement of muscles in his back and shoulders as he serenaded the keys. Did everything he does have to seem so effortless? she asked herself. Muttering a disgruntled sigh, she forced her attention to the student paper at the top of the stack.

"I thought it was a tape when I first heard the music,"

Nat said over the improvisation. "You've gotten a lot stronger since I last heard you. Your left hand has caught up with your right. Now, there's an awesome power in your playing." Stopping play to look up from the piano, he said, "You've mastered man's instrument, Jenine."

With a hollow chuckle, she replied, "Don't give me that chauvinistic dribble about the piano being a masculine instrument that can only be controlled by the strong hands of a man. I don't buy it."

"You can deny it all you want, but generally it's true," he said, laughter floating up from his throat. Turning back to the piano, he began to play the introduction to "My Favorite Things."

He hit a wrong note. Believing he did it deliberately— for he again sought her reaction, an intrepid light beaming in his eyes—Jenine snapped the paper in her hand and plunked down in the chair as if about to busy herself with grading.

Nat picked up where he'd left off on the piano and in thought, as well. "I never expected to hear that kind of music in small-town Texas," he said.

"You'd be surprised at what you'd find in small-town Texas," she replied grudgingly to his back.

Regarding her with a mysterious gaze, he replied softly, "Yeah," shaking his head. "No doubt about it," before biting down on his smiling bottom lip.

Jenine forced herself to ignore him, kept her gaze focused on the paper, though she couldn't get past the student's name at the top of the page.

"Do you sing as well?" he asked.

In a bored tone of voice, she replied, "I can carry a tune, but I'm not about to abandon my piano."

"Good for you," he declared. "Everybody wants to be a singer these days." He turned back to the piano, picking out notes to play.

Jenine made a face at his back. Snob, she thought.

Suddenly, dropping the paper on the desk, she realized she couldn't concentrate on her work, or much else. Getting to her feet, she asked, "Where's Natasha?"

"In her playpen," he replied over his shoulder. "What was the name of that tune you were playing? I'm not familiar with it."

Heading for the door, she replied, "Just a little something I've been working on."

"Hey," Nat said, running to catch up with her in the family room. "Come back here and play that song for me again."

"No," Jenine replied, picking Natasha up from the playpen. "Hi, sweetie," she said, kissing the baby on the nose. Natasha giggled, and Jenine held her close to her bosom for an affectionate squeeze.

Nat sat next to them on the couch and took Jenine's hand in his. Examining the strong-fingered, soft hand, he said softly, "I'm sorry if I insulted you, okay. Sometimes," he chuckled introspectively, "I suffer from this disease called foot-in-mouth. Still friends?"

Jenine merely nodded her reply. She didn't trust herself to speak, not while her heart was tumbling in her chest. With her hand now her own again, she set Natasha on her knees for a gentle ride.

"What have you been doing all day?" Jenine asked Natasha.

"Oh, a little laundry," Nat replied. "We washed the car. My mother is home now, so I called to find out if anybody had called or come by looking for me."

Jenine stilled, ending the galloping movement of her legs. "And?" she asked, her breath suspended in her chest. "Has someone tried to get in touch with you?"

"I didn't get an answer," Nat replied, stretching out his legs. "Then I called my agent to let him know I'd be out of touch for a while, and got somebody to keep an eye on my place. Oh, I almost forgot. I called your lawyer friend Robbie Franks. She's out of town, but her daughter said she'd be sure to have her call me when she gets back."

"She will," Jenine said. "Karyn is good about delivering messages." More to herself, she added, "I need to talk to her, too."

"Is something wrong?"

Forcing a smile to her countenance, she replied, "No," shaking her head.

"Are you sure, Jenine? Is my being here causing a problem for you at school?"

Laughing, Jenine replied, "We're small-town, but we don't do witch hunts on single females."

"That's not why I asked. I want you to be okay," Nat said. "How was your first day back? In fact, how was your trip? We never got around to talking about it. Was it for the school or personal?"

"School, and it was great, thank you," she replied, a tad of excitement spilling into her tone. "My students won second place in the International High School Jazz Band Competition in San Francisco."

"Congratulations," he said, applauding softly with his hands. "What got you over?"

Nat would know about the stress and rigors of jazz-band competitions, having once belonged to the TSU Jazz Ensemble, whose clean-up victories at the Notre Dame Jazz Festivals were well known. "A little number I wrote a long time ago," she replied.

"It wouldn't happen to be the little number that also won you the BMC's award, would it?" he asked slyly.

Staring at him with surprise, she asked, "How did you know?"

"Just a good guess," he replied, before sheepishly adding, "I'm afraid I went poking around in your study and saw the trophy. I know what it means to receive that kind of recognition. You should be very proud of yourself."

She noticed he looked as if he wanted to say more, but changed his mind. She filled the silence. "What about you? Haven't seen your name gracing an album jacket in a year."

Nat chuckled, "Yeah, I know. I've been busy on the road and in the studio. I was in the midst of producing an album until," his voice trailed off. "It's a collaborative project, but I'm more than pleased. But boy, do I wish I had some drums now."

"There are drums we could borrow from school, but . . ." Jenine's voice trailed off. "How long will you . . ." She couldn't finish the question.

"Drumming helps me think, Jenine. I need to think through this problem with David Cissoko. I need to know the right thing to do," Nat explained. "Is it too late to get them now?" he asked with a sly smile.

Laughing, Jenine said, "Now, as in *right* now?"

Later that night, Jenine sauntered into the kitchen, headphones around her neck and a portable cassette player hooked at her waist. Looking through a drawer, she retrieved a pack of batteries. Dumping the dead ones from the player in the trash, she installed the new ones.

She had just put Natasha down and wanted to get in some playing before she called it a night herself. That tune was in her head again. Plus, Nat was still drumming his heart out in the other room.

They couldn't get to the Academy fast enough for Nat, she recalled, heading for the study. Though the campus had been nearly deserted, she solicited the help of the custodian in loading the trunk and back seat of Nat's car with an entire drum set, as well as a conga and bongo drum. Following a side trip to a fast-food restaurant, they returned home. Nat immediately went to work setting up the drums to his liking in the spare bedroom she had yet to furnish for lack of interest, time and money.

Standing outside the door of her study, she listened to him playing in the room across the hall. He hadn't even come out to eat. Now that he had his drums, it was as if the problem with his father-in-law no longer existed. She envied him the ability to shuck off everything else for the sake of his music.

That was what she had to do, she told herself. At least give herself another chance to fail. Maybe she would find contentment in knowing she'd tried again.

Picking up on the silence, Jenine walked inside her study and closed the door.

Chapter Three

In an office high above the street on Embassy Row, the African sat in practiced repose behind a large desk. Except for the small desk light, the room was dark, casting him in a silhouette.

He knew Nat couldn't prove a thing. As with the boy who cried "Wolf!" no one believed his story of a kidnapping attempt. And every American knew as what happened to the boy would happen to Nat: he would be destroyed.

The knowledge brought a smile to his lips, but only for a second. Recalling all the time he'd wasted, feeding his self-pity with inertia, an angry scowl settled over his features.

A man lesser than he had been permitted to rob him of a long-held dream. It was unthinkable that an American, a lowly musician at that, had bested him.

But it wasn't over between them. It was just the beginning. The American would pay. And pay dearly, he thought, rising from his seat to stroll around the side of the desk. He stopped in front of an armchair that held a black, sturdy plastic bag. It sagged in the seat.

He stared at it with a quiet smirk.

"You and your mother have ruined my plans for the

last time." He spoke—referring to his daughter and her mother, both deceased—in a foreign accent reflecting both his African ethnicity and his English education. "But you shall not go unpunished. As your mother did not escape. May your soul drift forever and know no resting place."

Abruptly, he pivoted, returning to the desk. He pressed one of the buttons on the bottom of the phone. Seconds later, a slim, powerfully built man entered the room quietly. He stood at the door, awaiting instructions.

"I have said my good-byes. You may take her to the airport now."

"Yes, Minister," the servant replied, but he didn't move.

"Well?"

"Minister," the servant said hesitantly, "he left the city."

"He did what?" the minister asked with shock and disbelief. His face contorted into a profoundly spiteful mask.

The servant repeated weakly, "He and the baby are gone."

Though it was late and her body was fatigued from long hours of work, Jenine was much too excited to sleep. However, knowing she had to get up in the morning, she turned out the light in the study, filled with a wonderful sense of satisfaction over her accomplishment.

Opening the door, she bumped into Nat, getting to his feet. "Nat," she exclaimed, mildly surprised. "What are you doing here?"

"Listening to you," he replied. "I knew you wouldn't let me sit in, and this was the only way I could get to hear that song again."

Laughing, she said, "You idiot."

"Idiot, am I?" he said, playfully backing her up against the wall. A whiff of the sweet flower fragrance of her scent jolted him for the reaction in him, a shaft of electrical currents coursing through his veins. Distancing himself, he leaned with his back against the opposite wall in the narrow hallway and folded his arms across his chest. "I'd have you know, Ms. Jones, that I know a hit when I hear one."

The flattering words delighted Jenine, and the proximity threatened to propel her own excited state into orbit. Yet, she sensed a sudden reserve in him, but was grateful for the space he put between them.

"How . . . how did you like the drums?" she asked.

"They're wonderful," he lied convincingly. For a young drummer, the drums were more than adequate. They could never compare to his personal set, but he would never tell Jenine and risk hurting her feelings.

"Liar," she chided laughingly. "I happen to know you swear by a certain set, and I'm sure the manufacturer keeps you amply supplied."

"Guilty," he said, admitting defeat with laughter. "You saw the ad in a couple of musicians' magazines. Still, I appreciate your going to the trouble. Thanks."

"That's more like it," she replied. "Well, I'm turning in. See you in the morning."

Halting her retreat by grabbing her wrist, he said, "Wait up, what's your rush?"

"It must be nearly one in the morning," she replied. "I'll be a zombie when the alarm goes off at six. I stayed up longer than I intended."

"Don't go yet," he said softly.

Jenine studied his face intently, searching for the reason for the need she heard in his voice. "Nat, what's the matter?"

"Nothing," he said lightly, with an embarrassing shrug. "I just wanted a little company, that's all. But you're right; you have to get up in the morning and I don't."

"I guess a few more minutes won't matter," she replied.

He beamed. "How about a cup of hot chocolate?"

"Sounds like a good idea," she replied.

"Good," he said with a pleased light in his eyes. Gesturing in gentlemanly style, he extended a hand in front of them, and said, "After you."

Jenine led the way to the kitchen and climbed onto a stool at the counter. She watched as Nat set out the makings for two cups of hot chocolate.

With his back to her, pouring milk in a pan, he said, "Sounds like you were making good progress with the piece."

"It's coming," she replied, tempering the excitement in her voice. It wouldn't do to encourage his prodding for a change of careers.

He smiled over his shoulder at her. "Modesty is not a musician's trait," he said.

"How do you know until you try it?" she quipped.

Nat turned on a burner, then set the pan on the stove before facing her. "How do you know you wouldn't like being a musician full time?" he challenged.

Returning his headlong stare, "I think we've traded enough quips for one night, don't you?" she said with a hint of warning.

"You're something else, you know that?" he said quietly.

"What makes you say that?" she asked, matching his tone. In addition to a hint of mirth, there was a look in the depths of his eyes she couldn't define.

"You've just changed. Not like I expected. Well, maybe a little bit," he amended chuckling.

With a cheeky curiosity in her tone, she asked, "And

what did you expect?" folding her arms on the counter-top.

"You know, I really don't know," he replied, his mouth twisted in contemplation. "Maybe that you'd still have long hair . . ." he said, dumping a package of instant chocolate into the milk.

"And be overweight," she added laughing at herself.

"Banish the thought," he grinned, wiggling his brows lewdly. "I certainly wouldn't have expected you to enjoy teaching. Well, on second thought, I guess I can see where you would be drawn to teaching. Heaven knows you were always willing to help somebody, even when you didn't want to."

"I did have a problem saying no, didn't I?" she said. That wasn't the only problem she had, she thought.

"Oh, I wouldn't call it a problem," his brow rose in amusement, "or Natasha and I would be at some hotel or something."

"It's not too late," she said, her eyes bright with teasing.

"I expected I would have heard about Jenine Jones the song-writer or something," he said, pouring hot chocolate into two mugs. He passed a cup of the steaming brown liquid to Jenine. Blowing over his cup, he said, "I certainly heard that person playing today."

Jenine ducked her gaze from his to take a cautious sip of the chocolate. She knew he was waiting for an answer, but she wanted to forget the past, the time she wasted nursing a bruised ego and indulging in self-flagellation. She looked up at him; his look indicated he was still waiting for her response.

"It just didn't pan out," she replied softly, taking an-other drink of chocolate.

Jenine began to grow uneasy under his rapt stare; his eyes, fire-warm embers, were stirring havoc in her. The silence strained against her ears; she wanted to speak, to break this quiet that was both frightening and comfortable at the same time. She felt under a magician's spell and was reminded—not that she needed a reminder—of why she must not let Nat get too close.

Sliding off the stool, she sauntered into the den, her hands wrapped around the mug. She eased onto the couch, crossing her legs at the thigh.

Nat watched her intently for several moments before following. "I asked you before if something was wrong and you said no. Are you sure?" he asked, his deep voice laced with concern.

She tried to speak, but her voice faltered. How could she tell him *he* was what's wrong? Or, more honestly, her response to him. "I swear it's nothing," she said.

"You'll tell me if there is?" he said. "Promise me."

Nodding her head, "Promise. At the first sign of trouble I'll come running to you faster than you can beat out a drum roll," she said, setting the mug on the coffee table.

"This is serious stuff, lady," he said seriously with a smile. Placing his mug on the table, he sat on the floor near her, with his knees raised to his chin. "Hopefully, Robbie will be back in town tomorrow and we can get the ball rolling so Natasha and I can hurry and get out of your hair."

Jenine opened her mouth to deny she was disturbed by their presence. But in addition to being too revealing, the truth was that his presence did disturb her, though not the way he thought. Still, she clamped her mouth shut.

"Do you really think he will try and find you?" she asked.

"I would be surprised if he didn't," he replied with a sardonic chuckle.

"How well do you know him?"

Nat shrugged. The man was a control freak, for one, he thought, taking a sip of chocolate. Born into a powerful and monied family—David enjoyed unlimited resources. He had been a shrewd, manipulative father.

"Mostly what Netta told me," he replied at last. Then, speaking slowly, as if feeling his way, he said, "I know he ran for the presidency of his country, oh, maybe five or six years ago, but he ended up dropping out of the race. I'm not sure why."

And, if he remembered correctly, Netta's mother had escaped his clutches only to be tracked down in London before she was mysteriously killed. Though Netta never said it outright, it was implied that David had something to do with her death.

"I know he didn't approve of our marriage," he continued. "He thought I wasn't good enough for his daughter. Normally, a trait inherent in all fathers, I would imagine," he added musingly. "But I didn't find out just how much he disapproved until after we were married."

"How did that happen?"

"Well, according to Netta, he was away in Africa on business, so he didn't attend the wedding," Nat replied. "When I finally did meet him—it was at one of those diplomatic parties—he had plenty to say on the subject. And believe me, he didn't bother hiding his dislike. But Netta was pregnant, so there wasn't much he could do about it." Setting the mug on the coffee table, "But that didn't stop him from trying. Even after we were married, she was expected to play hostess for his many social functions. He seemed quite possessive of her."

"Wasn't that a little difficult? I mean, weren't you living in New York?" she asked.

"It wasn't physically difficult, but tiring for Netta, who traveled back and forth on the train," he replied. "I tried to get her to just tell him no, but she was a dutiful daughter."

But not a dutiful wife? Jenine asked herself, hiding her

opinion by taking a drink of her chocolate. Watching Nat from the rim of the mug, she wondered at the thoughts behind his somber expression. She had more questions about the woman who had been his wife and mother of his child, but kept her counsel.

"I've been thinking," Nat said, resting his chin on his knees.

"Oh, really," she replied with a slightly raised brow and amusement in her tone.

"Ha-ha," he said mockingly. "I figure there must be a pretty good daycare in town."

"I imagine there is," she replied carefully.

"Maybe I'll enroll Natasha in one," he said. Looking up into her face, "What do you think?"

Masking her curiosity under a demure smile, Jenine wondered what he was leading up to. For someone who didn't expect to be around too long, such a move seemed questionable.

She blurted her initial thoughts on the subject. "What about your ex-father-in-law? Aren't you afraid he might try something?"

"No doubt he would if he could find us," Nat chuckled in a one-upmanship tone. "On the real side though," he said seriously, "I've thought about this. I need space and time to work out a plan to save Natasha from any danger her grandfather may cause, legal or otherwise. As I've recently discovered, taking care of a baby is not an easy job," Nat said with a wink. "I feel relatively confident that he won't be able to find us, considering how long it took me to find this town myself and I'm more familiar with this part of the country than he is. The faster I can get protection for her, the sooner we'll be out of your hair."

Jenine felt a pang of heartache as Nat continued. "David Cissoko doesn't want publicity, so I think a reputable and secure daycare center would be too public for him to try anything funny. I plan to give very explicit instructions and make sure they understand that Natasha is not to be picked up or even visited by anyone, except you and me."

Seeing that Nat was convinced he had covered all bases, Jenine felt she was in no position to argue. "Well, . . . I'm sure . . . If that's what you want to do, it should be fine," she said.

"Can you recommend someplace?"

"Uh, I know a couple of people I can call," she replied. Sipping chocolate, "How soon would you like to do this?"

"As soon as possible," he replied.

"All right," she said. "I'll check at school tomorrow and call you back and let you know."

"Okay. That'll be good." He downed the remains of the chocolate, then looked momentarily at the bottom of the cup. "Maybe you ought to call it a night," he suggested.

Jenine noticed him staring up at her in a faraway gaze, as if he was looking right through her or not seeing her at all. He was turning into a giant question mark.

"That sounds like a good idea," she replied, though she suspected another night of tossing and turning was in store for her. He had merely increased her level of confusion.

Rising to his feet, he said, "Thanks again for the drums. You're a lifesaver. Good night, Jenine," he said in a pondering tone of voice. Leaning over to kiss her on the cheek, "Pleasant dreams."

Too stunned to move, Jenine nodded her head woodenly. With the cup at her lips, she watched him disappear as abruptly as he first appeared.

* * *

When Nat made up his mind, there was no stopping or changing directions, Jenine discovered. She called him from school with the name of a good daycare, and he called back a few hours later to inform her that a very displeased Natasha was deposited with her new caretaker Mrs. Givens, director of Kiddie Preparatory.

Weaving through the crowded hallways to her office, she couldn't help thinking that in the few days he had been in town, Nat hadn't lost a beat. He had acquired a set of drums, located a daycare for his daughter and was probably having the time of his life.

Compared to him, she had been standing still. And if she didn't want to get left behind, she had better move.

The encouraging refrain repeated itself throughout the day.

Standing by the piano, Jenine stared across the room at the faces of her students. With their instruments held in rest position, they sat in tiers of steel folding chairs in the band rehearsal hall. Bewildered expressions stared back at her.

"Look kids, I'm sorry," Jenine said. She was embarrassed and ashamed as well. Never before had she allowed her personal problems to enter a classroom and lashed out at her students.

These students, members of the jazz band were not the only ones who suffered unfairly from her unusually bad temper, she recalled. She had been extremely hard in all of her classes today, justifying her harsh criticisms as her high expectations for the students to do better. When Nikki went flying from the room in tears a few moments ago, she was forced to admit that her behavior had nothing to do with student performance at all.

Appalled by her lack of professionalism, she decided at

that moment to pursue a course of action that was as distasteful to her as she knew it would be to John Sawyer the principal. She was going to ask for—demand if need be—time off. John would not like it, but he would get over it, she thought, her lips pressed together in a determined set.

"I've been a witch," Jenine said with a self-derisive chuckle. "And I use that word in deference to your tender ears, instead of the one that fully describes my attitude today."

The students joined her in laughter. Relief edged the mirth, aided by applause and whistles. They understood full well what she meant.

"Nikki, I want to apologize to you especially. You're a heck of a piano player, and don't let anybody, including me, tell you otherwise. I hope you'll forgive me."

Nikki's eyes were watery with tears and forgiveness as she got up and shared an embrace with Jenine. "It's okay, Ms. Jones."

"Thank you, sweetheart, but it's not okay," Jenine said, a twisted smile on her mouth. "And it won't happen again."

Releasing Nikki who returned to sit on the bench at the piano, Jenine turned to the rest of the class. She looked at the wall clock at her back; it was 4:45. Then she faced the students again.

"Have I worked you hard enough, or do you want more?" she asked.

"More of the old Ms. Jones, or the witch?" one of the trumpet players on the top row wanted to know.

Laughing with them, she replied, "The old Ms. Jones. Consider the wicked witch dead."

Knowing this would be her last teaching session for a while, Jenine put a tight lid on her inner turmoil and continued class with the teacher the students had grown to respect and love. She pointed out errors, fussed about repeated mistakes, encouraged improvements and praised their successes.

At the end of rehearsal, Jenine returned to her office. Looking around the room, she felt a twinge of anxiety, but none of the sadness she expected. She had feared it would be harder, breaking an eight-year-old routine of coming to school every day. Instead, she felt a sense of relief over her decision. It was as if a light had clicked on in her head, helping her to locate the source of the discontent she'd been feeling lately.

She was going to put in more time writing. She owed it to herself, she thought, gathering the things she would need at home.

Taking a final look at the room, she silently affirmed that she wasn't doing this for Nat. Yes, he had been the impetus for her decision, but for the first time she could recall in a long time, she was going to do what was in her best interest.

With her briefcase and coat in one hand, Jenine locked the door and left the room, heading for the principal's office. The main office was empty when she arrived. It was after five, and it seemed everyone had gone home.

She suffered an anxious moment, fearing John had left as well. Walking past the waist-high swinging door, she walked deeper into the area, toward the door with the word PRINCIPAL overhead. A light shone through the cracked opening.

Knocking as she walked into the room, Jenine said, "May I come in?"

John, a former professional football player was reared back in the chair behind the big desk, staring absently out the window. "By all means," he said, straightening in his chair. "To what do I owe this visit from my favorite music teacher?"

"John, I need some time off," she said in a rush as if fearing she would change her mind.

"Sure," he replied, riffling through files in a bottom drawer. "How much time?" he asked, opening a folder on the desk. "A day, two days, what?"

"Indefinite," she replied, holding her breath.

Negotiating a leave with John had taken longer than Jenine had originally thought it would take, she reflected as she returned to her office. Before he finally agreed, John insisted that she prepare a schedule that would permit the other music teachers to cover her classes until a suitable substitute could be found. It was the least she could do since she was leaving them in the lurch, he had argued.

After getting the additional items, Jenine relocked the door, then headed down the long hallway, heels clicking against the brick tile flooring.

She heard another sound, the rapid steps of someone wearing flat-heeled shoes, and Nat's fear became her own. Quickening her pace, she stuck her hand inside her purse, searching for her keys: they weren't there. She then dug inside her coat pocket, shifting the briefcase to her other hand.

With keys in one hand, her other hand on the door handle and a cautious semblance of relief inside her, she heard, "Hey, Jenine, wait up."

Turning to face him, Jenine said peeved, "Bruce, you scared the life out of me." She sagged against the heavy metal doors.

"Serves you right for staying here so late by yourself," he replied.

"Obviously, I'm not alone. You're still here."

"But you didn't know that," he said.

"I don't feel like arguing with you, Bruce," she said, struggling to push open the door.

He easily shoved the door open, and they walked out into the dark, nearly black night. "Good, because neither do I. I need to talk to you."

"I need to talk to you, too," she replied. They stayed on the sidewalk path.

"Not here, I'm starving," he said. "Let's get something to eat, and I'll tell you over dinner."

"Bruce, I need to get home," she replied. "I have a lot of things to do."

"That's right," he said, snapping his fingers. "I forgot there's a man in your life now. You've got to check in."

Jenine opened her mouth to issue the standard reply to the numerous inquiries and comments she had received since Nat arrived, but waved it off. "I don't have to check in with anybody, but I do have some very important work to do in a short period of time," she said.

"That's what I like," Bruce replied, "an independent woman."

"You're trying to bait me and I know it," Jenine said. Looking at her wristwatch, she said, "You win this time, but I can't stay long."

"Want to go in my car or yours?"

"We meet at last."

"Yes," Nat replied, locking the door.

He was standing in the entrance hallway of Jenine's home, Natasha in his arms. Robbie got out of her coat, dumped it in Nat's free hand, then took Natasha from his arm.

"This must be the baby I've heard so much about," Robbie said.

"Yes," he said, his face in a frown, looking after Robbie

who had vanished to the den with Natasha. He hung the coat in the hall closet, then hurried to the den.

"Jenine's not back yet," he said. "I guess she got held up at school."

"That's fine," Robbie replied, riding Natasha on her knees.

Nat stared intently at the woman who was playing with his daughter. Expecting someone younger and more aggressive looking, he felt uncomfortable by what he saw.

Robbie Franks looked gentle and serenely wise. Like his mother. He guessed her to be in her mid-to-late fifties, though he couldn't be sure because her sweet-smelling ivory skin was smooth on her round face. She had a genial mouth and sparkling blue eyes that were entirely too full of warmth and kindness. Her reddish-brown hair was twisted on top of her head, held in place by a delicate comb that complimented the lavender suit she wore.

In an instant, he concluded Jenine's attorney friend was certainly no match for the dirty job that had to be done.

"Hey, look, Ms. Franks, this is nothing personal you understand."

Robbie looked at him from the tip of her eyes, a brow raised slightly.

"I'm sure you're a competent, no, a very good attorney," Nat amended quickly, "but uh, I don't . . . Oh, this is not coming out right."

"If you have time to waste looking for other counsel, I'd be more than happy to provide you with a list of male attorneys in the city, Mr. Padell," Robbie said tartly.

Nat's head snapped in surprise. Her blue eyes were suddenly icy glaciers boring into him and the gentle tone that had greeted him only minutes ago chilled him to the bone.

"No, I don't have the time, as you've pointed out. And

it seems I was mistaken, anyway, Ms. Franks," he said humbly with a hint of a smile alight in his eyes. "Can I get you some coffee or something? I don't know what's keeping Jenine."

Chapter Four

Nat was going out of his mind. It was after ten, and Jenine had yet to arrive. As he paced the floor in the den, horrible scenarios filled his head. Each scene pitted Jenine in danger, and each new picture portrayed one more frightening than the last. Had David Cissoko found them?

The hands on the kitchen clock played an equally cruel game, barely seeming to move when he checked every few minutes. Yet, the time passed with no signs of Jenine.

He was probably worrying needlessly, he told himself. In all likelihood, Jenine was safe and having a good time, drinking with some of her co-workers or something. However, the image didn't sit right; he couldn't see Jenine in some smoke-filled tawdry tavern, with a drink in her hand in the mixed company of a boisterous band of teachers.

But she was an adult, an inner voice reminded him, and not the cute, chaste teenager he once courted with care. Definitely a grown woman, and quite an attractive one. He felt a fluttering in his heart, and a smile, like one that marks a man's thoughts when he finds a woman worthy of taking home to meet his parents visited his visage.

Suddenly, all pleasure left him. Conscious of where his thoughts were leading, Nat told himself he had to fight any sign of an attraction between them. He owed Jenine more respect than below-the-waist sensations, he chided himself silently.

"Jenine, where are you?" he asked, looking over his shoulders to the clock on the wall: only a minute had gone by. Natasha began to squirm and he hurried to pick her up before she rolled off the couch. Shaking her back to sleep, he decided to put her in bed.

Returning from the bedroom, he stopped at the front door. Though he knew it was useless, he opened it and stepped out onto the porch. Standing under the small yellow beam of light, undaunted by the cold and rain, he looked anxiously up and down the dark, lifeless street.

Jenine's neighbors were locked in for the night. It was never this quiet in his adopted town, a promised land that beckoned platoons of aspiring talent. The harsh weather if not the hour matched the night he returned to his apartment for the fright of his life, he recalled.

Staring into the still night, his senses filled with the ambience of New York. He could almost touch its energy, see its ugly face, feel its exciting mystique. And relive its dangers. His memory came crowding back, like a hidden current engulfing him.

He and the two fellow musicians, Joel and Marty, had called it quits in the studio. They were supposed to drop him off at his place on their way home, but ended up inviting themselves up for a nightcap.

He walked into the apartment first, calling out, "Ms. Cramer, it's just me." Receiving no response, he loped to Natasha's room where he expected to find Ms. Cramer asleep in the rocking chair.

He was struck from behind, but the blow grazed his shoulder. Surprised, he didn't react swiftly enough to ward off the right hand that connected with his jaw, sending him crashing into the dresser. Shaking off the punch to clear his vision, white lights flashing in his eyes, he saw the man leaning over Natasha's bed.

With a warring cry on his lips, he raced across the room, landing a well-placed, flying kick, buckling the intruder's legs under him. He fought his opponent with deadly intentions, but the man was up to the challenge, bigger, better trained in self-defense and driven by self-preservation.

Hearing the commotion, Marty and Joel came rushing to his defense, but they were even less a match. The intruder knocked them into each other like in a slapstick comic routine and made his getaway from the apartment.

The police officer who came to the apartment was polite and seemingly efficient, taking their statements and looking for fingerprints. But he offered little hope in catching the guy. According to the policeman, Nat should consider himself lucky nothing was stolen and no one was seriously injured.

Ms. Cramer, who was hysterical when they had found her gagged and tied in the kitchen, had quit that night. She insisted on staying at a hotel and called the next day with a forwarding address to receive her possessions.

David also called that day, ranting and raving that Natasha would be better off with his people 'back home,' he recalled. Wasting no time, Nat notified the officer who had given him a pat on the back for being a concerned parent. His statement was taken, but a few days later, the policeman delivered only apologies.

The cold penetrated his light clothing. Nat shuddered, then returned inside. Locking the door, he heard the crisp peal of the telephone bell and sprinted to the kitchen to answer the phone on the island counter.

"Hello, Jones residence."

It wasn't Jenine, but one of her co-workers, a Gloria

somebody or another, inviting them to dinner. He promised to deliver the message and hung up.

The niggling voice in his head persisted. Guilt compounded his fear. Any man with an ounce of pride would never have let this happen, he reminded himself. If harm came to Jenine, it would be his fault.

With visions of her in the clutches of David Cissoko, Nat picked up the phone to call the police. As he punched the second of the three-digit emergency number, Jenine walked in through the kitchen door.

"Where in the hell have you been?" he demanded, dropping the receiver in its cradle.

Stunned, Jenine didn't respond right away, except to stare at Nat with a profoundly curious expression. She wasn't expecting the irate-husband tone of voice, nor the tense drawn face that greeted her—both of which were out of tempo with her spirits. She took her time locking the door behind her.

She stared guardedly as Nat marched around the counter to stand inches from her. With her gaze roaming over him, an appreciative moan nearly escaped her lips. The buttoned down blue and black striped shirt he wore was opened at the neck, revealing his smooth fine dark chest beneath. Lowering her lids, Jenine nervously licked her lips and walked around him, heading toward the couch.

"Natasha and I have been sick with worry that something terrible happened to you," he shouted at her back.

Holding on to her temper, Jenine asked softly, "Where's the little darling now?" She tossed her coat across the back of the couch.

"Jenine, what's this all about? You didn't say anything about being late, and you didn't call. Didn't you think we would worry about you?"

"I know I should have called, and I'm sorry, okay?" She tried to look apologetic; instead, her eyes flashed a gentle, but firm warning, conveying that she wanted this conversation to end.

"What were you doing that you couldn't stop and call? Where were you?" he demanded angrily.

Her antennae zeroed in on the barely audible high pitch of strain in his voice, and her eyes moved up to lock with his in combat. Closer scrutiny showed desperation lurking in the depths of his glittering olive-brown eyes, and she understood the reason for his outbursts.

She'd never mattered to anyone before, Jenine thought, a thrill shivering through her senses. Pleased by his open concern for her, she forgave him for acting out an irrational fear. After all, she scolded herself, she could have called. It was a simple courtesy she neglected to perform because she had gotten carried away with Bruce, whose reason for talking to her piggybacked her own plans.

Sauntering to stand inches from him, she reached out her hand to caress his tight jaw. "Nat, I'm sorry. I didn't mean to scare you," she said.

The warm glow in her eyes and gentle touch took the fight out of Nat, replacing anxiety with an emotion infinitely more disturbing. Despite the evidence that she was safe, he felt a keen need to touch her, and did, holding her palm still on the side of his face. Though cool and soft, it seared his flesh. Staring down into her face, his eyes fastened on her mouth, the slight parting of her lips. He knew he should let her go, but the prohibition of touching fueled his excitement.

Silence loomed loud in the room. The tension between them altered, a prelude to longing.

Jenine felt the giveaway heat in her face under the scorching intent of his gaze. The voice of reason was abandoned to desire. She wanted Nat to kiss her . . . to see if memory made more of his kisses than reality, she told herself.

When he bent his head, she met his lips halfway. The tingling effects of the contact spread through each like wildfire.

A small sound of wonder came from her, his lips massaging her mouth with provocative insistence. The kiss was more persuasive than she cared to admit, even more intoxicating than she remembered. Moving against him in a suggestive body caress, Jenine pulled his head closer to her, wanting the kiss to go on forever.

With streamers of sensations unfurling in him, Nat pressed every inch of her body to his. He didn't realize the depths of his hunger, and felt himself losing control. He pulled away with tearing reluctance, leaving them both unsatisfied.

Drawing a ragged breath, Nat stepped back from her, shaken and amazed. He couldn't make himself meet her eyes, distressed by his behavior. He walked away to the den as if in a rush to do something he had forgotten. What he forgot was his promise not to complicate Jenine's life any further—he chastised himself.

Mortified by her behavior, Jenine studied the patterns in the rug under her feet. Her fear of the known had been justified, she thought, her body temperature still warm with want for him.

At least Nat was gracious enough to act as if nothing happened between them, she thought, drawing a deep breath. And nothing did, she told herself. They merely shared a simple kiss that changed nothing. He was still leaving; she was rediscovering her music.

"Robbie came by," Nat said.

Although she strolled across the room to stand behind the couch, Jenine wanted nothing more than to run off to her room with her shame. Watching Nat staring into his own thoughts, she asked dutifully, "How did it go?"

"Not as well as I expected," he replied, bending to pick up the colorful foam duck off the floor. With the baby toy in his hands, he paused thoughtfully before he spoke again. "Robbie was great," he said, tossing the duck on the table. "At first I was a little skeptical. She didn't look like the lioness you'd described," he said, some of his initial skepticism slipping into his voice. "It didn't take long for me to learn otherwise. She grilled me like a drill sergeant."

His hollow laugh was joined by an equally empty one from Jenine.

"Then she proceeded to sound like a defense attorney, picking my story apart until I was starting to wonder if I hadn't dreamed the whole incident," Nat continued. "The bottom line is that I have no proof that David was behind the kidnapping attempt or that it really was a kidnapping attempt in the first place."

"So Robbie couldn't help you at all?" she said, hope sinking from her voice.

"Yes and no," he replied. "It seems there is a lack of uniformity from state to state in terms of the law on parental kidnapping, and mine is complicated because I can't prove it."

"Can't you file an injunction, or peace bond, or something?" she asked.

Nat chortled, thinking they shared similar beliefs. Both of them had been fooled by the so-called power of the law.

"Yeah, I thought it was that simple, too," he said. "But to do that, would mean announcing where we are, for starters. And I'm not ready to do that. Two, I would have to prove to a judge that David had either harmed Natasha in some way, or will harm her. So, with no proof, that's out of the question."

"But," Jenine started perplexed, "didn't Congress pass a law several years ago about parental kidnapping?"

With his sense of humor taking over, Nat laughed in retort. "You get an A in current affairs, Miss Jones." He dropped back into the chair. "I hadn't heard of that law until Robbie proceeded to explain how little benefit it offered to my situation." He sounded dismally defeated. "Yes, to your question, there is a law. However, it seems I prevented the very crime that would put me in an even more hopeless situation."

"I don't understand."

"It all comes back to the fact that I can't prove attempted kidnapping, and since Natasha wasn't kidnapped, no law has been broken. If, on the other hand, she had been kidnapped, there are three requirements for getting the police—from the FBI on down to the local authorities—involved. But," he emphasized, making the point with an index finger, "before that can happen, parental kidnapping must be a felony in the state where it happened." Jenine groaned. "My sentiments exactly."

"So, what are you going to do now?"

With a note of admiration in his voice, he said, "That Robbie has a devious mind. She gave me a few options to consider. We're going to build a case against him."

"How?"

"One," he said, "we're going to engage the services of a private investigator to look into the glamorous lifestyle of a man representing one of the poorest nations on the continent of Africa."

Amazed, she asked, "There's a private investigator in Highland Heights?"

"No," he replied, laughing at her expression. "Robbie is going to contact someone in Houston. She's used him before on other cases."

"What will he be looking for?"

"Nothing in particular, everything in general that will paint an unstable grandfather who couldn't possibly be a good influence on a child."

"You sound hopeful that the investigator will find something incriminating," Jenine said.

"Oh, I am. Short of confronting David myself, hope is all that I have at the moment," he replied wistfully, a thoughtful glaze in his eyes.

"It's just so amazing that with all the laws we have, in the end there's so little a parent can do to ensure his child's safety."

"Well, I'm finding out that in more instances than not, the law's hands are virtually tied behind its legal back," he said. With a disgusted snort, "Even grandparents have inherent rights."

Jenine could think of nothing to say. She merely looked at him with a sympathetic half-smile on her lips.

"There's nothing to do. But wait," he said as if speaking to himself. Changing the conversation, "Enough about my problems. How was your day? Are you hungry? I left a plate for you in the oven."

"Thanks, but I'm not hungry," she replied. She couldn't eat a bite even if she were, she thought, wanting only to get to the privacy of her room. "I think I'm going to call it a night."

"Jenine?" he called, halting her exit.

"Yes, Nat?" she replied. She noticed sad apology on his face, and held her breath in waiting.

"Good night," he replied.

With a smile on her mouth that didn't reach her eyes, Jenine nodded her head, then turned and left the room.

The brilliant ringing of the phone intruded upon the dreams of the sleeping man. Groggily, he sat up, reached over to the lamp on the table next to the bed and clicked on the light. A glance at the round, gold-rimmed white porcelain clock showed it was after midnight.

The phone rang again, and he answered, snatching the receiver off the hook. "Yes," he replied.

"It is I, Minister," the caller replied.

"Yes, Bede," the minister said, sitting up in the high four-poster bed. "You have news for me," he said, his eyes brightening with excitement. "What have you found in Atlanta?"

Bede paused a second before he replied. "We have found nothing, Minister."

The minister's voice was controlled, almost tight, like the expression on his face when he spoke. "You wake me in the middle of the night for nothing?" he reprimanded.

"But Minister, you told me to keep you posted." Bede defended himself in a calm, reasonable voice. "We have staked out his brother's home for two days and we haven't seen a sign of him or the baby. Shall we proceed to Houston where his mother lives?"

"Yes, yes, by all means," the minister replied. "And you were right. Keep me posted at all times. And Bede," he said with prompting, his voice trailing off.

"Yes, Minister?"

"Do not fail me," he said, a silken thread of warning in his voice. He did not wait for a reply before severing the call.

He might have ruled as once the great Candaces who were his ancestors ruled. It was his mother's last wish on her deathbed, that a Nubacushian lead their country back into a rebirth of its former greatness.

Men and strategy had been in place five years ago to ensure his victory. But his wife, she, the nosy one, saw something she shouldn't have, heard something he never meant her to hear.

Only three of them knew the entire plan, he recalled. One died defending his actions; she, the other, had to be neutralized. Those who would have committed the actual crime were to be mere hired hands with no ties to him.

Oh, she promised not to tell, but he couldn't take that chance. His wife ran away from him, and finding her became supreme. The frantic activity in his ambitious political campaign attracted the attention of election watchers. Speculations about a coup d'état surfaced, and he had no choice but to postpone his dreams.

He used the announcement of his wife's unfortunate death as an excuse for withdrawing from politics. Another loyal and dedicated Nubacushian stepped forward, taking the blame for the botched plot, leaving him free to try again.

The present leaders were wary of him, but they had no proof. In their attempt to show the world a humanitarian face, he was given a title to go with a powerless, diplomatic position.

But the dream didn't die. He had been biding his time. Only, he had intended to rely on a different weapon, his beautiful daughter.

He stared unseeingly, his eyes narrowed, his lips folded in his mouth. "Mukarramma." He whispered his daughter's African name with disdain.

Mukarramma had known that her father intended her to marry the second-in-command of their country. Within the ranks of recognition, he would have been her counsel. Power would have been but two mere men away from him, a clear path to the throne, as their deaths would have been arranged as neatly as the others. But his daughter had married an American, and now she was dead.

Thwarted again, he thought, shaking his head bitterly with a silent curse.

Instead of returning to Nubacush as a man of high stature, he remained exiled in America as second-in-command of the diplomatic corps of a country that got poorer as the seasons changed.

He had nothing to comfort him in the coming seasons except revenge. But he would not suffer alone. The burden and brunt of his unforgiving nature would be borne by Nathaniel Padell.

"A daughter for a daughter," he whispered, then turned off the light and snuggled in bed, a confident smile on his face.

Chapter Five

With a folded slip of paper in her hand, Jenine looked into the master bedroom. She intended to leave the note on the dresser for Nat, explaining that she would be late again tonight.

Today was the first day of her new life. After dropping off the temporary class schedules with John, she was going straight to Bruce's studio. She planned to write and play until her fingers ached, she thought, smiling at the prospect. Later, she and Bruce planned to go over the music before the other members of the newly assembled band arrived to meet one another and have a light rehearsal.

She felt an electric sparkle—like knowing you're soon to go on holiday—as she tiptoed into the room. Seeing Nat asleep, buried under the covers, she felt her excitement curtailed only by a sense of guilt for keeping her plans secret from him.

She set the note prominently on the dresser, then looked across the room where Natasha, tangled in the covers in her bed, was stirring awake. With another glance at Nat to assure herself he was really asleep, Jenine tipped to the baby bed to pick up Natasha.

"What are you doing up so early?" she mouthed smilingly to the baby before kissing her on the forehead.

Grabbing a pre-folded diaper from the table, Jenine left the room quietly with Natasha. In the den, she set the baby on the couch to change the diaper.

"Are you hungry?" she asked Natasha. "I'll feed you as soon as I finish, so be patient," she said when Natasha began to squirm, growing impatient.

Moments later, Natasha was strapped in her highchair while Jenine was standing at the counter to feed her. Enjoying her breakfast, Natasha began clapping her hands, missing more often than bringing the two still-uncontrollable limbs together.

"You're making me late," Jenine scolded playfully. "You know that, don't you?"

Responding, Natasha mimicked Jenine's conversation with her own baby language.

"Well, I missed you, too," Jenine replied. "You should have waited up for me last night. You knew I was coming."

With Natasha, Jenine felt at ease, comfortable with her emotions and actions. She wished a similar manner were possible with Nat, she thought, spooning oatmeal into the baby's mouth.

With a shiver of vivid recollection, her mind turned to last night. Mechanically she went over and over the scene—the thrilling kiss, the ecstasy of being held against his strong body and the aftermath of her humiliation. Her dreams and sojourns into the past had caught up with her, she thought.

As she had taken action to devote more time to composing, she had to do likewise to bolster her personal restraint, Jenine told herself. She simply couldn't afford to be distracted by romantic notions. The time she had to accomplish her goal, coupled with the late-night rehearsals would go a long way to toughen her resolve, forcing her to concentrate less on Nat and more on her music, she thought, satisfied with her plan.

Beating the tabletop of her highchair, Natasha jolted Jenine back to the present.

"Sorry," Jenine said, resuming her duty. "You know what, Natasha," she said pensively, "adulthood complicates life. Yeah, that's right," she said, replying to Natasha's comment. "Enjoy your childhood for as long as you can," she said, scraping the bowl. "Here's your last bite," she said, feeding the baby. She got up to put the empty bowl in the sink, then returned. "Now," wiping Natasha's mouth, "you're all finished. I'm going to drop you back off with your daddy, then I'm going to work."

Unstrapping Natasha from the chair, Jenine picked up the baby. She started for the bedroom, intending to return Natasha to her father, but froze in her steps. Nat was standing in the doorway, bare-chested.

With her lips parted in a startled gape, Jenine stared as he advanced upon them, moving as usual with languid grace. He was a testament to virility in the flesh—tall, mustached, swarthy, his skin as dark and smooth as black velvet.

Yawning, he said cheerfully, "Good morning ladies."

Hesitant in her reply, Jenine finally got out, "Good morning," lowering her gaze from his chest. The man was exquisite. There was no other word for it, she thought, swallowing the lump lodged in her throat.

Natasha babbled joyfully at the sight of her father. Jenine felt her insides reveal an equally foolish reaction. Though in her, it wasn't cute, she thought, irritated at the thrilling current moving through her.

"Hello, pumpkin," he said, bending to kiss Natasha on the cheek. Looking at Jenine from the corner of his gaze, he noticed she was dressed more casually than usual for school—in a bulky turquoise and blue knit sweater over designer jeans molding her shapely hips. Except for the dab of wine on her lips, she was wearing no makeup. Surprise heightened her coffee-and-cream complexion, her big brown eyes sparkling bright like diamonds and lips, parted invitingly so.

Starkly sexual melodramas suddenly filled his head, and his heart began to thud like a kettledrum in his chest. Realizing he was staring, Nat feigned a yawn.

With his hand over his mouth, he said, "Excuse me," propping himself on a stool. "Why didn't you wake me? I guess I was sleeping so hard I didn't hear Natasha wake up."

"I was just about to return her," replied Jenine. "We're all changed and fed."

Nat yawned again; this one was for real. He rubbed his face hard with his hands, as if trying to rub the sleep out. He hadn't gotten much of it last night, he recalled. A pair of brown, doe-shaped eyes, staring at him wider than usual with accusation, haunted his dreams. Nor had he allayed his concern that he would be leaving Jenine for the second time in their lives. Guilt possessed the better part of him, he thought.

"Well, I better get going," Jenine stammered. She felt awkward passing Natasha to Nat while trying not to look at him at the same time. Walking to the couch to get her coat, she said, "I'm going to be late tonight, so don't worry and don't wait up for me."

"You're going to be that late?" he asked. "What's up?"

"Band rehearsal," she replied, slipping her coat on.

"You have another competition coming up soon?" he asked.

Swinging her purse over her shoulder, she replied, "Uh, yeah."

"Well, we'll see you when we see you," he said.

"Okay," Jenine said, with a nod of her head. "Bye, Natasha," she waved.

Guiding Natasha's hand, Nat said, "Tell Jenine bye."

Trailing her exit out the back door with his gaze, Nat thought he had to shake the sensations growing like wild weeds within him.

"It's time for you to get ready for school, pumpkin," he said to Natasha. "While you're learning whatever it is they teach you at that school, I think I'll start learning the city. We may be here longer than I thought. What do you think about that?" he asked his daughter, returning to the bedroom.

The lunch hour found Jenine in her office at school. She was standing at the side of the piano, a half-eaten sandwich in her hand. With a disgusted sigh, she slapped it on the plate, folded her arms across her bosom and began pacing about the room.

Not only had her plans been changed, she couldn't write anything worth putting on paper, she fumed silently, her brows knitted in a frown. She should be at Bruce's studio this very moment, not still on campus, with two more classes to teach before the day was over.

School policy had put a pin in her plans, calling for the support of two board members before her leave of absence was finally approved. She blamed herself as much as John for the oversight that hadn't come up when she initially spoke to him. Maybe he'd known about it all along and was placating her, believing she would change her mind overnight. Or at least, in the few days it would take her to round up two people, she thought.

She had already placed a call to Robbie. More than a friend, Robbie had been her mentor and confidante since her arrival in Highland Heights.

Robbie was also her last hope to secure the leave, for she was hesitant to call Ethel Cobb, who initially hired her. She believed Ethel would side with John. After all, as founder of the school, Ethel was even more protective of its standing than anyone else. Since Robbie and Ethel were tight friends, she was hoping to get Robbie to convince Ethel to support her.

Just one more day, Jenine told herself, sitting at the piano. There was a knock on the door before she resumed play, and she turned to face it. "Come in," she said.

The door opened and Robbie walked in.

"I got a message you were looking for me," Robbie said, closing the door behind her.

"Yes," Jenine said with relief, getting to her feet. "I'm glad to see you, as always, but even more so today."

"I'm here," Robbie replied, setting her burgundy leather briefcase on the desk.

"John told you I want a leave of absence," Jenine stated.

"Yes," Robbie replied hesitantly. She smacked her lips together thoughtfully. "And he made a good case for himself."

"He's against it," Jenine said with defeat in her demeanor.

"Well, can you blame him?" Robbie replied. "You're head of the Music Department, one of his best teachers, and he's afraid you won't come back."

"That's nonsense," Jenine said.

"It doesn't change how he feels," Robbie said.

"Robbie, I need this time off," Jenine said beseechingly. "Believe me, if I didn't, I wouldn't have asked for it. I haven't been good in the classroom lately. My mind has been wandering off. My attitude is lousy. Ask any of my students," she said hugging herself.

With an intense look in her blue eyes, Robbie asked,

"Does this new attitude have anything to do with Nathaniel Padell?" She accepted his case because Jenine asked her to, but she had yet to make up her mind about him.

"No," Jenine replied emphatically. She felt like a soldier surrounded by enemies: from the outside, she faced those who would deny her her music; and inwardly the warm sensations which continually weakened her resolve every time she was around Nat. "It's all about me and my music."

"I see," Robbie replied cryptically.

"Robbie, I need your support on this," Jenine said.

"Tell me more," Robbie said, sitting behind the desk. "Why is this leave so important? And why does it have to be indefinite? That makes it difficult. The new semester just started, and not counting this last week in January, there are four months left in the school term. What are you going to do about the jazz band? And don't you have that annual competition coming up this spring in Houston at TSU? Then there's the Teacher Talent Show which everyone counts on you to coordinate."

"John really got to you, didn't he?" Jenine said with a bitter chuckle.

"He talked; I listened," Robbie replied. "You know I care about you like you're one of my own children, but this is a school-board matter and as a member, I'm expected to act in the best interest of the school. Give me something to help me act in your best interest, as well."

"Can't we just call it teacher burn-out and let it go at that?" Jenine asked.

With a half-smile on her face, Robbie looked at Jenine expectantly, her arms folded across her bosom. "Is that what it is?" she asked quietly.

"In part," Jenine replied. She eased onto the piano bench as if tired and weary. Her face collapsed into a complex set of wrinkles, pondering an explanation that Robbie could comprehend.

None of the three people she considered her friends—Gloria, Bruce or Robbie—knew everything about Jenine Jones . . . who she was, why, and what she secretly aspired to, she mused. Rather, they each knew bits and pieces of her private self—that she wrote music and used to submit her songs.

But not even Robbie, the most perceptive of the trio and the only one knowledgeable about the failed relationship with her late mother, could have fathomed the depths of the scars she'd suffered over the rejections. Against all advice and even knowing better, she had taken them personally. As if they had come from Elise Jones herself.

As a result, teaching became her panacea. As the years went by, she buried her aspirations a little deeper under mounds of excuses.

She had always worn her game face, even for Robbie, who knew her as a forthright and confident person without an ounce of insecurity. She wondered what her friend's reaction would be if she admitted she had been a coward with an overwhelming fear of failure.

Breaking the silence, Jenine said simply, "I need to devote some time to my music."

Two beats passed before Robbie spoke. "How far are you willing to take this?" she asked.

"I don't understand what you mean?"

"I mean," Robbie replied, placing her elbows on the desk, hands clasped together, "are you willing to quit your teaching position if the leave is not granted?"

Shrugging indecisively, Jenine replied, "I don't know. I hadn't thought about it in such a dramatic fashion. I never believed it would come to that."

"Start thinking about it in those terms," Robbie replied, "because I don't think you're going to get the needed support on this. Ethel called me shortly after John called her. I'm sure you were counting on me to get her approval."

With a winded sigh, Jenine replied, "Yes." Pushing herself up to her feet, she said, "So, it's come down to this. My choices are either to quit altogether or stay." Shaking her head, with an expression of bewilderment, she said, "I've worked here for eight years and I haven't missed a school day except for school-related trips. Then I ask for some time off to pursue my dreams, and the school waves a policy mandate in my face. It's not fair," she said with exasperation.

"You know the old saying," Robbie replied.

Jenine started to ask Robbie her opinion, but clamped her mouth shut, lips pressed together. She knew Robbie would counsel her only after she made a decision, not before.

"Have I been given a deadline?" she asked.

"Not as long as you're teaching while you're thinking about it," Robbie replied, her lips pursed in displeasure.

"Okay," Jenine said with confidence, knowing what she must do. Robbie was right. If she were as serious about pursuing her music, she had to be willing to take risks. "Okay. Thanks, Robbie."

With apology in her blue eyes, Robbie said, "Don't thank me. I feel as if I've let you down in a way." However, she wanted to encourage Jenine to follow her dream, but kept her counsel.

"No, you haven't," Jenine replied. "You've only made me think. As you usually do," she said, smiling through her dismay. She never believed it would come to this, she thought.

Getting to her feet, Robbie said, "Well, I guess I better be moving along."

"Wait for me," Jenine said, hurrying to retrieve her handbag from the drawer and her coat from the metal tree.

"Where are you going?"

"I suddenly feel sick," Jenine replied. "I think I'll start using some of those days I've accrued." Opening the door, "After you."

Robbie winked at Jenine before preceding her out the room.

Sitting at a back table in the downtown diner, Nat stared absently beyond the glass window. The words "Scotty's Corner" etched in bold red letters, obstructed his view.

But there wasn't much to see, he thought with amusement stretching his mouth in a smile. Still, he was more pleased by what he didn't see. He took a bite of his greasy hamburger.

After dropping Natasha off at the daycare, he thought he would return to Jenine's to practice his music. However, he gave in to a stronger voice, an anxious soul that was teeming with unleashed energy, and he had taken a driving tour of the city.

There were none of the disfigurements of urbanization. Instead, a country feeling prevailed, from the endless stretch of white-blue sky to the picture-postcard-looking town with its unique stone and wood buildings. Clean, wide paved streets with bigger sidewalks; no buildings over ten stories high. The lone four-star restaurant was located in the hotel, also the tallest building in town. The hotel also had a gym where Nat managed to wangle a couple of complimentary future visits at his convenience.

Highland did have a mall, however, he recalled with a musing chuckle. It had an old-time pharmacy with a soda fountain; several fashionable boutiques, a music shop, and a department store that sold everything from furniture to lawn mowers. The store did a booming mail-order business.

In addition to serving food, Scotty, the diner owner, as well as waiter, cook and washer, had also served up quite a wealth of information about Highland Heights.

The town boasted a population of less than nine thousand people. A fourth were either students or employees of the Highland Heights Academies. Though public, they were run like private institutions. Another eighth of the populace represented the professions in law, medicine and auto mechanics. They were the pool from which city council aldermen and women were selected. A larger number of the residents were die-hard Texans who had moved from metropolitan areas to escape the pollutants of city life.

The biggest crimes demanding the attention of the three-man sheriff's department were fast-driving teenagers who had nothing else to do on the weekends except go to a movie or the skating rink. The last major crime was committed over ten years ago when a woman tried to leave her husband, and he shot her in the foot. She left anyway, according to Scotty.

There was no airport, except for a private landing strip for those with the money to support expensive recreational flying or the call of out-of-town business. He would have to have his drums bused into town.

He recalled teasing Jenine about small town, Texas. But, all in all, Highland Heights was not a bad place to live.

"Hey, Nat, how you doing?" Scotty called from the window behind the counter. "Need some more coffee?"

"No, I'm fine Scotty, thanks," Nat replied, thinking the people weren't so bad, either.

*   *   *

With the key Bruce had given her last night, Jenine let herself through a side door into the garage-turned-studio behind his house.

After signing herself out at school, she had come straight here. Although this was her second visit, she was still amazed by the amount and quality of the equipment Bruce had amassed.

The walls, ceiling and elevated floor were insulated, providing a near-perfect acoustical studio for recording. The control room, sealed off from the actual studio, was not much bigger than a regular-sized closet, but the room contained state-of-the art signal processing equipment mounted in racks from the ceiling to the floor. Twin, gray-encased monitors were carefully placed on each side of the twenty-four channel mixing console.

Sauntering into the actual studio, on the other side of the thick-plated glass, Jenine was careful not to trip over the long, thick black cables on the floor that ran to the control room. She took a cursory look at the microphones of all sizes and the drum set, but was heading straight for the black baby grand piano.

Setting her briefcase on the floor, she sat before the piano and played a riff from one end of the keyboard to the other.

"Perfect," she exclaimed, her hands together in delight.

Suddenly assailed by a bittersweet sensation, Jenine stared absently at the keyboard. When Nat left, maybe her despair would be assuaged here, and she could create new dreams.

Redirecting her thoughts, Jenine pulled sheets of music from the briefcase and set out to work harder than she'd ever worked before.

Chapter Six

Jenine and Natasha were sitting on a colorful patchwork quilt on the floor in the den, surrounded by an assortment of toys. Feeling lethargic, as if the life had been siphoned out of her body by a suction pump, she watched Natasha chatting delightfully in her baby tongue, trying to master control over the toys. Jenine had no inclination to interfere, but retrieved the foam ball that Natasha tossed away unintentionally.

For more than a week now, she had fastidiously followed a pattern she was confident met her requirements for more music and less contact with Nat. However, the old saying, "out of sight, out of mind," didn't work as effectively as she'd first hoped, she thought, dutifully putting a ball within Natasha's reach. Even while she was lost in her playing, he inevitably crept into her mind. And her music, she thought, squirming uncomfortably.

Nevertheless, she stuck to that schedule, rising early to dress and spend time with Natasha over breakfast. Every morning she called in sick to the school, then dashed off to the studio until Bruce arrived with dinner, followed by rehearsals lasting late into the night. When she returned home, Nat and Natasha were usually asleep. Although there were a couple of times when they weren't at home.

Nat never failed to leave a note, informing her of their whereabouts, usually at Robbie's playing Nintendo.

Sniffing pitifully, on the verge of tears, Natasha captured Jenine's attention. Pulling Natasha in her lap, Jenine said, "You had enough of these hard-to-manage toys?"

Kissing Natasha on the head, Jenine held the baby close to her and began stroking her back. "You got up too early, huh? I know the feeling." Natasha popped her little head up, squirming in protest to be released. "All right," Jenine said, setting her down. "Off you go."

Glancing at Natasha with a maternal glow in her eyes, Jenine rested her head against the couch. She could tell the baby was sleepy, but was fighting it. Like she had been fighting her attraction to Nat, she thought with the rueful acceptance of a terrible knowledge.

She simply must not cave in to daring thoughts and yearning sensations. Both were fantastic to dream about, but it was fatal to think about their becoming a reality.

His departure—unlike his arrival—was expected, she thought. With a despondent glaze falling over her eyes, she reminded herself that the feeling he retained for Annette was another concern she shouldn't forget. Annette was the mother of his child, searing a permanent bond between them. But first, Annette had been his soulmate.

Assailed by twinges of envy, Jenine shuddered with humiliation. She had to force herself to get actively involved with Natasha.

Holding up the yellow foam toy, she said, "This is a duck. Duck. Can you say duck?"

The rainbow-colored square followed, preceding the brown bear. But the ruse wasn't entirely successful. Every few seconds, Jenine caught herself glancing toward the entry. She wondered what Nat was doing. Though he usually gave them this time together alone, it was mighty quiet on the other side of the house.

"Ball," Jenine said, holding up the soft red toy dutifully. She clapped her hands in praise when Natasha grabbed the ball. "Good girl!"

Natasha laughed, but it was more a prelude to tears than happiness for her achievement. She stuck the ball in her mouth before rubbing it across her eyes and began to cry.

"Oh, come on baby," Jenine cooed sympathetically, cuddling Natasha next to her bosom. Getting the bottle off the coffee table, she inserted it in the child's mouth. "You're sleepy. Let's see if this will help."

Standing in the doorway unnoticed, Nat stared at his child cradled in Jenine's arms. The sight opened the door to a rush of emotions he'd tried to bury.

Except for perfunctory exchanges, he and Jenine had barely spoken to each other all week. It had caused mixed feelings in him. He was at once relieved by her absence, while longing for her presence. The latter gripped him now.

There was no basis for him to feel the way he felt— proud and protective like the father he was, but the husband he wasn't. He couldn't deny the feelings were real. Real and building with frightening intensity. He felt he would burst with them because he couldn't, didn't dare, share them.

It had been that way fifteen years ago, he mused, and his memories opened like a curtain ripping apart.

The Padell home used to be the hang-out for Nat and his friends, a practice that continued even after he started college and was living on campus. They lived in a sprawling modern home right off MacGregor Bayou. The house was big enough to host the impromptu jam sessions that most visits evolved into, without disturbing his parents, who made everybody feel welcome.

The last of the Padell children living in town, he went home regularly, often inviting band members for some home cooking. Even a sandwich at home tasted better than the food served in the dormitory.

So his mother hadn't been surprised when he brought Jenine home. As a matter of fact, she seemed to enjoy having Jenine over. He didn't know what it was that made Jenine special to his mom; he just accepted it without question.

About the fourth or fifth time he had taken Jenine home, his mother pulled him off to her bedroom. "What's the matter, mama?"

They were standing in the invisible divider that separated the sleeping from the sitting area in the large room. The furnishings were fairly new; his mother had redecorated after his father died two years before. But the room still retained its warm and inviting feel, with a floral smell to go with the floral pattern in the carpet.

"You know I like Jenine," Dorothy Padell said. "She's a sweet girl. But she's just that, a girl, Nat."

"Yeah, I know," he had replied. Though he didn't show it, he was curious about where this conversation was going. "We just dropped in to get a bite. I'm broke," opening his empty pockets inside out.

"I don't care about you coming home to eat," she had said, waving aside that concern. "I do care about that girl's feelings and what I want to know," she continued without pausing to take a breath, "is whether you do, too. Or is this just one of those hormone things?"

"Mama, you know I'm too old for that," he said with

indignation in his voice. "I like Jenine. A lot. You don't have to worry. She's not like the others."

"She's tender, Nat," Dorothy added as if he hadn't already been aware of that fact. "Don't you hurt that girl, do you hear me?"

"I hear you, mama," he replied. "And I have no intentions of hurting her. She could be the one." He winked at her with teasing.

"I said she was tender, not stupid," his mother had quipped. But she had seemed satisfied with his intentions. "I got half a smoked turkey out in the freezer. Y'all can thaw it out and make some sandwiches if you want."

Nat inhaled deeply through his nostrils, the past receding to its place, his thoughts to the present. He had answered his mother's concern honestly, he mused. The answer held true today. Hurting Jenine was the last thing he intended.

He hadn't realized the truth of his declaration until he had been forced to say the words aloud. Jenine had never demanded anything from him.

While he couldn't have listed specific qualities accounting for his feelings for her, they indeed had been different from those he felt toward other women he dated. He had only known she had to be special to him: they only kissed and held hands. He had courted her slowly as if composing a sentimental ballad that would never lose its charm.

Maybe that what was it was. She hadn't been a woman in the sense of knowing the score. Her innocence was real, and she was all the more alluring because of it.

Besides, he was quite familiar with her mother's belief that he was after one thing. It made him all the more determined to prove her wrong, so he never pressured Jenine to assuage the ache in his loins that grew proportionately with his growing want of her.

In one of those short bouts of disconnected thoughts, he

pondered the possibility that Natasha was missing something by not having a mother, wondering about her future without a mother to guide her—and whether Natasha, at her young age, cared about such things as emotional security. He was concerned about the effect it could have on her when they left, and she no longer had Jenine.

With his usual arrogance, he had believed at one time he was enough family for her, he thought, drawing in his lips. But witnessing the growing bond between Natasha and Jenine was forcing him to alter his views on parenting.

Quelling all thoughts about a time not yet come, Nat pasted the semblance of cheerfulness on his face and made his presence known.

"Why don't you girls go back to bed?" he suggested in a humor-lined voice.

Lifting her head, Jenine softened her dark brown eyes at the sight of him, and his eyes drooped sensuously at the corners. Her gaze tracked his approach, and a tremor of desire warmed her to the bone as he sank in the nearby chair, the tangy scent of his cologne forming a halo over her. She silently sucked the air in her dry throat and drew her lips together in a tight smile.

"We thought you were still asleep," she said. Masking her nervousness, she looked down at the bundle in her arms and a whole new set of feelings washed over her. Noticing the power of her grip around the bottle, she schooled herself to relax.

"I wish," he replied with a soft chuckle.

Gently pulling the bottle nipple from Natasha's mouth, Jenine said, "She finally gave in."

Leaning over to take the bottle, Nat replied, "Knowing Miss Nosy, I bet she put up a good fight." He held the bottle in his hands momentarily, just staring down at his daughter, the corners of his mouth tilted up in a small smile.

"Yes, she did."

Jenine positioned Natasha on her shoulder. Patting the baby on the back, she risked a glance at Nat. The chair was a throne to his majestic presence—sitting there, leather jacket opened to reveal the powder blue turtleneck tucked in the waistline of camel slacks; knees apart, taking up lots of space. He caught her roving gaze, and her heart flip-flopped in her chest. She ducked her head into Natasha's warm body, shivering in memory of his oblique, half-shy look. Like a cat coveting the canary, she thought.

With his arms outstretched, Nat said, "Here, let me take her." He put Natasha on a corner of the quilt, stroking her until she resettled in sleep, then scooted back in the chair.

Jenine began to grow uncomfortable under his toneless stare. Realizing for the first time that he was dressed to go out, she felt a creeping uneasiness at the bottom of her heart. Robbie must have some news about the case, she thought, believing Nat was going to meet with the attorney. She was dressed in her usual, around-the-house, worn-out gray sweats, and a big hole just above her left knee revealed a portion of her desire-hot flesh. She certainly presented no inducement for him to stay, she mused before chiding herself for inviting trouble by mere foolish thinking.

Because she could take the lingering silence no longer, Jenine asked the question whose answer she dreaded. "Has the investigator come up with anything?"

"No," he replied. His brows drew downward in a frown. "Nothing yet," with a weary sigh.

Though she was measurably pleased by his lack of news, Jenine wondered if she should feel guilty for the sense of relief that came over her. Fingering the hole in the sweat pants, she looked up at him in a furtive glance.

"This waiting must be driving you crazy," she said, as if making amends for feeling as if she had been given a bonus.

"It is," he replied, picking at an invisible piece of lint on his slacks. "But Robbie assures me these things take time." He fell silent for a moment before he spoke again. "I hope we're not getting on your nerves too badly."

Unable to think of a suitable reply, Jenine merely smiled ambiguously, leaving the interpretation to his discretion. She lowered her lids so that she could see out, but he couldn't see in. If he could, he would probably pack right now and run as fast and as far away from her unrequited sensibilities as he could get.

"You're mighty quiet, what are you thinking about?" he asked.

"Oh, nothing in particular," she replied.

"Anything interesting happen at school this week?"

Knowing Nat assumed she had been going to school every day and that the late rehearsals were with the Academy's jazz band, Jenine feared choking on the lie. She wet her lips with her tongue, clearing her throat.

"The usual," she replied, gazing at Natasha. Despite the guilt growing like a sore within her, she had no intention of telling him differently. At least, not now. When the time was right, she told herself, though she had no idea when or if that time would ever come.

Nat palmed his thighs before he spoke. "Jenine? You know, I've been thinking." He reached out to grab her foot playfully.

The innocent touch unfurled streamers of sensations in Jenine, causing her to sip air in a quick breath. There was something intimate about his touching her foot, and her uneasiness grew.

Nat attended her foot with his gaze, then turned it over in his hands to examine both sides, the lines, the textures. Natasha's feet would be bigger than hers one day, he thought. He left it at that.

Flustered by the extended contact, Jenine demanded, "What are you doing?" in a hands-on-her-hip tone, forcing a playful look on her face to hide the urge to know his touch on more places than her foot.

Though tempted to maintain his possession, Nat released her foot, gently setting it back on the floor. It was time to direct his attention to the present.

"I was just thinking," he said more confidently than before.

Folding her foot close to her, Jenine cut him off. "When are you going to realize Natasha and I are the smart ones around here?"

"Well, smarty, why don't you tell me what I've been thinking?" he said.

"Uh, let's see, what would your feeble mind come up with?" she said, a finger poked in the indentation of an active dimple on her face. And then she made the mistake of looking up into his visage, his olive-brown eyes were humorous and tender, and it caused an oddly primitive warning to sound in her brain. Suddenly, the game was no longer fun, for it required a lightheartedness she no longer felt.

"You've been thinking you can hardly wait to leave this place and get back to your music," she said in a rush.

"That's been on my mind, but that's not it," he said at last, then fell silent before adding, "I think I'm beginning to like it. The town, I mean."

Jenine didn't realize she had been holding her breath until her heart began to beat so hard in her chest she had to regulate the air she drew into her lungs. Feeling a declaration of war with her hardheaded heart not to read anything else into his behavior, Jenine told herself he was just making polite conversation.

"Good schools—you know all your neighbors—and there's no crime to speak of," he continued. "It's a good place to raise children."

Jenine couldn't stand it any longer, wondering where this conversation was going. Her stomach churned from the internal struggle between a pining for her dream to come true and despondency because reality demanded it. Believing that freedom came with knowing, she asked as casually as she could manage, "Nat, what are you trying to say?"

Nat knew the idea within him was not acceptable. But that was not strong enough reason to uproot the seed of his attraction to her that grew a little more with each passing day. He was like a piece of iron, incapable of escaping the magnetic power she possessed.

"Nat?" she prodded.

He looked at her intently, missing nothing, not even the tenuous cast of anticipation in her eyes. She had no idea how engaging he found her; not just on the surface, but on the inside, as well. But he had no promises for a future, bright or otherwise, to give, he reminded himself with frustration clouding his expression. Hell, he couldn't make any promises to himself right now. He averted his head to look up at the ceiling, so that she would not see the wounded look that tore from inside him.

"I don't know, Jenine," he said at last, pushing himself to the edge of the chair. She made it so easy for him to forget why he had come. Yet, his conscience demanded that the confession remain locked inside him. "Just wishful thinking I guess," he said on a sigh, angling his body to look her squarely in the face.

"Are you sure?" she queried. "If you have something to say, just say it."

"I wish," he started as if testing the idea, before cutting off the words which reflected an idle indulgence.

"You don't owe me anything, Nat. All I ask is that you be honest with me," she said calmly, with no lighting of her eyes, no smile of tenderness. Though she felt let down that he apparently was not about to favor her secret desires with the words she wanted to hear, she refused to allow any misplaced sense of gratitude on his part to further complicate their delicate situation.

"That's all," she added softly with sincerity rather than disappointment on her countenance.

Nat hesitated, measuring her for a moment. "You know, there have been a couple of times when I felt I didn't know you at all."

Jenine smiled wordlessly before she spoke. "Did you want to, Nat?" She raised her knees up to her chin and wrapped her arms around her legs. "Did you want to know the woman I've become, or were you more comfortable with the eighteen-year-old kid you remembered?"

"Oh, the eighteen-year-old kid I remembered was easier for me to deal with," he said with a melancholy chuckle, getting up to stand in front of the stereo unit.

"Because she was naive," Jenine retorted with self-derision for the starry eyed teenager she had been.

"No, it wasn't because of that," he denied quickly. "Even then it wasn't easy for me," gazing directly into her eyes, "despite what your mother told you."

Jenine couldn't argue, for he spoke the truth. Her mother hated Nat, not personally, but in general. He was a man, a person whom Jenine could lose her mind over and become helplessly dependent upon.

"Leaving you was more frightening than striking out for New York on my own," he admitted in a tone of fresh feeling.

"Then why did you leave me?" she demanded, unable to keep the fifteen-year-old hurt from creeping into her voice.

"I believe you already know the answer to that," he replied and reached out to take her hand in his. She nodded solemnly. "You were too young, and I wasn't emotionally or financially stable enough to offer you anything but grief."

"And now? Do you feel you know the woman?" she asked before she could stop herself. The question out, she could only hope she didn't sound as if she was begging.

"I'm proud of the woman," he replied, editing out how lately she's been in his every waking thought and how he felt she was filling an emptiness in his life he barely realized existed. "I have a lot of respect for her. I'm not sure I understand her all the time," he said on a lighter note, "but that's nature's heavily guarded secret."

With her mouth pressed together and eyes deliberately expressionless, Jenine nodded. Inside, a pain squeezed her heart.

"She's a caring person, a good friend to have. Yes. I like her," he said softly. Suddenly, in a brisk, businesslike manner, he said, "I need to run out for a while." Realizing how curt he sounded, he modulated his tone and expression. "That is, if you don't have something to do and can keep Natasha."

Gazing with a sweet musing look at the sleeping baby, Jenine replied, "No problem."

"I won't be long," he said, feeling anxious, yet reluctant to leave.

"That's fine, Nat," she said in a light voice. Staring absently at the hole in her pants, she didn't see creamy brown flesh, but an empty void.

* * *

With her hands under her chin and elbows on the counter, Jenine was perched on a stool in the kitchen. Robbie, who arrived shortly after Nat left, was in the kitchen making herself a cup of coffee.

"I thought I would have heard from you before now," Robbie said, her back to Jenine.

Jenine smiled at the mildly scolding tone in Robbie's voice. Dressed in a plum-colored corduroy jumpsuit and her hair in a ponytail at the nape of her neck, Robbie looked far younger than a mother of four grown children.

Facing Jenine, Robbie asked, "What did you decide to do?"

"As far as resigning is concerned, I've made no decision one way or the other yet. So far, I've only been calling in sick. I have six weeks' worth of those excuses left," she chuckled. "I might as well get paid until I either secure another source of income or figure out how to do both, write and teach."

"You know John is not fooled," Robbie said, stirring sugar in her cup of coffee.

Shrugging, Jenine said, "I know. But I don't care. There's nothing he can do about it at this point. I went back and read the policy manual," she added smugly.

Blowing over the hot dark brew, Robbie sauntered into the den, leaving Jenine to follow. She sat on a chair opposite the couch where Jenine plopped down.

"How are things working out so far?" Robbie asked. "Are you satisfied?"

Burying her fingers in her hair, Jenine replied laughingly, "So much so it scares me." With melancholy overshadowing her features, she said, "I had forgotten how gratifying it is to have the time to devote to writing, listening to music by other writers for my own benefit and not to rework a program for the kids to perform."

"Have you decided on your next move as far as your

music is concerned?" Robbie asked, taking a careful sip of coffee.

"I have two pieces in particular I plan to do something within the next week or two," Jenine replied. Rising to her feet, "One piece in particular, I'm thinking about sending to a singer who I think could really do justice to it." Laughing at herself, "Listen to me. I sound as if my word carries some weight. But anyway, that's what I plan to do. If it's not wanted, then . . ."

"Unscrew your face, it's not becoming," Robbie said in her motherly tone.

Playfully wrinkling her nose, Jenine sank into the couch, swinging her legs over the end.

Eyeing Jenine over the rim of the cup, "Where's Nat?"

"He had to go out," Jenine replied. "Did you need to see him? He said he wouldn't be long."

"I have some papers for him to sign, but I can just leave them," Robbie replied. "How are you two getting along?"

Reading more than casual interest into the question, Jenine pondered her reply. Casually speaking, she mused, they got along fine considering they were hardly ever alone together for any length of time. Maybe Robbie knew something she didn't know.

Slowly, Jenine sat up prim and proper-like, hands in her lap, eyes narrowed suspiciously. "I know you. You don't do or say anything without a motive."

With a half-smile lifting her brows a fraction, Robbie replied, "I'm not that predictable, but I am concerned about you. Now answer the question."

Jenine got up, busying herself picking toys off the floor. "Why wouldn't we get along?"

"Are you under a strain here?" Robbie continued to pry, in a nonthreatening tone.

"No," Jenine replied. With an armload of toys, "Why

would you think that?" Setting the toys in a neat pile in a corner of the couch, she searched the room for something else to do.

"Because every time I speak with Nat and ask how you're doing, I get, 'I guess she's okay. Haven't seen too much of her lately.' Then I have to come all the way over here to see for myself because you haven't called me. That's not like you."

Jenine looked apologetic. "I'm sorry. I've just gotten so involved with my music that I guess I have been acting a little out of character."

"You're acting exactly in character for somebody on the run," Robbie quipped.

Feeling duly trapped, Jenine dropped onto the couch. "I don't know, Robbie," she said, with a gesture of her hands mimicking her bemused tone.

"You have a tendency to do that when you're troubled about something," Robbie added knowingly. "You were the same way before the trip to California—very active, yet distant and preoccupied. I thought you just had the jitters about the competition. But you come back home, triumphant and equally discontented. At least I know why now," drinking her coffee. "What I can't understand is why you waited so long before doing something about it."

Jenine looked at Robbie stunned by her analysis.

"Thought I hadn't put two and two together?" Robbie replied. "It wasn't too difficult to figure out where you got some of your notions from. Anything short of perfection means failure—and independence is supreme. I'm a mother, too, remember? My kids love telling me that my expectations of them are unreal. It must be a mother thing," she said, smiling in her cup as she took another sip of coffee.

Jenine chuckled.

The smile waned from Robbie's face as she looked at

Jenine from a sidelong speculative gaze. "And I'm also wondering," she said slowly, as if maneuvering a minefield, "what role Nat played in this change."

"None," Jenine replied hastily, but her reply lacked the ring of certainty. She fell silent and thoughtful. It was a little late for denials of any sort, she told herself. "A little bit," she conceded, facing Robbie headlong. With her lips in a self-derisive twist, she said, "To your first question, I guess I was just scared."

Robbie nodded knowingly.

"Even before he arrived, I was feeling the pangs of dissatisfaction," Jenine said softly. With her brows drawn in an agonized expression, "Then Nat showed up and I . . ." Her voice wavered to silence. She remembered the adventurous anticipation they'd had in youth, an obsessive clamor for adulthood.

Guessing what Jenine didn't say, Robbie twitched imperceptibly. "I know," she said as if speaking to herself. "Sometimes I find myself recalling the follies of my own youth. Some were good, but we generally drum up the bad memories and make them worse, or better than they actually were. I'm just glad it's all behind me," she said, sipping her coffee.

With a melancholy glaze over her eyes, Jenine said, "I'm just trying to catch up with my own plans." Looking at Robbie with a lopsided smile, she added, "Not compete with his success."

"So his coming has been a good thing for you," Robbie surmised.

Before Jenine could reply, the doorbell rang. Looking at the time on her wrist, "I wonder who that could be," she wondered aloud with a curious expression on her face.

"Nat?" Robbie offered speculatively.

"No. He has a key," Jenine replied. "I'll be right back,"

she said, strolling from the room. She returned shortly with Bruce as Robbie was getting into her coat.

"Hi, Mrs. Franks," Bruce said.

"Hello, Mr. Richards," Robbie replied.

"You don't have to leave on my account," he said, with a chuckle. "It won't take long for Jenine to break my heart."

"If she hadn't broken it yet, I doubt that day will ever come," Robbie quipped. She embraced Jenine and said, "We'll talk another time."

"Okay," Jenine replied, shaking her head.

"I'll see myself out," Robbie said. "Take care."

With Robbie gone, Jenine turned to Bruce, arms folded across her chest. "Okay, what's so urgent you couldn't call?"

Rubbing his hands together with relish, he replied, "We got a gig."

"A gig?" Jenine echoed, dropping her hands.

"Yeah, you know, a performance," he said.

"Where? When?"

"At Pirates," he replied. With his features contorted in a grimace, "Tonight." He held his breath.

"Oh no," Jenine said, gesturing with her hands. "I never agreed to that. I'm just filling in until you can find a permanent pianist, and helping you develop the sound for the group."

With his hands together in a praying position, Bruce said, "Please, please, pretty please."

"Aw, Bruce," Jenine moaned. "I don't know," she said hesitantly, a forefinger in her mouth.

Noticing the indecision on her face, Bruce looked at her in a serious headlong stare and took her hands in his. "This opportunity is not going to come our way again," he said in a near whisper.

His words reached Jenine, and she nodded with resigned agreement.

"Please don't turn your back on us now. If you find you really don't like it, I'll find somebody else as fast as I can. Though heaven knows from where. But please give it a chance," he said with pleading in his voice.

"Hello," Nat said from the doorway.

Chapter Seven

"Nat," Jenine exclaimed in a whisper.

Though she was innocent of any crime, she certainly felt guilty. With her pulse rocketing to outer-space limits, she massaged her hands: Bruce had released them so abruptly they hurt. Then conscious of the implications of the gesture, she put them behind her back.

Drawing a calming breath, although her heartbeat refused to return to earth, Jenine said as casually as she could muster, "I didn't hear you come in."

"That would seem apparent," Nat replied.

Caught off guard by a hint of censure in his tone, Jenine turned her head with a jerk, her eyes seeking him in a headlong stare. His flat, unspeaking eyes prolonged the moment, and the only knowledge she gained was an increased awareness of his masculine appeal. Flicking her tongue over her lips, she thought she must be imagining things and cast aside her suspicion. She felt Bruce's wide wary gaze on her, reminding her of the social custom she had yet to perform.

Stepping forward to make the introduction, she said, "Nat, I want you to meet Bruce Richards. Bruce, this is Nathaniel Padell, my house guest."

"Nat," Bruce said manly. "Jenine and I are co-workers

at the Academy," he added for safe measure, thinking, She should have warned me about her jealous lover. "It's a pleasure."

So this was the reason for the late-night rehearsals, Nat thought, with a bitterness stirring inside him. Taking inventory of the stranger he caught touching Jenine, his expression carefully devoid of emotion, he silently snarled his disapproval. Shrugging in thought, he guessed women might find pretty-faced men with laughing eyes attractive. Of sturdy build, Richards was average height for a man, but not much taller than Jenine.

Watching the exchange, Jenine felt embarrassment, annoyance and confusion collide into one another inside her. She was also pissed, watching Nat behaving rudely. Finally, he accepted Bruce's hand in a grudging and limp handshake, which riled her a few more percentage points.

With his expression as deadpan as his voice, Nat replied, "Bruce."

Dropping the younger man's hand, Nat dismissed Bruce as handily as he greeted him to stare at Jenine. The air between them was charged with electrical sparks. Not all were powered by the vexatious exchange.

Shoring up disinterest to his countenance, Nat casually stuck his hands in the pockets of his jacket. A piece of advice was trying to forge its way through the foggy mist of his brain, but he couldn't discern it, wondering what Jenine saw in this shrimp of a man. She was fuming, he noted. Her brown eyes were shooting daggers at him and her posture was stiff, defensive; she was spoiling for a fight.

With dislike writhing in his stomach like a dinosaurian snake, he wanted to give it to her. He felt another sensation coursing through him. Its name was jealousy.

Jenine must really like this guy. A lot, he thought. He was out of line and knew it.

"Where's Natasha?" he asked in a tone harsher than he intended.

"She's asleep," replied Jenine. She didn't try to bridle the anger in her voice. She didn't know what had set Nat off. Nor did she care at this moment. "I put her in bed," as if daring him to challenge the wisdom of her decision.

"Well, I need to run out again," he said, backing up to leave as he spoke. He had to hurry and get away before he made a complete fool of himself. "But you don't have to worry about it, I'll take her with me."

"Nat, you don't have to . . . ," started Jenine. He was gone before she finished lamely, ". . . wake her up."

As soon as she got rid of Bruce, she was going to give him a piece of her mind. How dare he treat her guest like that? she fumed silently.

"Hm," Bruce muttered curiously. His gaze shifted from the empty entry to Jenine, watching her shoulders rise and fall with deep breathing. He waited for the peeved frown to melt from her expression before he spoke. With a disappointed shrug, he said, "I guess this means I can count you out tonight, huh?"

For a second, Jenine stared at him with an absent look in her eyes before realizing he had spoken. "Wait a minute," she said.

It suddenly occurred to her that Nat's foul mood could be attributed to some bad news he'd gotten about his father-in-law. He had to have run into Robbie. Maybe she gave him some disturbing news that she couldn't tell Jenine because of client confidentiality.

Why couldn't he just say he needed to talk to her, she wondered. Forgetting all about Bruce, she stalked off in the path Nat had taken.

"Jenine," Bruce called louder than normal, halting her

exit. With a half-smile wobbling on his mouth and regret in his eyes, he said, "Let me call you later."

"No," she said firmly. Pointing a commanding finger, "Just wait here," then marched off. Rounding the corner into the hallway, she silently cursed the small minds of men, namely the proud one she found stuffing diapers in the baby bag when she got to the bedroom.

"Nat, do you need to talk to me about something?" she asked, with some of the irritation she felt in her voice.

Shaking his head, his back to her, he replied succinctly, "No."

"Are you sure?"

Nat shot her a penetrating look over his shoulder. A shadow of annoyance crossed his expression, then wordlessly he resumed his task.

With her brows bunched together in a frown, Jenine heaved a frustrated sigh. "Then what is your problem?" she said in a three-finger-snap and head-roll tone of voice.

"I don't have a problem," he replied.

Irked by his cool, aloof manner, Jenine walked around to stand inches in front of him. "You were rude to my guest." She shoved the accusation at him.

"Did I hurt the teacher's feelings?" he said in a light saccharine tone, lacking in sincerity and full of mocking.

Seething with anger, her body trembled with the emotion. Not a word to express it came to her mind, so she glowered at him speechless. Clenching and unclenching her hands at her sides, she wanted to slap that smug, condescending look off his handsome face.

Reading her thoughts, Nat warned, "Don't try it."

Rising to the challenge, she snapped, "That's right, resort to violence when you can't communicate." Nat shot her a withering look, but she didn't falter, physically or in temper. Snatching the diaper from his hand, she shouted, "Damn it. I want to know what's wrong with you."

Grabbing a baby blanket from the table, he walked around her to the baby bed where Natasha was sleeping soundly. "Go entertain your company, Jenine."

His response was full of impatience, weary with the subject, but Jenine ignored the advice. She felt uncharacteristically driven to get to the truth and clear the air.

"A simple explanation will do," she said, her hands spread wide as if expecting him to put reasons in them. "And why are you going to wake this baby, Nat? It doesn't make sense."

"She's my baby," he retorted in cold sarcasm. "I do what I damn well please as far as she's concerned." He regretted the words as soon as they were out, but it was too late to take them back.

Scooping Natasha onto the blanket, Nat folded it around her. The baby didn't stir. Neither did Jenine.

Shock and fury yielded to a hurting so deep, she felt bereft and desolate. Her heart squeezed in anguish as she realized at last that her energies were wasted against his proud, granite stand. With tears beyond pain threatening to fall, she bit her lip until it throbbed like her pulse: But she refused to let him see the results of the malignant insult.

"Fine." She spat out the word contemptuously, then stormed from the bedroom.

In the hallway, Jenine drew a deep breath and wiped away the tiny drops of water forming in the corners of her eyes. She deserved what she got for her troubles, she scolded herself. Before reaching the den where Bruce was standing in front of her stereo reading an album cover, she had imposed an iron control over herself.

"What time should I be at the club?" she asked.

Startled, Bruce jumped. With his wits returning, he

stared with open-mouthed astonishment, wondering if he had heard right.

Somewhere between the bedroom and here, Jenine made the snap decision. Watching Bruce staring all agog at her, she felt a momentary bout of panic and folded her bottom lip in her mouth.

"Don't tease me, Jenine," Bruce said.

It was too late to back out. It was too late for a lot of things, she thought, her heart quivering in her bosom.

"What time?" she pressed with a nervous smile.

"Between five-thirty and six," he replied in a rush as if expecting her to change her mind.

"Fine," she said. "What are we doing?"

"Well, uh," Bruce hedged, "I was hoping we could make some selections while I'm here, but I guess that's not possible now."

"It's now or never," she replied. "Everything's in my study," she said, walking off. Reaching the opening, she stopped and turned to face Bruce who hadn't moved. "Are you coming or not?" she asked with exasperation in her tone.

Looking at her with a half-wary, half-amused expression, he replied, "Are you sure it's safe?"

They heard the front door slam shut.

Jenine wanted only to run off to her room and indulge the misery enshrouding her like a steel weight. Instead, she replied, "It's safe."

"Minister, I think we're on the right trail," the tall, slender Bede Ndakwa said into the phone as he paced the floor in the small space between the double beds in the hotel room at the Hyatt Regency in downtown Houston.

Listening to the minister lecture him on taking too long to get in touch, he glanced across the room to his fat companion Mubari, a man of wide proportions, downing a can of beer. Turning his nose up disgust, he grunted an affirmative sound into the phone. "Yes, Minister."

Holding the receiver to his ear with his shoulder, Bede scribbled the number he was given on the pad of white paper on the lamp table. The hotel's name was etched in black shiny lettering across the top.

"Yes, Minister," he replied to whether they were close to finding the minister's son-in-law and grandbaby. Though he had no idea whether they had a line on their quarry or not, it wasn't advisable to tell that to Minister Cissoko. The man was not the best of employers, but the money was sufficient and would finance his law-school education the next term.

"No, we've only been in Houston a few hours." That, too, was a lie, for they had been in the city for several days, but the minister didn't need to know otherwise.

Houston was a surprise to them. Filled with movie versions of the Good Old West, they expected to find vast undeveloped land and men on horseback. They had seen both, but neither matched their images. The city was typically metropolitan and sprawled all over the place, with as many bayous as tall skyscraping buildings; people from a wide host of ethnic backgrounds, even some of his kinsmen; and cars as thick as a colony of ants, idling in long lines of traffic.

Stifling a chuckle, he recalled how their first view of the city came after driving around Loop 610 twice before realizing they were merely going in a circle. At least, the winter temperature was mild, matching what they were accustomed to back home.

"Yes, we've placed one call already to his mother, but there was no answer," he replied into the phone. "We're getting ready to go by her home."

Thanks to the friendly people they met, the Padell

family home was easy to find. In a well-to-do neighborhood on a street called North MacGregor, it was adjacent to a bayou and running trail. Pretending to be joggers, he and Mubari had been able to keep a vigil on the comings and goings at the house. There had been no activity, but Mubari needed the exercise, he thought, casting an amused glance at his companion.

"Yes, Minister, we'll keep you posted. No, Minister, we will not fail you."

Holding the hotel stationery pad, Bede stared at the phone numbers he had written down, each fronted by a different area code. The minister was about to embark on a six-city tour, promoting the educational exchange program between Nubacush and U.S. schools.

Finally, Minister Cissoko was doing the work he had been assigned to do, Bede thought sarcastically. Tossing the pad on the lamp table, he mused that Houston was possibly his and Mubari's last stop in the state. Maybe their last job for the minister from Nubacush as well.

With his mouth twisted sourly, he said, "Mubari," then exhaled a lengthy breath, "there has to be a better way to earn a living in America."

"Can we go to dinner, now? I'm starved," Mubari replied.

Jenine's eyes rested briefly on each of the seven band members crammed in the long, rectangular-shaped dressing room of Pirates, the restaurant turned club where they were soon to perform. With her back pressed against the wall, sitting on a wooden bench, she smiled as the saying about musicians came to mind.

Bass players were laid back. That had almost been true of Paul Gardner. Being the father of four daughters may have accounted for some of his ease, she thought with a chuckle.

Drummers were wild and crazy; the description fit Clarence Case to a T. *Horn players were cocky*, and Bruce made that statement a scientific fact. The saying was doubly true for Josh Taper who played saxophones and flute. Guitarist Tony Maupin was a classic egotist, while on the other end of the scale was the shy Clifton Segaro. A closet jazz lover and classical-music teacher at the Academy, Clifton played the electric violin.

And last but not least, she came to herself where the word was that *pianists were assholes*. With a soft smile brightening her features, she recalled that each of them had had a moment during rehearsals where the descriptions fit like a pair of comfortable shoes. And she had loved every minute of it. More than she imagined.

With a bemused sigh, she closed her eyes and rested her head against the wall. Nat had been right. Taking this chance made her feel as if a whole new world were opening up to her. After tonight, she would possibly know definitively her true calling.

Shifting, she tilted her shoulders one way, her hips another. Why couldn't she read Nat as well as he seemed to read her, she pondered.

Damn him! she thought, recalling their heated exchange. Her anger had abated somewhat, lessened by the excitement for the challenge she was about to undertake. Nothing was going to spoil tonight for her, she thought, with determination etched on her face.

Unable to let the incident go so easily, she was soon replaying it in her mind and everything that led up to it. She recalled that Bruce was trying to talk her into performing tonight. She had been indecisive, wondering if she wanted to go that far with her music. Looking at her with a combination of pleading and wisdom in his eyes,

Bruce had then taken her hands in his. The next thing she remembered was Nat's voice.

In hindsight, he'd spoken in an even deeper register than normal. At the time, her heart was beating crazily furious in her chest at the mere sight of him that it didn't register.

The only other reason that came to her mind accounting for his behavior was that he'd overheard their conversation. But even that didn't make sense, as Nat was always encouraging her to perform.

Unless, she thought, covering the surprised shape of her mouth, he was upset about Bruce. Her pupils widened with shock as her gaze flew to Bruce, who was talking with Josh and Clifton across the room. Wrinkling the silk fabric of her dress over her chest where her heart was threatening to jump right out of her body, Jenine vehemently shook her head from side to side.

It couldn't be. She must have misread the jealous indicators in his behavior.

Within seconds, her breathing returned to normal, her heartbeat slowed and a gorgeous battlefield of wrinkles broke out across her forehead. She had to believe the error was hers, for otherwise, it was a dangerous game she played with her mind, putting faith in a feeling that was not nor could ever be substantiated.

"Everything okay?" Bruce asked, breaking away from the guys as he approached her.

Forcing a smile to her face, Jenine moved her head with an affirmative nod in reply.

Sliding onto the bench next to Jenine, Bruce asked, "You and Padell finally get squared away?" He spoke in a soft-toned voice, glancing across the room to make sure no one was paying attention to them.

Wetting her lips with her tongue, Jenine pondered her response before she spoke. She knew Bruce was bursting with wrong assumptions, but wasn't sure which ones needed to be corrected.

"We're fine," she replied at last, deciding the less fanfare, the better. And it was a harmless lie as far as Bruce was concerned, she thought.

"You know," Bruce said, rubbing his hand across the lower half of his face to rest on his chin, "I got the impression he didn't know you haven't been to school."

"He doesn't," Jenine replied, her gaze straight ahead to the wall across the room. The paint was chipping on the ugly lime green walls.

"I see," Bruce replied. He rubbed his hands together as if nervous, then shoved them under the armpits of his red sports coat. "Well, I don't, but I guess it's none of my business."

With laughter in her voice, she retorted, "I guess you're right."

Laughing, Bruce ducked his head, then rubbed his palms across his slacks. "Okay," he said. Looking at the time on his wristwatch, he said "I'll leave it alone." Getting to his feet, he clapped his hands together, "Everybody ready?"

To the response of, "Ready," he ushered them out of the dressing room, but not before holding Jenine back.

At her inquiring gaze, he replied with a lopsided smile on his face, "You look good, babe."

Bruce was a nice guy, Jenine thought, looking at him with a fond expression. He was uncomplicated and handsome in his own way. Why couldn't she be attracted to somebody like him, she wondered.

Because he doesn't make your heart sing, replied the cynic in her head.

Returning his smile, she curtsied, holding the side ruffles of the glimmering gray and burnt orange silk caftan. "Thank you."

"Nervous?"

"A little," she replied with a smile, wrinkling her nose.

They heard the cue. "Good evening, ladies and gentlemen."

Squeezing her hands affectionately, Bruce said, "All right, let's go and give 'em a show."

The first set ended with a robust version of "The Last Time I Saw Jenine" at 10:45. It had gone better than even Bruce expected. He was walking around like a cheerleader, praising everyone's performance. They were back in the dressing room sipping soft drinks and trying to cool off.

Jenine fanned herself with her hand, the silk dress was sticking to her body like a second skin. Bruce pulled a stool next to her. "You were fantastic, Jenine."

"Yeah, you were great," Clifton echoed.

"Thanks, Cliff," she said, resting her head against the wall behind her. To Bruce, "You were pretty good yourself. For a minute, I thought Miles Davis had joined us on stage," she added, laughing at the cocky grin on Bruce's face.

"I hope you thought to bring a change," he said, noticing her discomfort in the dress.

"Yes, Dad, I brought something else," she replied amused.

"Well, you better go and get ready. We have about eight minutes before the second show starts."

"All right, slave-driver," she retorted, allowing him to help her up.

"Quit complaining. You know you love it. I can see it in your eyes."

*   *   *

Nat was sitting at one of the tables in the back of the crowded restaurant-turned-club, waiting like everyone else in the audience for the entertainment to resume. Seated next to him was Trina Matheson, his date. He had met the pretty young woman while waiting at a bus station for his instruments to arrive. She was a jazz fan and had recognized him. Nat was flattered and somewhat attracted to the lovely woman, but lately his thoughts had been overrun with images of Jenine. When he returned home and changed into more comfortable clothes, he found her phone number on a book of matches that had worked its way into his jacket pocket. When he called, she could barely keep the squeal out of her voice.

Nat never mentioned that he'd sent for his drum set to Jenine. It was a risky move, but he needed his instruments. Jenine would understand.

He took another sip of his drink and turned his attention back to the woman sitting beside him.

Trina was in her early twenties and very attractive. Yet, he was questioning the wisdom of his decision to bring her here. They had arrived in the middle of the first set. Though he was far from disappointed in the musicianship he had heard so far, he could tell the music wasn't Trina's favorite.

Still, she had come in handy, he thought, feeling a tad guilty for using her. Seeing Jenine with Bruce had driven him to ask Trina for a date. An impulsive act he now regretted. It wasn't the only rash thing he had done today, he chided himself.

Burying the reminder, his thoughts spun back to his ugly mood. With a barely perceptible shake of his head, he cursed his abominable behavior, wondering how he was going to apologize to Jenine. And Bruce, he added silently. There was nothing more between them than music, he thought, relieved, smiling to himself. Too bad he hadn't realized that before now.

But damn it, it was Jenine's fault! She was infuriating, with her secrets. She could have told him what she was up to. She knew he would have supported her in this, even offered his help in other ways, he thought. But she had said nothing.

Still, he couldn't argue against the sense of satisfaction he felt, knowing he played a small role in her decision to do more with her music than teach. As he suspected, she had a dynamic stage presence, and it went without saying that her playing was impeccable. Pleasure returned full blown to his countenance.

"Nat," Trina said in her girlish voice.

"Oh, I'm sorry, Trina," he replied politely. "Would you like another glass of wine?" He wished she would remove her proprietorial hand from his arm.

"No thanks, I'm fine. I was just wondering where you had gone off to," she said, with a flirtatious look.

He was annoyed, but hid it. "Sorry," he replied. She flashed a brilliant smile at him. All he saw was a perfect set of white teeth, for another smile was haunting his thoughts.

The waiters discreetly disappeared and the lights dimmed, signaling the start of the second set. A mid-tempo jazzy number with a syncopated rhythm opened the show. He recognized the melody instantly as the song Jenine had been working on. But she was nowhere on stage.

Disappointment fell over him like a heavy tent when he saw the guy who had played the electric violin sitting behind the keyboards. Then a spotlight came up downstage to his right, throwing a shadow in front of woman holding a microphone. The circle of light widened, and he saw the woman in the center of attention was Jenine.

Untangling himself from Trina's hold, he sat up, almost on the edge of his seat. Staring, he felt appreciably stunned, not only at her dress—a blue metallic voluminous cocoon jacket topping a sexy cami-topped outfit— but the rich contralto of her voice, hinting at a wider range on either side of the vocal register when she began to sing.

Jenine was poised and commanding—of the music, the audience and Nat, as well. He picked up every nuance of her sultry voice like a tape recorder; his eyes were a high-powered telescope, sighting her in rapturous fascination. So captivated by her naturally sensuous showmanship, her body swaying to the beat of the suggestive lyrics she belted out, he forgot all about his date.

"I searched for love in all the wrong places; I searched for joy in all the wrong faces. Until I looked into your eyes, and then I knew; All the love I desire is mine with you. It's because of you, I'm a fool no more; Because of you, I found what I've been searching for. Because of you, my baby; Because of you . . ."

Before the end of the set, Jenine also sang a duet with the guitar player, scatted with a foursome of the group, and belted out an old love-gone-wrong ballad. Nevertheless, the lyrics of the very first number haunted Nat for the remainder of the show. He never knew the title or that there were words to the song, but he would never forget the refrain. So sweet, so loving and so clearly directed to someone, he wondered who.

He was among the first to leave, rushing to drop Trina off and go home.

Home.

Funny, he thought to himself. Jenine's place was his home now, and he wanted to be there when she arrived.

Chapter Eight

The show over, the club was closed. The bartender and two other employees were moving about like quiet beavers, cleaning up in preparation for tomorrow night. Except for Bruce, the other guys in the band had already left.

Winding down from the excitement over the performance, Jenine made busywork for herself on stage. As she was looping the synthesizer cord, her thoughts returned unhindered to the subject from which they never strayed too far: Nat—his name an echo in the stillness of her mind. Her last image of him was his preparing to leave, and she was curious of his whereabouts.

Sliding the synthesizer in its black carrying case, she wondered if he had returned to the house. Or had his bitter exit been the last time he intended setting foot inside her house?

Feeling a total understanding of her current status, she expelled a deep breath. She had proved two things to herself tonight. While performing had given her a temporary thrill, it wasn't what she wanted to do for a living. Weekends were okay, but not day in and day out.

It was helping to mold future musicians that gave her a greater sense of satisfaction, she mused, with a half-smile on her face. It was a short first place behind the gratification she felt for writing.

And number two, she thought with sobering realization, she loved the tall drummer-man. Despite the cruel words of his parental rights that cut her in half, she accepted the dreaded truth.

As a teacher, she was accustomed to accepting a parent's decision as final. Even though it may not have been in the best interest of the child. But the extent of her responsibility and obligation ended after assessing a situation and making a recommendation. Often, she could do no more than that.

Her musings were interrupted by Bruce, hopping onto the stage. "You about ready to go?" he asked.

Snapping the case closed, "Just about," Jenine replied. She placed the case in the large silver trunk slightly off-stage behind the curtains and returned to pick up a large plastic covering. Bruce helped her slide it over the piano.

Looking at the nearly empty stage, Bruce said, "All right. Let's get out of here. Where's your stuff?"

Jenine pointed to a front-row table on the floor level, then descended the stairs on the side of the stage. Bruce jumped down, reaching the carryall and dress bag before she did.

"I'll take this," he said. "What's the matter? You don't look too happy about something."

Jenine smiled weakly. "That's exhaustion you're looking at," she replied, slipping into her overcoat.

"You're not afraid to go home are you?" he asked, pinning her with a concerned look. "I mean," he said embarrassed, "you and Padell did iron things out?"

She could tell Bruce the truth—that she hadn't the faintest idea where Nat was, that she didn't know whether he was even still a houseguest, that she was reluctant to go home to an empty house. Though she was still angry with Nat, tonight, she would prefer his hostile company to none at all.

"You're so sweet," she said, treating him to a fond smile.

With an aw-shucks expression, Bruce replied, "I'm not sweet. I am worried about you."

"There's no need to be," she replied. She rubbed his arm affectionately, then walked off, leaving him to follow.

"Oh yeah?" he quipped at her heels. "If thoughts could kill, I'd be a dead man. I don't know what you're doing to the man, but he is hell-bent on making sure you don't do it with anybody else," he continued with a chuckle in his throat.

Stunned, Jenine stopped walking. She spun around to look at Bruce, her eyes shining bright with amazement. But she didn't really see him, for hope blinded her gaze and created life in every nerve ending in her body.

"Don't tell me you didn't realize that he was jealous," Bruce asked and stated.

His mocking grin jolted Jenine back to reality, a practical reminder. Bruce was no more right than she had been, reaching the same wrong conclusion, she told herself.

Shaking his head, he said, "Jenine, Jenine, Jenine," with a bemused smile.

With a tsk, Jenine replied, "You don't know what you're talking about, Bruce." Again, she turned to leave, heading for the side door at the back of the club.

She pushed open the door against a brisk wind, leading the way into the cold, starless night. Three cars remained on the well-lit parking lot. Her Volvo was closest to the door. Jingling her keys, she unlocked the car. Bruce put her belongings in the back seat, then helped her in the front seat under the wheel.

"Be careful," he said, his hands on the top of the car.

"I will," she replied, buckling the seatbelt. "Thanks, Bruce. I'm glad you talked me into it."

Laughing, he said, "Thanks to Padell for making it easy."

"You're hopeless," she replied cheerfully. "I'll see you tomorrow."

"Tomorrow," he replied with a salute, stepping back from the car as she brought it to life. "Don't forget rehearsal at noon," he yelled at the moving car. "Hey, Jenine!" he called after her, waving his arms.

She stopped the car and rolled down the window. "What did you say?"

Giving her a thumbs-up, he said, "You were great tonight. It's just the beginning."

Wordlessly, Jenine nodded. She backed the car in a circle until it faced the street, then drove off the lot. Unbuttoning her coat, she turned on the car heater to full blast.

Except for tall lampposts spitting beams of yellow lights, the streets were dark and deserted. The club was an exception to the businesses that stayed open past midnight, and it was now after one-thirty Sunday morning. The late hour and the melancholy within her made Jenine feel unstrung, at loose emotional ends.

"Lover man, oh, where can you be?" she whispered soulfully. She sang the refrain of the song popularized by Billie Holiday in the 1930s. She wished hard to find Nat at home with Natasha.

Humming to herself, she was spiritually in tune with the meaningful lyrics, as well as the glory and destruction of the woman who crooned them so elegantly. Jenine smiled in spite of the despair chipping away at her innards like a chisel.

But he's not your lover, a little voice in her head said.

"I know," she replied, with a combination of regret and wistful defeat in her voice.

One minute, she was floating on champagne bubbles, and the next on turbulent waters without an anchor. Maybe they were the same, she thought. The result was pure confusion.

Coming upon the town's biggest hotel, Jenine slowed the car, thinking about checking in. The inside lights invitingly spread out to the sidewalk from the wide revolving door.

But what if Nat were home? she asked herself.

So what? replied the cynic in her head.

Just because he was driving her out of her mind, didn't mean she had to let him drive her out of her home, too, she chided herself. Go home, Jenine, she told herself. This wasn't the first, nor would it be the last time you shared your loneliness with a house.

Bright lights appeared—reflected in the mirror, and Jenine veered the car into the slower lane to let the trailing car pass by. It was a dark-colored Cadillac, either navy or black. She couldn't read the license plates and had no idea who was driving. But it didn't pass. Instead, it closed the gap between the two cars, right on her tail.

Feeling threatened by the strangeness, Jenine bore down on the gas, her foot trembling on the pedal. The driver behind did likewise, and she gave him a name. David Cissoko. Nat's former in-law had found them, she thought fearfully.

Looking down at her speedometer, Jenine swallowed hard. She was doing seventy-five and inching upwards in a thirty-mile speed zone. Her heart pounded at double the climbing speeds in her chest.

The driver behind did another curious thing by blinking his bright light. The powerful flashing beams were like a signal. Then the car switched lanes, pulling up alongside her and the driver honked the horn.

Looking over to the phantom car, the passenger window rolled down, Jenine noticed Bruce behind the wheel. Relief, irritation and curiosity blended inside her; anger came out.

Rolling down her window, she chastised him in a peeved tone of voice. "Bruce! What are you doing?" He'd scared the daylights out of her with that stunt. And what was he doing in somebody else's car? she wondered with mild interest.

"Your lights," he was shouting. "Turn on your lights," pointing toward the front of her car.

Embarrassed, Jenine indicated she understood with a nod of her head. She turned on her lights and watched as Bruce pulled off in front of her, speeding away.

She had been so preoccupied with worrying about Nat that she put her own life in jeopardy, she scolded herself. Was his love worth it?

Moments later, Jenine drove into a town-house complex and parked alongside a sporty little car in front of the house. The porch light was on; another one showed in the picture window behind the curtains.

She knew what she was letting herself in for, she thought, getting out the car. But she felt pleased with her decision, for she feared the mere thought of spending the night with her wretched solitude. Clutching her purse and keys, she hurried up the steps to the door and rang the bell.

Within seconds, a sleepy voice from inside inquired out, "Who is it?"

"Gloria, it's me. Jenine," she replied.

"Jenine," Gloria exclaimed. Pulling open the door,

"What are you doing here? What's the matter?" she asked anxiously.

With a sad, embarrassed smile, Jenine replied, "I, uh . . . Can I spend the night?"

"I don't want you to work," he said firmly.

"Teach, you mean," she retorted angrily. "You don't want me to teach!"

Jenine and Nat were having what had become a standing argument between them.

"All right, teach!" he conceded. "I want you to stay home. I don't want some strangers taking care of Natasha."

Jenine stormed angrily from the house, taking Natasha with her. She jumped in her car, heading no place in particular, with the baby strapped in her carseat.

She ended up at the school, and though it was night, all the lights were on inside the building. She walked straight for her office as if filled with purpose. Opening the door, a . . . a . . . a Thing, leaped for her.

She fell backwards, with Natasha squeezed in her arms, crying from the jolt of their landing on the concrete floor. With eyes frightfully wide and a terrible scream stuck in her throat, she scampered from the Thing. Ten feet tall with the body of a man, it had to stoop to get its crocodile head under the door.

She made it to her feet, still clinging to Natasha, and narrowly escaped its claw-like hands, grabbing for her. She ran as fast as she could with the baby in her arms. Racing around the corner of one corridor, she saw Nat standing at the end of the hallway.

"Hurry, this way," he shouted, beckoning her to him.

The monster was still on her heels. The closer he got, the bigger he loomed in her shadow. Yet, no matter how fast she ran, the farther away Nat seemed, as if he was fading away in front of her eyes. Capture was eminent. Thick, pinching claws dug into her shoulders.

Jenine screamed.

The light from the bedside lamp clicked on, and Jenine, springing up in bed, looked up to see Gloria standing over her, a nervous look on her face.

"Gloria," Jenine whispered in both relief and surprise. "What are you doing up?" she asked, a hand over her racing heart. The front of the gown was damp and she felt perspiration lining her forehead.

"I heard all that racket and thought it was a party going on in here," Gloria replied, attempting humor.

"I'm sorry, Gloria," Jenine said, genuinely embarrassed. She didn't realize she had actually cried out.

"Well, since you're awake, and now, I'm awake, we might as well chat," Gloria said. "How about something to drink? You're probably parched from all that screaming."

"Yeah," Jenine replied nodding, her hand at her throat. She smiled appreciatively at Gloria who then left the room.

She was safe, Jenine thought as her eyes swept over the alien room. Half of Gloria's spare bedroom contained the bare necessities, while the other half subbed as her home office. In addition to desk and chair, there was a trio of bookshelves filled with theater books.

"No monsters lurking about," she said in a soft relieved voice.

Nothing about the dream made sense, she thought, wetting her dry lips with her tongue. If anything, the show at Pirates should have played in her subconscious. She doubted it was a premonition. Her mind, in its infinite state of confusion, had merely conjured a series of incredible events that could only happen in one's dreams. Or nightmare, she corrected silently.

Bede was sitting behind the wheel of the car, folding a map closed. They should reach their destination by night-fall, he mused, sticking the map in the side pocket next to the driver's seat. He planned to push for an earlier arrival.

The car was idling in the parking lot of a truck stop, sandwiched between two eighteen-wheelers. Mubari was inside ordering breakfast. Bede wished his partner would hurry.

He rubbed his hands together and blew his warm breath into cupped hands. Even though the heater was turned up full blast, he couldn't thaw the chill in his body.

It was a little after eight, Sunday morning. They had been driving non-stop from Houston since yesterday morning, following an urgent call from the minister.

"What a stroke of luck," he recalled the minister saying with glee. "The ichneumon is about to devour the snake."

Further instructions had put them on Highway 27, heading into the hilly region of Texas. The temperature had changed drastically. Though the sun was smiling happily in the endless stretch of wide blue skies, it was twenty degrees outside. He had to buy a heavier coat, Bede thought.

The door opened and Mubari squeezed his hulking frame in the front seat with over a dozen bags. The smells of greasy foods teased Bede's nostrils, and his stomach turned over.

With irritation borne out of weariness, he watched Mubari juggling the bags while trying to slide into the seat comfortably. He didn't offer to help; he wanted no part of that meal.

"Where's the coffee?" Bede asked.

"Oh," Mubari said with a wide-eyed look. "I forgot."

Bede groaned.

"I'll run back inside right quick."

"Never mind," Bede grumbled, putting the car in the drive. There was a town up ahead. Hopefully, the stores were open.

At eight-thirty a.m., Jenine walked into the den of her home. Tossing her belongings on the chair, she dropped onto the couch and stretched out. She had left Gloria's place even more exhausted than before, and sleepier.

They had stayed up for hours, talking about nothing significant, until Gloria finally dozed off. Even though questions bubbled inside her, Gloria surprised Jenine and didn't ask one of them, Jenine recalled, a smile flitting across her lips.

She knew she should get up and go to her bed, but she was too tired to move. Closing her eyes, she remembered she had a rehearsal in several hours, to be followed by an early evening show. She needed rest and a good hot meal.

Forcing her body to move, she slowly pushed herself up to a sitting position. Yawning, she kneaded the stiff muscles in her shoulders, then rolled her head in a circle.

"I see you finally came home."

Jenine heard the insolent insinuation in the tone before angling her head in the direction of the voice. Nat, a slim, trim silhouette, was standing on the edge of the room. Suddenly, light filled the area, further defining his mood. His jaw was clenched, his eyes slightly narrowed.

Heart thumping against her rib cage, Jenine followed the barefooted approach of his long, lean form with a guarded look in her eyes. The rich outlines of his shoulders and chest strained against the white T-shirt, his muscular arms bare. He wore leggy, rainbow-colored exercise pants, the drawstrings swaying with his movement.

With common sense skittering into the shadows, Jenine felt the soul-deep flaw of her ill-fated desires, a wild urge to throw herself into the fire of his arms. He settled in the chair across from her, elbows on the armrest. She could feel the angry warmth of his nearness.

She had caught this act before, staring at him unimpressed by his temperament. It was a spin-off of their previous bitter duel which she had lost. She had had enough of his quick flashes of temper. She smacked her lips together. The inside of her mouth was dry as hard paste.

"Good morning," she said for lack of anything else to say.

Nat grunted sarcastically in reply. His hands opened and closed into tight fists before he stilled them, gripping the ends of the chair.

"Where have you been all night?" he asked. A chill hung on the edge of the words.

He wondered if she intended all along to spend the night away from home. Or had he driven her into Bruce's bed? The thought had plagued him all night, he recalled, taking in the outlines of her slender body in the sweater pants and matching top, accented by tiny pearl buttons down the front. Absolutely stunning on her, the black clinging fabric heightened the beauty of her honey complexion. It was the kind of outfit that wouldn't call undue attention to a woman leaving a man's place the next morning. Yet, sexy enough to stir the blood of any healthy male.

He began to seethe in silence with the images building in him: Of Bruce ogling her. Of Bruce touching her. Of

Bruce, comforting and caressing her through the night. Feeling his nature rise in proportion to his jealous anger, he balled his hands into steel fists. He had to force complacency to himself lest his inner turmoil erupt and make a mockery of every argument of why he should stay away from Jenine.

Jenine noticed Nat holding himself under tight control. She could destroy it completely with a lie. But she wasn't up to playing games. She hoped the truth would end this one.

"Gloria's," she replied, looking at him in a headlong stare.

"Right," Nat said.

The one word carried a stiff sentence of guilt, but he believed her. Still, it wasn't enough to mollify him and he sprang to his feet to pace about the room. He motioned to put his hands in his pockets, but there were none, so he folded them across his chest.

After dropping Trina off, he came back here, expecting Jenine to show in any minute. Instead, he had waited for nothing, until the waiting had become unbearable. He left to pick up Natasha from Robbie's, then drove back by the house. She still hadn't returned. Scared and worried something had happened to her, he had driven around for several hours looking for her.

"If you're not going to believe me, why bother asking?"

Ceasing his restless movement, to glower at her, he retorted, "I'd say you've given me enough grounds to suspect your trustworthiness."

Jenine sat with her back against the back of the couch so as not to strain her neck looking up at him looking down at her from his arrogant height, looming over her like a contentious giant. Even in anger he was a sight to behold, standing post-still, arms hanging rigid, legs braced, all waiting. Reproach was a living thing in his olive-brown eyes. Refusing to be intimidated, she returned his look with a stubborn, defiant one.

"You let me believe all this time that your late rehearsals were with the school band," he said with hot accusation. "Then I find out, quite by accident, that your students are not students and don't need a teacher. And to make matters worse, you haven't even been to school."

"You were at the show?" she asked in a stunned whisper. He quickly vanquished her excitement.

"Yes, I was there," he snarled, poking a finger in his chest. "You seemed to enjoy yourself. I guess you're going to tell me you still enjoy teaching more," he added, daring her to deny it.

Disappointed that no comments or compliments about the performance were forthcoming, she said in a tight voice, "I don't have to tell you anything."

Jenine was right. She was always right, while he was always in the wrong, he thought, the hairs of his mustache bunching over his tightly pressed lips. He had tried hard to let their friendship remain platonic. After all, he was leaving, going back to New York, his home.

No, not home, the realist in him argued. It was simply a place he returned to at the end of another day or night from his office—the stage or a studio. It couldn't compete with what he had discovered in Highland Heights, made even more attractive by a bewitching woman empowered to destroy his principles, tempting him into believing he could have it all.

Jenine just had to have known how he felt about her, he thought, slapping his hands together explosively.

"When are you going to stop playing games, Jenine?" he demanded, frustration surfacing through his harsh tone.

Jenine got stiffly to her feet. She debated for a moment whether to cross his path to get to her clothes or go around the back of the couch. She passed right in front of him as if he didn't exist. Hard to do considering his presence permeated her senses, as well as the entire house, she thought, collecting her belongings from the chair.

"Don't you have something to say?" he yelled to her back.

With the dress bag folded across one arm and the carryall in her other hand, she replied, "No." Let him get a taste of his own medicine, she thought, walking off.

"That's right, keep running," he shouted. Furious, Nat ignored the inner warning to let the matter rest. He went on gamely, "That's all you've been doing for the past eight years. Hiding out in this nowhere town, going nowhere, finding glory in teaching."

Jenine had reached the door on the way to her room. Pushed beyond her limits, she decided to dispense with her seemingly calm, unaffected attitude and meet fire with fire.

"You're a fine one to talk," she said, her brown eyes clawing him like talons. "And what the hell do you care how I've lived my life for the past eight years?" she shouted, with aggressive machine-gun speech. "Or even the last eight minutes. It's no concern of yours. I granted you and your daughter a place to stay; not the place to tell me how to live my life." Waving her arms, making the dress bag and carryall swing in the air with the violent motion, she said summarily, "If you don't like it, the both of you can leave."

"That song," he said . . . " 'Because of You.' You wrote it."

The quick change of subject jolted Jenine into utter stillness. So he remembered, she thought, but felt no joy in the awareness.

Looking into his face, a need-to-know look in his eyes, she remembered Bruce laughing at her, teasing her for not figuring out that Nat was jealous of him. Twice she discounted her suspicion as a figment of her wishful longings. But the desperation in his demand unleashed something within her. A hope she was afraid to rejoice in, quivered in her stomach, though she felt a wavering in her judgment.

"Did you write it for him? Bruce Richards?" he asked with an ugly tone in his voice. "Or me?"

The alternative was spoken as if as a prelude to commitment, a proposal. Jenine stood rooted in the spot. Flustered with indignation and to her utter embarrassment, arousal, she merely stared at him with her mouth open and brown eyes as wide as saucers. Of all the arrogant, egotistical conclusions, she thought.

"Don't flatter yourself," she hissed savagely on her way out.

Jenine neither saw nor sensed the attack coming. Nat lunged for her and she didn't give a thought to her possessions, dropping them to the floor. She needed her hands to push at the limbs and body parts assaulting her senses and personage from all sides. His mouth was brutal, trying to fasten on hers, the full length of his body plastering her into the wall, his hands dancing with hers to pin them to her sides.

As quickly and unexpectedly as the hostile encounter began, it stopped, changed altogether. The once-punishing mouth gentled, and his persuasive firm lips caressed hers, the once-gruff hands delivering tender touches. His hard body remained pressed against hers, but with an amorous touch, a delectable eroticism, a leg inserting itself between hers. The combination coaxed and drugged her senses into a sensual skirmish that delighted her body.

Nat lifted his mouth to speak, his forehead against hers and his breathing hard. "See what you've turned me into," he said.

Humiliated by her wanton capitulation to his aggression, Jenine silenced the contempt in her throat. Her body was still hungering for his touch. With her forehead against his chest, she felt resistance-drained. Her defeat had been inevitable, she thought.

"We have to take responsibility for our own actions," she said softly, looking up into his face. She had already accepted responsibility for her own hurting, a pain she was sure would last long after he was gone.

An indulgent smile flitted across his mouth and a sardonic chuckle rumbled in his chest. She had no idea that as far as she was concerned, he had no control over his own actions. But as painful as the admission was to him, he knew Jenine was right.

"Okay," he said. He backed away from her, his hands held up as if he were a surrendering criminal.

Looking into his gaze intently, Jenine saw regret in his eyes. He was sorry for making an advance, one that was governed by a show of masculine strength and superiority. The interpretation stretched the size of the hole in her heart.

Quietly, she bent to pick up her fallen possessions, then risked a final glance at Nat. He had already turned to leave.

Nothing had changed between them. She and Nat would always be going in opposite directions. Nothing had changed, she told herself over and over as if denial were a cure to the hot throbbing in her body, as she proceeded to the bedroom where she had become the guest.

Flipping on the light switch, she surveyed the blue-flower-pattern papered room absently. Tossing her things across the regular-sized bed, she sat on the footstool at the end of the bed to pull off her ankle boots. She tossed them toward the closet; one landed against the wall and hit the floor with a thud. She shrugged in its direction, then pushed herself up to stand in front of the dresser.

Staring at her reflection, she began to unbutton the sweater. She was not surprised by what she saw. Her brown eyes were tinted equally by the remnants of sexual anticipation and sadness over a missed opportunity. She felt dissatisfied with herself, more of a failure than ever before.

Nat bolted into the room. "Jenine, I can't leave things like this," he said in a rush, then fell silent, uncomfortable-looking. "I'm sorry," he said imploringly, as if apologizing for all the sins in the world. "Jenine! Say something!"

With her gaze lowered to the floor, Jenine opened her mouth to speak, a confession on the tip of her tongue. She had nothing to lose, not even her pride, she thought. "I . . . ," she started.

Nat never allowed her to finish. As if it were more important to get this off his chest, he said, "Annette wasn't right for me, and I wasn't right for her."

With a jerk of her head, Jenine looked up, intense astonishment in her eyes. His reflection appeared behind and above hers. His eyes were serenely compelling, pinning her with long, silent scrutiny.

"It wasn't real love," he said soberly. "I realized too late she was not the woman for me."

Imbued by a deep longing to believe what she'd heard, Jenine spun to face him in the flesh, seeking his gaze for confirmation. His eyes, sparkling with a tender glow, answered her unspoken question. They told her she was the woman for him.

Chapter Nine

Taking her turn at honesty, a liberating disclosure, Jenine said softly, "It was all because of you."

With joy spreading through her like a sunrise bursting onto a horizon, Jenine felt transported back in time, a breathless girl of eighteen. But it was with a woman's eyes that she viewed him now, a maturity that sensed his eagerness and heightened her own. She realized that everything that had happened between them had been leading up to this point, and she was no longer afraid of her emotions.

Stroking her cheek with great tender fingers, Nat said, "God, I've missed you."

Jenine shivered at the fervor in his voice—accompanying the mesmeric eyes gazing at her with a covetous look. Reacting to the unspoken sign, she walked into the circle of his embrace. He held her reverently, and she felt a great exultation fill her chest to bursting.

Nat tilted up her chin to stare down into her face. Her doe-shaped eyes fixed on his in a tender look, bits of topaz shining in their depths; her lips soft and moist, seeming to be in wait of his kiss. But, for now, he was content just looking at her, sharing heartbeats with her.

"I tried to keep my distance, Jenine," he said softly.

"You ought to kick me out right now. I'm probably more trouble than I'm worth. Definitely more trouble than you deserve."

A look of sad waiting came over his features. As if he expected her to do as he said—which she had no intention of doing—Jenine thought. She didn't want to talk about deserving, nor of her sending him away. Now, finally, she knew exactly what she wanted.

Raising herself on her toes, her hands slipped up his arms, bringing him closer. Her mouth moved over his in a series of slow, shivery kisses that elicited a small sound of wonder from his throat. Then the pressure of her hungry warm lips increased, and she demanded entry into his mouth with her tongue. He let her possess his mouth in a thorough and tender kiss, and all thoughts of leaving left his mind.

Their tongues danced together in a sweet melody. A duet of ardent sighs from their light hearts filled the quiet spaces and banished the shadows of doubts and future recriminations. Two mouths melded together like hot irons, sealing a commitment that transcended words and thoughts.

Taking control of the kiss, Nat smothered her mouth in a wild kiss that performed magic with her senses, and her hunger burst forth in a heated gush. His lips traipsed leisurely along her neck, up to her ear where his tongue dipped into the center. Like a thief, it stole her breath away, then retreated to attack again over and over, until she felt like little more than a organism of sensations.

Whimpering with sheer need, her hands went wild and frantic; they pulled and tugged at the offensive shirt denying her access to the true warmth of his flesh. Severing the contact of their mouths, he ripped off his shirt, abetting her desires. Her senses throbbed with the strength and feel and scent of him as her hands explored the planes of his back, skimming both sides of his waist to his thighs.

His tormented groan was a heady invitation of approval, and her lips mastered over his, her tongue probing the inner recesses of his mouth in the sweetest kiss he'd ever succumbed to. When her hand descended the length of his body to the bulge in his pants, he felt a want so deep that he thought he'd die from it.

With wonder sparks shooting through him like rapid-fire bullets at the contact, he released the primitive yearning within him in a moan and buried his head in the nape of her neck.

"Jenine, Jenine," he murmured, drawing her against him until she was aware of his entire length. In a flash, he lifted her off the floor and eased her down onto the center of the bed, partially covering her with his body.

They lay facing each other inches apart Jenine smiled into the ardent light in his eyes, cherishing the moment of being near to him, of having her wildest dream come true. She cradled his strong sun-kissed face between her tremulous hands, and with her thumbs brushed his brows, then his mustache, enjoying the friction of the short wiry hairs against her hands.

Capturing a finger between his teeth, his tongue teased its sensitive tip, causing a hot energy, like liquid electricity to ooze through her. Closing her eyes, she savored the sensation, spreading like wildfire through her.

With an errant hand trailing down the center of her bosom to the lace of her bra, he unclasped it. She inhaled sharply at the contact. Her response pleased him, drove him to proceed. Slipping his hand inside the sweater, he outlined the tips of her breasts with his fingers. She sucked in a deep breath and held it but for a second, as he elicited convulsive gasps from her, for his hand began to roam intimately over her breasts, her stomach, then down inside her pants.

He slid the sweater off her shoulder, and she arched to completely discard it. But that was minor to Nat for now, as he lowered his head to the satin bodice of her brown body to kiss a taut nipple, rousing a melting sweetness within her.

"Tell me it's true," he murmured, his hot breath fanning her stomach. Gazing into her eyes, dilated with ecstasy, he said in a deeply affected voice. "Tell me you're mine."

For seconds she couldn't speak, couldn't think, for his hands never stilled on her, tracing a worshipful path over her bare skin. She merely stared with wonder into his eyes.

"Yes," she said in a tone as pure and natural as truth.

His mouth swooped down to capture hers. The kiss was surprisingly tender. Jenine whimpered when he deprived her of the kiss, leaving her mouth burning with fire. He removed the sweater, then tugged the pants off her hips. Her entire body blushed as his possessive gaze caressed her nakedness with appreciation, and she felt her pulse beating in her throat. He removed his pants, tossed them onto the floor, then kneeled upright over her thighs.

She stared entranced at his proud and magnificent wide-shouldered, rangy physique. His sun-baked flesh, silk-smooth, and olive-brown eyes illuminated with unquenchable desire.

A dream-like aura encircled them. The air teemed with sexual tension, waiting with bated breath for their lead.

He leaned over her, his hands flat on the bed near her head. First, he kissed the tip of her nose, then her eyes, and, finally, he satisfyingly kissed her soft mouth while his hands explored the planes of her body. Though her thin panties separated his palm from her pulsating treasure, the contact was no less arousing.

The exploration of her soft flesh transported Jenine to a paradisical setting. Nat was driving her mindless with his sedulously sweet assault, awakening a new and passionate woman inside her. And she wanted to unleash that hunger and satisfy it.

Pulling him over her until his naked chest melded to hers, she nudged her tongue against his lips and painted the roof of his mouth with strong, impelling strokes.

She was hot under him, a stimulant to his own amorous sensibilities. He felt the steadily tightening coil in his lower regions; her frantic caresses were pushing him over the threshold. He pulled away slowly to regain some semblance of control, fearing he wouldn't be able to carry out the pleasure he wanted to give her. She deserved nothing but the best from him, and he intended to spoil her with his love.

Jenine helped him make short work of removing the rest of their clothes, as eager and excited as he to experience his possession, a refrain from which she'd never tire. When he returned to her, a mutual shudder ran along their length.

He pinned her hands under her as his tongue began a journey down her satin brown body, tormenting her flesh along with way. He stopped at the short, wiry hairs between her legs, then held her buttocks in his hands while he placed painfully, delicate bites on the inside of her thighs.

Whimpers that Jenine couldn't identify as her own escaped her throat as she tossed her head from side to side, writhing uncontrollably. She didn't know if she were pleading for the end, or for more of the sweet torture.

"Please, Nat. Please. Please, Nat."

He responded to her plea, for it mirrored the want

which he craved, and lifted himself to allow her to guide his silky hardness into her womanly treasure. His deep lusty moan mingled with her fervent cry at the slow possession he enacted. And when he was buried in her warm center, felt its tightness surround him, he called out her name reverently.

"Oh, Jenine. My little Jenie," he exclaimed repeatedly, creating a melody with his andante thrusts into her body.

The moderate rhythm became unbearable for Jenine, her body spinning like a rondo refrain, the end reached only by sharing a duet with Nat, her love, her life.

"Nat! Oh, Nat, I, it's . . ." There were no words to describe the remarkable sensations she felt, like millions of notes singing through her, and she clung to him tenaciously.

"Let it go, baby. Let it go, I'm here for you," he ground out above her, adjusting his pace to match the andantino passage of her hips under him. "I'll always be here for you."

In perfect rhythm, each propelled the other up the scale to the highest octave of love, seeking a harmonious finale. Jenine cried out passionately as her body shook with the intensity of her release.

"Oh, God, Jenine."

Nat belted out the exclamation as his body tightened abruptly, then fell limp, reaching the climatic end.

With glistening wet bodies still clinging to each other, Nat and Jenine collapsed on the bed. For a long time, neither spoke nor thought of anything except the supreme contentment they felt.

Leaning on his haunches, Nat gazed down into her face. Their eyes locked as their breathing slowed in unison.

"I miss you when you're away from me and torture myself watching the clock until you get home," he confessed. "Sometimes, I just lie in bed to keep your fragrance on me. As though I'm likely to forget," he said with a self-depreciative laugh. "Then, like a kid trying to cover up something before he gets in trouble, I hurry up and make up the bed before you come home." He laughed at himself, then bit down on his lip. "I'm crazy."

"No," she said, shaking her head.

Bobbing his head up and down, he replied, "Yes, I am. Crazy in love with you."

A choked cry escaped her throat. Jenine wanted to shut him up and edge him on at the same time as tears formed in her eyes. No matter how much she wanted to believe him, she couldn't forget what little she knew about love, she thought. It had to be founded in reality, and their reality was tenuous. Still, feelings of joy won out over reason.

"If I had known I'd have that kind of effect on you, I'd have kept my mouth shut," he teased.

"Don't you dare," she said, crying and laughing at the same time. Through her tears, she saw his Adam's apple bob as though the words he wanted to say were stuck in his throat; the significance of it made her heart dance. She held him dearly to her before seeking his lips for a painfully sweet kiss. Releasing his mouth, she laughed with her joy and stroked the side of his face with her loving eyes and hands.

"What time is rehearsal?" he asked, a sly grin on his face.

"Noon," she replied. "What time is it now?"

"At least another hour to make good use of our time," he replied, seductively. She giggled like a girl, but offered no objections to the suggestion of his gaze. "I've ached for you so long," he offered as explanation for his greed as he kissed the pulsing hollow at the base of her throat.

The doorbell rang.

Lifting his head, he groaned. "You expecting company?"

"In a way, yes," Jenine replied, half groaning, half laughing.

"May I please get that in English?" he asked with a chuckle, nuzzling her neck.

With a trembling breath, she replied, "It's either Robbie or John North," she replied. "John is the principal at the Academy. He was at the show last night."

Looking into her face with a puzzled look. "So?"

"I've been using my sick leave for the past weeks. I think the boom is about to be lowered."

Moments later, Jenine strolled into the den. She sent Nat to entertain her unscheduled, but expected, visitor while she took a quick, hot shower and changed. She was dressed to leave for rehearsal soon after Robbie departed. She found her friend and school board adviser sitting on the couch, inspecting one of Natasha's rubber toys.

"Where's Nat?" Jenine asked, looking around the three-room area.

Examining Jenine closely, Robbie replied absently, "I think Natasha woke up." Noticing something different about Jenine, she added, "I came at a bad time."

Mildly embarrassed, Jenine flashed a shy smile. "No," she replied, though she knew Robbie guessed the secret of her body's delight. She slid onto the edge of an armchair and crossed her legs at the knee. "We have a few minutes before I have to leave for rehearsal. But, before you begin, I have to tell you something."

"Okay," Robbie said, sitting with her back against the couch.

"I've made my decision." Robbie nodded wordlessly. "I've decided to return to school."

Exhaling a deep breath, Robbie was visibly relieved and Jenine smiled. "When did all this happen?" she asked.

With a knowing look on her face, Jenine studied Robbie's person. She looked curious, but patient and calm, hands crossed in her lap casually. Jenine wasn't fooled. However, despite her decision to return to school, she had to know whether Robbie had been sent to plea bargain or deliver an ultimatum.

"Who called you?"

A barely perceptible look of approval flitted across Robbie's features, then her face split in a wide grin. "John called me," she admitted plainly. With humor lining her voice, she said, "And very early this morning, I might add."

"He was at the show last night," Jenine said.

"Yes," Robbie replied. "You scared him pretty bad."

With a puzzled expression, Jenine replied, "How so? He didn't even stay afterwards to speak."

"Let me see if I can remember his exact words," the attorney replied with a smile atop her thoughtful look. ' "She's good, Robbie. She's damn good and we can lose her," ' she recanted. Looking headlong at Jenine with an impressed smile, "That's a direct quote."

"But why should that frighten him?" Jenine asked. "I'm replaceable."

"He doesn't feel that you are."

Jenine gestured her disbelief, flicking the air with her hand.

"To lose you would be a blemish on his record that he doesn't want to have," Robbie explained. "Ethel suggested to him that maybe his management style needs some work." Both women laughed. "Your turn."

"After the show," Jenine replied, licking her lips, "I

realized that I enjoy teaching more. At least more than performing."

"And your writing?"

"I want to drop one of my classes permanently," she replied promptly. That was her compromise. "I have too many. Heading up the department with all the paperwork that's involved, on top of the planning period and teaching five classes is getting to be too much."

"All right, what's a good number?" Robbie replied, ready to deal.

"Three," Jenine said.

"Four," Robbie countered.

"Then more money," Jenine replied.

"An extra one-fifty per month."

"I see you've already worked out all the details," Jenine said with a chuckle.

"Almost," Robbie said. "Will you return next year?"

"When will these new changes start?" Jenine wanted to know first.

"The next reporting period," Robbie replied. "That will give him enough time to make the schedule changes. And next year?"

"I'll be there," Jenine replied.

"Anything else?" Robbie asked.

"What else is he offering?"

"That's all he could offer without board approval," Robbie replied. "But if there's more, you better put your cards on the table now."

"No," Jenine said, gesturing with her hands. "That's it."

"Good," Robbie declared, breathing a deep sigh of relief. "When do you intend to return?"

"Tomorrow," Jenine replied.

"That soon?"

"I miss my students," she confessed.

The phone rang, interrupting the flow of the conversation. Jenine looked across the way, and it stopped. She guessed Nat must have answered in the bedroom.

"They miss you, too, from what I hear," Robbie said. "John says he has had to field complaints from the students about the substitute every day. But I have a sneaking suspicion it's not the sub's fault."

"It's nice to know I have a loyal group of followers," Jenine said.

"Now, for more pleasant conversation," Robbie said with a conspiratorial gleam in her blue eyes. "What's new with you and Nat?"

"Jenine," Nat called before he appeared, carrying Natasha in his arms. "It's for you."

"I see we'll have to finish this another time," Robbie said, getting set to leave. "It seems we're always interrupted when I get to the good part," she said, with a wink in Nat's direction.

Getting to her feet, Jenine replied, "Like you say, another time. Hi, pretty baby," she cooed to Natasha, who reached out to be taken.

"I'll see Robbie out," Nat said. "Don't forget the phone."

"I won't," she replied. Guiding Natasha's hand, "Wave bye-bye to Robbie."

"See you kids later," Robbie said, leaving the room with Nat at her side.

"Did you have a good nap? Jenine asked Natasha, walking across the room to the phone on the counter. "Hello," she said into the mouthpiece. "Yes, this is Jenine Jones." Within seconds she realized she didn't want to be bothered with this call. "I'm not interested, thank you." She sighed in exasperation. "Look, I don't have time to take part in a survey. That's fine, but I don't have any children." Natasha took that moment to start babbling and grabbing for the phone. "Good-bye," Jenine said firmly, slamming the receiver in its cradle.

After seeing Robbie out, Nat returned to stare at Jenine, her back to him. Recalling her passion and the delights her delectable body delivered only a short time ago, he felt his nature rising and was already regretting her departure. He could hardly wait for her return and she hadn't even left yet, he thought with a chuckle, sauntering to stand beside her.

Natasha switched her allegiance, reaching for Nat. It was then that he noticed the lines of deep concentration etching her forehead.

"What's the matter, baby?" he asked Jenine, taking Natasha in his arms. "You look like you failed a test or something."

"Maybe it's nothing, but that was a strange call," she said.

"Yeah?"

Staring into his concerned gaze, her train of thought was momentarily interrupted, and she smiled with fond recollections of being held against his strong body.

"Jenine," he prompted, laughing, guessing at her thoughts.

With an embarrassed smile, she replied, "They asked me to participate in a survey on household products."

"What's so strange about that? Companies do that all the time."

"When I told them I wasn't interested, they kept on and on about how I could win a year's supply of baby diapers," she replied.

Nat threw back his head and broke out laughing. At Jenine's raised brow, indicating a sign of pique, he clamped his mouth shut and draped his free arm around her shoulder.

"I'm sorry," he said, leading her into the den. "I'm not

making fun of you," mirth still in his voice. "But you're worse than I used to be." They eased onto the couch simultaneously.

"Well, damn it Nat, I can't help it," she said. "I got a funny feeling about that call, and I think it's something to be concerned about."

"Let me tell you something," he said, taking her hand. "I'm fairly certain that David is not going to take a round-about approach like a phone survey to find us. He's a little too forward for that."

"So you expect him to find you?"

With a succinct nod of his head, he replied, "Yes." Most definitely, he thought assured, a frown darkening his expression. "I almost wish I had stayed in New York," he spoke his inner thought aloud.

"And who would have cared for Natasha?" Jenine asked softly, the baby now in her lap again.

Nat smiled down into her face with an entranced gaze, then bent his head for a quick peck on the cheek. He caught her lips instead, and a lingering kiss. Lifting his head to stare into her fire-warm eyes, he first thought the words that had become a fixture in his mind, his heart, before he spoke. "No one as good as you. And that goes double for me, too."

Beaming with joy, Jenine left home feeling as if she were riding a cloud of good fortune. Her effervescence came as a surprise to the guys in the band; at least, all but Bruce, who guessed at the reason for her uncharacteristically buoyant mood.

The glow lasted through rehearsal, and later during the performance, where it shone brighter than the spotlight that followed her on stage. It was evident in her voice when she sang as she dazzled the audience regardless of the song. She could have sung the alphabet and still held them entranced in the palm of her hand, her voice emoting with power and confidence, and that rare quality that separated mere singers from entertainers.

Following the close of the show, Jenine informed Bruce she was returning to school. He was disappointed, believing such a move would interfere with her creativity.

She didn't linger around the club to debate the point with him, still carrying the delight in her heart, the memories of Nat's touch and the two little words he had murmured to her before she left. "Hurry home."

She raced to do just that.

Nat greeted her at the door and carried her to their bedroom, the master suite. Natasha and her possessions had been moved to the guest room. Jenine felt as if it was the first night of their lives together. She felt like a bride, totally disregarding the reminders of Nat's imminent departure.

Chapter Ten

"You're going to school," Nat both asked and stated, grinning down at into Jenine's smiling face.

They were standing in the opening between the dining room and kitchen, arms wrapped around the other's waist. Part in celebration of her return to school, Jenine was bedecked in a pencil-slim suit in burnished gold, while Nat was still in his bathrobe. Neither wanted to part.

Aware of what he was referring to, Jenine smiled. "Yes. I'm going to school."

"I'm going to miss you." He kissed her on the mouth, then squeezed her to him.

"I'll be back before you know it," she said into his chest, revealed to her between the open folds of the white robe. She inhaled the clean smell of soap on his smooth ebony flesh, and remembered she shared his scent, for they had showered together this morning.

With her face burning in memory of what else they had done together this morning, Jenine felt as if she had lived in a dream world for the past twenty-four hours. She was as reluctant as he to leave that place even for the short time they had to part.

"I'll know it, all right," he replied laughingly. "I'll keep a vigil on the clock all day." Then he grew serious. "You don't have to return, you know. To school, I mean. Teaching."

With her heart pounding, Jenine stared wordlessly up at him. She wondered what game he was playing. What did he mean exactly by, she didn't have to return to teaching? "Nat, what are you saying?"

"If you want to pursue your music, I'm more than able to . . . to . . . ," he said, unable to find the right words.

"To what?" she asked with annoyance that he was making her go through this with the skill of pulling teeth.

Reading the hesitation on his face, Jenine knew the answer. She didn't want to believe what her heart was telling her, had told her time and time again before now.

"Be kind of like a sponsor," he said at last.

The subject broached, Jenine couldn't ignore the future which had been so easy to forget when she was in his arms. It was time to start facing reality, she thought, stepping out of his embrace, her expression marred by thought.

And when you're gone? she wanted to ask, but the words stuck in her throat.

"Jenine, it's not what you're thinking," he said in a rush of speech. "This doesn't have anything to do with gratitude and stuff like that. I have money now. You don't have to worry about the bills, or house-note or anything like that. I'm financially able and willing," he tagged on with emphasis, "to take care of those little things. It's the least I can do for you, and it would mean a lot if you let me."

Nat sounded like a salesman on commission, trying to sell her a used car. Good mileage, but no guarantees it wouldn't break down the second or third time she cranked it up, she thought, unable to suppress her unhappiness by a sarcastic snort. Some women might have been elated that he thought enough of her talent to make such an offer. She felt as if all pleasure had been siphoned from her body.

Swallowing the lump that had lodged itself in her throat, Jenine struggled to hide her pain from him. Busying herself to leave, she sauntered to the den to get her coat.

"I better go, or I'll be late," she said somberly.

She let him help her into in the coat, then retrieved her briefcase and purse from the couch. She wanted to cry, but held back tears of disappointment before turning to face him, a sad smile on her face. "I'll see you later."

Pulling her into the circle of his embrace, Nat held her tenderly next to him. "Please don't be angry with me," he said with pleading in his voice. "I wasn't trying to insult you or anything." He kissed her on the top of her head. "You know I wouldn't do anything in the world to hurt you. Please believe that. Tell me you believe that," he said, tilting her chin to look up into his gaze.

Wrapped in the warm bunting of his strong embrace, she could believe anything, she thought, pining with her hurt. Again, they were at crossed signals, which was probably for the best.

"I believe you," she replied sincerely.

They held each other tightly before Nat loosened his hold on her. "Do you have a band rehearsal tonight?" he asked.

Clearing her throat, she replied, "No. Not until Wednesday night."

Nat nodded.

"Kiss my baby for me," she said.

"I don't think I'll take her to school today," he said. He felt a flash of loneliness stab at him and desperately wanted some company. Since he couldn't have Jenine's, Natasha's would have to do.

Jenine merely nodded, then turned and walked out the back door.

On the drive to school, Jenine didn't notice winter was receding, teasing the weather with the promise of a new season. A white blur of sun stood fixed in the blue, chilly skies.

She was rehashing the shock she had received from Nat. A professional, not a personal relationship, Miss. Jones, she said to herself mockingly.

What did she expect? she demanded of herself silently, hitting the steering wheel. She had only herself to blame for believing pledges of love issued in the heat of passion. When hot bodies parted, the warmth waned and vows were washed away in the showers that followed. Nat's only commitment was to pleasure her body with caresses and kisses. Because he did so with such incredible satisfaction, she had let herself believe love was an essential part of the act. Now, she had to decide whether less than what she expected was enough.

Love was a grown-up game, she reminded herself. And the rule was that there were no rules. Often no winners, just losers. She was a grown-up and she had already stepped onto the playing field. As far as she could see, she had two choices. She could spend what little time she and Nat had left making their lives miserable. Or she could build upon her memories. The choice was hers.

Arriving at school, Jenine hurried inside the building to the main office. It was her first day back to school in two weeks and little had changed. The place was noisy with the hustle and bustle that typified the beginning of the school week. Teachers, students, secretaries and support personnel were going about their normal, harried, Monday-morning routine. She went straight to the counter to sign in.

"I hope you're feeling better."

Lifting her head, Jenine looked up directly into the principal's knowing gaze. John was standing on the other side of the counter. She shifted uneasily, not sure what to expect from him despite Robbie's assurances that he really wanted her back at the Academy.

"Yes, I am," she replied, staring back at him with no hint of guilt, chagrin or apology for the lie she had told nearly two weeks running.

"Good," he said, knocking a knuckled fist on the wooden counter top. "Mrs. Cobb wants to see you in the conference room."

"What about?" she asked hastily before she could temper the note of annoyance in her tone. She had already agreed to come back. She was anxious to get back to her students. What more did Ethel Cobb want?

"She's so excited, I'll let her tell you about it," John replied with a wise look on his smiling face.

"Okay," she replied agreeably, though she began to feel slightly uneasy. She lowered her gaze to the sign in, but felt John's lingering presence. Slightly uncomfortable, she stopped writing to look up at him. "Is there anything else?"

"She's waiting now," he replied. "Mr. Richards will take over your class until you're finished."

"Fine," she said.

Before turning to leave, John said, "By the way, I caught your set the other night. I probably shouldn't tell you I was impressed," he said with a grin, "but I will. You were fantastic. And I truly mean that."

"Thanks, John," she replied.

"But I'm glad you made us a priority," he added before walking off.

A half smile flitted across her lips. Completing the sign-in, Jenine left the main office. All the way to the conference room on the second floor of the building, adjacent to the library, she wondered about the summons.

While Mrs. Cobb looked the part of a pampered society matron, everyone knew she was genuinely concerned about the education of young people and was forever scheming to provide the best for the students in Highland Heights. Her husband's money had afforded the former educator the opportunity to build her dream school in the elementary and secondary academies, with the number-one goal of providing a private-school education in a public-school setting. Ethel Cobb usually got her wish.

Although she was fairly certain her job was secure, Jenine felt a thread of apprehension course through her. She swallowed it, telling herself Ethel Cobb could do nothing to her that she wouldn't allow. She remembered Nat's offer, thinking she might have to take him up on it.

She passed through a maze of narrow passageways before reaching the conference room. It was a functional, spacious room with few amenities. Well-tended, potted plants sat on the sills of the four windows with beige, pull-down shades lining the north wall; the brown carpet was inexpensive, but clean.

Seated at the head of the wooden table surrounded by high-back, leather-covered chairs was the founder of the Highland Heights's academics, Ethel Cobb. She was dressed in a lavender designer suit, with pearls at her neck and ears. Her full, dark hair, graying at the temples, was worn in its customary chignon. With reading glasses perched on the edge of her nose, she was looking over some papers.

Jenine braced herself at the door and quietly drew a deep breath. "Mrs. Cobb," she said, stepping into the room. "Mr. North said you wanted to see me."

Ethel Cobb looked up; a charming smile spread across her coffin-shaped, elegant face. She pulled off the reading glasses while getting to her feet. "Yes, Miss Jones." Gesturing to the chair at her left, she said, "Have a seat."

Seated, Jenine wasted no time getting the discussion underway. "What did you want to talk to me about?"

The day was passing quickly; already it was noon. Three classes completed, two more to go. Jenine was sitting behind the desk in her office. She made a note in the green grade book before her, then flipped it closed.

Rearing back in her chair, hands behind her head, she marveled at how well she had been able to keep the two parts of herself from colliding, for Nat had certainly left her feeling split in half. Ms. Jones the teacher had successfully steered clear of Miss. Jones the temporary lover. Love only came every fifteen years, she mused mockingly.

Righting herself in the chair, elbows propped on the desk, Jenine planned her bleak future in her mind. Work had merely been a scapegoat for her in the past, she realized. In the future, she would need it as an elixir of life. She was counting on getting lost in it—and she had plenty—to help her survive again. In fact, there was so much for her to do in order to catch up, she was resigned to staying after school to finish half of it.

Pushing herself up from her desk, she walked across the room to the piano. She hunched over it, one knee resting on the bench, as she played while reading from the score of music atop the piano. The song had been selected by the chemistry teachers to dance to for the upcoming Teachers' Talent Show. It was one of the subjects she had discussed with Ethel Cobb.

Mrs. Cobb wanted her assurance that it would be the best ever. A group of education bigwigs was coming to town and Mrs. Cobb wanted to impress them with the versatility of the Academy's teachers. Jenine reassured her the program would go off without a hitch.

She had chaired it enough to do it in her sleep, Jenine thought, closing the score of music. This number was so simple that one of her students could play it with minimal rehearsal.

Scanning a folder of music scores, she began looking for the piece she was required to play for yet another group of teacher performers, but couldn't find it. As she crossed the room back to her desk, several hard raps sounded on the door. She opened it to John.

"I hope you haven't come with yet another 'little thing' you want me to do," she said laughingly. "I'm swamped as it is."

Grinning boyishly, he replied, "I just wanted to check and see that you were okay."

"As you can see, I'm okay," she replied. Returning to her desk, she asked, "What's going on?"

"Several teachers reported a suspicious-looking man walking around the parking lot," he replied. "They thought maybe he was trying to figure out which car to steal."

"I'm not even worried," she quipped laughingly. "I wish somebody would steal mine. Heaven knows it's time for a new one."

Laughing with Jenine, John agreed. "I know what you mean. Unfortunately, nobody wants the piece of junk I have, either. Hell, it would probably break down before they got it off the lot anyway."

"Is the man still hanging around?"

"No. At least he wasn't when I went out to check. I called the sheriff and he's sending somebody over to check it out just in case. Meanwhile, keep your door locked." He looked over at her desk, littered with papers and file folders. "Didn't you have a phone in here?"

She grimaced and looked at him with one eye open, shaking her head up and down. "I took it out."

John shook his head and smiled at her indulgently. "I know you hate interruptions when you're practicing, but emergencies do crop up, and it's not always easy for someone to run down here to get you. I would certainly appreciate it, Miss Jones," he said in a stern voice tinged with humor, "if you would take the phone out of hiding and put it back where it belongs."

"Yes, sir."

"Carry on," he said, opening the door. "Oh," he turned to face her, "I know Mrs. Cobb told you about our guests."

Laughing, Jenine replied, "Did she ever. There was also discussion about the possibility of establishing schools like Highland Heights across the country."

"Well, these guys have lots of money to spend," said John. "Hopefully, we'll get some of it to fund the new programs you teachers are always begging for."

"The engineering and music departments insist that you consider putting in a recording studio before you do anything else," she replied.

"Yes, I still have your proposal," he said, as if weary of the reminder, with humor in his voice. "How's the Talent Show shaping up?"

Jenine smiled at him to temper the warning note in her voice. "It will be good as usual," she said.

"All right, I get the picture," he said. "I'll leave it up to your capable hands. I know you always put your best foot forward, but point your toes for this one." Jenine nodded. "And don't forget to lock this," he reminded her before taking his leave.

Jenine locked the door after him, then returned to her

desk. Scanning its scattered contents, she forgot what she had been looking for. She couldn't shake John's warning of a stranger lurking about. Maybe she should inform Nat.

Bending behind the desk, she opened the bottom drawer and pulled out the square, black phone. After connecting the end of the cable into the wall, she set it on the desk. With the receiver held to her ear, she began to have second thoughts.

Again, she remembered Nat's offer to support her professionally. She was never likely to forget, for it was a far cry from the wish she harbored in her heart. She knew he sensed her disappointment.

But *she* didn't matter now, she argued silently. Her concern was for his and Natasha's safety. Yet, would he perceive a stranger on the school campus as a threat? she wondered. She didn't think so. It seemed there'd been nothing but miscommunication between them. It was highly possible Nat would read something else into her call. She didn't want to risk giving him the impression that she was somehow chasing him or in any way trying to make him beholden to her.

The buzzer sang for several seconds in her ear, like a warning din to her subconscious, then clicked off. Absently, Jenine replaced the receiver. With a faraway look in her gaze, she struggled to decipher the message still ringing in her subconscious.

Strolling to the piano, she sat on the bench, her expression set in curious thought. She felt as if she was overlooking something important. With her fingers poised just above the keyboard, that certain something clicked in her mind.

Her hands flew to her mouth as wave after wave of shock slapped at her. It wasn't the buzz in the phone, but the word 'beholden' that was trying to tell her something, she realized: she remembered she and Nat hadn't used any protection. With her thoughts veering slightly off track, she recalled that the birth control method stored in her bathroom cabinet was too old to be considered effective.

Clumsily, Jenine scooted off the bench and hit her knee. "Ouch," she cried out. "Serves you right," she said fussily, rubbing the sore spot.

She began traipsing through the room. How could she have been so careless? she chided herself testily, a fist at her mouth as if to suppress the scream in her throat.

Maybe she was needlessly concerned, she argued, visibly calming. With a chiding chuckle, Jenine shook her head, suspecting she was guilty of grasping at straws by which to keep his memory fresh in her mind.

But a baby was more tangible than memories, an inner voice cut through her thoughts to school her.

Feeling inundated with maybes and what-ifs, Jenine emitted a long, troubled sigh. It died under the shrill of the school bell, signaling the end of the lunch period and beginning of the next class.

"Special delivery for Mr. Nathaniel Padell. I need you to sign here, sir," said the uniformed mail carrier.

Nat was instantly wary as he stood in the door with Natasha in his arms. He knew it would serve no purpose to question the carrier. He shifted the baby to his other hip while the carrier held the clipboard for his signature.

"Thank you. Have a good day," said the carrier, darting away to his truck.

Nat closed the door and locked it, his eyes riveted on the brown, legal-size envelope. With Natasha secure in the crook of his arm, he tore open the letter.

Within minutes of reading it, Nat quickly bundled

them up in overcoats, jumped in his car and spun out of the driveway. He cursed and beat the steering wheel all the way to Robbie's. He turned in her driveway just as she was getting out of her burgundy Cadillac.

Jumping out of the car, "You're not going to believe what this son-of-a . . . ," he said, furiously waving the letter in the air.

"Whoa," Robbie overlapped calmly. "Why don't you get Natasha out of the car, and we'll take this into the house?" she suggested, digging for keys in her purse.

Minutes later, Nat was sitting on the bar stool in Robbie's large family room; Natasha was scooting across the blanket that had been spread over the carpeted floor. He watched the wheels turning in Robbie's mind as she read the letter. She was sitting on the leather couch, her shoes had been kicked off, and she was rubbing a foot with her toes.

"He got the jump on us," she said candidly, her brows drawn together in a disturbed expression.

Nat sprang from the stool as he banged his fist on top of the bar. Hatred blazed in his eyes as he strode angrily back and forth.

"If David thinks I'm going to honor that court order for visitation rights, he's one stupid bastard," he said hotly.

"Watch your language in front of the baby," Robbie said absently, not even looking up at Nat.

"I'm not going to let him within an inch of Natasha." He spoke vehemently, his outstretched finger accenting every word of his threat. "And no judge is going to make me. I'll see him in hell first." A tightly knotted fist crashed in his hand—the sound exploded in the air, startling Natasha.

"It's all right, baby," Robbie said reassuringly as she picked up Natasha and patted her on the back. "Calm down, Nat. Getting mad is not going to solve anything."

"And apparently neither is the law," he retorted bitingly. "Damn!" as he sat on the stool, drumming his fingers on the counter. This was not the action he expected.

"That's all right," Robbie replied confidently. She put Natasha back on the floor and placed the set of colored plastic keys between the baby's clumsy fingers. "We have some tricks up our sleeves, too."

Nat looked at Robbie anxiously. "Has the private investigator turned up something?"

"Yes," she replied, returning to her spot on the couch. "As a matter of fact, he phoned me at four this morning. I was going to call you this afternoon, but you beat me to the punch."

"Well? What did he have to say?"

"Hold your horses," she told him, pulling a yellow legal pad from her briefcase. "Some of this is very interesting, at least one part, anyway."

Nat was ready to scream: Robbie was taking too long, flipping through her pad, in his estimation, tormenting his temper. "Robbie," he said in an irascibly patient tone.

"Here it is," she said, folding papers over the back of the hard cover of the pad. "Seems your father-in-law is on the take."

"What? On the take for what?"

"You've heard the reports that all of the money provided for the African Relief Fund may not be getting to the people."

Nat shrugged indifferently. He was perplexed as to how that news affected his situation.

"The private investigator has picked up on bits and pieces that Minister Cissoko is taking money from some official or officials in Nubacush," she felt compelled to remind him, "to keep quiet about their selling supplies and pocketing the money."

"How in the hell is that going to help me?" he demanded, totally unconcerned about the relief money.

"Stop and think a second," she said sternly, growing impatient with his blinding temper. "What judge is going to allow visitation rights to a man who's stealing from the Relief Fund, preventing poor, starving people from getting the food and supplies this entire country has joined in providing? We probably won't even get to court," she said, speculating that David Cissoko would do anything not to have this information released.

"Yeah, but can we prove it? You taught me about that," he said, sliding off the stool to pace a circle around Natasha. The anger he felt had abated somewhat as he pondered the implications of using the private investigator's information in court. "If we go into court charging him with stealing and can't prove it, then hell, he'd damn near own me," he pointed out with truculence apparent in his voice.

"Where there's smoke, there's fire," Robbie countered. "We still have a month to come up with proof, or some other little tidbit that would discredit Mr. Cissoko before the court date. Hopefully, he'll be so busy trying to save his you-know-what that he won't have time to be bothered with a custody case."

Nat squatted near Natasha, weighing the plan Robbie outlined. It was skimpy, he thought, but he decided that a piece of something, even if it wasn't much, was better than a piece of nothing. Particularly considering his own miscalculation, he thought with a pensive shimmer in his eyes.

"Nat," Robbie said as if weighing her words carefully, "there's one more thing."

"Spit it out," he said. "Can't be any worse than this."

"Well, it may or may not have anything to do with David," she hedged, rifling through her briefcase. "The investigator thought it was interesting. Said it could give us more insight into the kind of man we're dealing with. But it could just be coincidence," she stressed. "I've been debating with myself all morning about whether or not to give it to you." Pulling out a clipped news article, she said, "Here it is."

"What is it?" Nat asked, crossing the room to her.

Passing him the article, she said, "I'll let you read it."

Nat scanned the article, a single-column story of no more than two paragraphs in length, his eyes riveted on the bold headline caption: BODY OF FORMER MODEL SNATCHED FROM GRAVE. His hands began to tremble, and his features twisted into a look of disbelief and rage.

The article went on to explain that the caretakers of the D.C. Glenhaven Cemetery discovered over the weekend that the remains of former model Annette Padell were missing. She was the late wife of percussionist Nat Padell. The musician could not be reached for comment. Annette Padell was also the daughter of the Nubacush's Culture and Education Minister, David Cissoko.

There was more, but Nat stopped reading. "When did this happen?" he asked, his voice as a maddening level, the article crushed in his tight grip.

"Two weeks ago," Robbie said softly. She sighed her regret and sympathy. "I'm sorry."

"He couldn't possess her in life, so he decides to possess her in death," Nat said, a haunted look coloring his expression and tone.

"You think David Cissoko took her body . . ." Robbie whispered. There was an audible gasp at Nat's slow nodding. "What kind of man is he?" When Nat didn't answer, she continued, hoping to divert Nat's attention from the startling revelation. "How did he find you in the first place? Did you tell anybody where you were staying?"

Cryptically, Nat replied, "Maybe he followed the drumbeat."

"I don't follow."

He looked down at Robbie, a sheepish expression on his face. "I had my agent send my instruments."

"Why didn't you take out an ad in the *Times?*" Robbie retorted as she got up from the couch to go behind the bar. She took two diet sodas from the portable refrigerator, popped the tops on each and held one out to Nat.

Accepting the soda, he said, "I thought I'd covered my tracks pretty well. I knew he was heading for California, so I instructed him to ship my instruments there, and from there, he would send them wherever I told him."

"All that cloak and dagger for nothing," she teased before turning serious. "Well, either your friend was trailed, which I doubt, or you were, my friend," she said, returning to the couch.

"You think he hired a private detective to find us?"

"You've employed one to find him out, I don't see why not," she reasoned, taking a sip of her drink.

Nat took a long thirst-quenching swallow from the soda, then set the can on the counter. He stared absently across the room, his expression guarded, quiet, contemplative.

"What is it, Nat?"

Slowly, he shook his head as if coming out of a daze. "Nothing." Not trusting himself to speak lest he say too much, he took another swallow of soda. "What do I do now?"

"Absolutely nothing," Robbie replied, setting the can on the coffee table. "Let me handle it," she added quickly, pulling the pad in her lap, a pen poised in her hand for writing. "That's what you're paying me a whopping fee to do. If Cissoko contacts you by letter again, or phone," she said, jotting notes on the pad, "I want to know about it immediately. I repeat, you do nothing, let me handle it."

Nat glowered at the advice, and his jaw ticked, before a mask of stone settled over his features. "Sure," he agreed solemnly, feeling like a kid who runs to his mama whenever in trouble. He picked up Natasha and began walking around the room, seemingly concerned only with making her laugh with his playful kisses.

Looking up from her notes, Robbie stared at Nat, suspicion in her look. "I mean it, Nat," she reiterated emphatically. "Don't do anything stupid. In fact, don't do anything." Still eyeing him intensely as if trying to guess what was going on inside his head, she advised, "I think you might want to consider having an alarm system installed."

"Jenine's going to kill me," he muttered to himself, imagining her reaction to the news of the security changes to her home.

"No, she won't," Robbie replied absently; she had already started scribbling more notes on the pad. "She loves you and that baby."

Nat froze, his eyes fixed on Robbie in an absent look. Jenine loved him? Liked him a lot, sure. Wanted him, yeah. But loved him?

"Did she tell you that?" he demanded of Robbie, the questions tumbling in his mind.

"Will you keep up with the conversation?" Robbie replied. "I'm trying to explain to you what I want you to do." She stopped writing to look up at him.

"You said Jenine loves me. How do you know?" he asked quietly, his searching gaze penetrating her serene one.

"Men can be so blind sometimes," she said, shaking her head. She exchanged pen and pad for the can of soda and took a swallow.

Remembering his offer to Jenine, Nat recalled she had

looked as if she couldn't bear the sight of him. He had thought it was because he came off sounding insulting, as if he were offering to pay for services rendered. That would explain the sudden coolness he felt from her, he told himself with an astonished look on his features.

Realizing just how grievous an error he had made in his thinking, he said, "I'm so stupid," slapping himself upside his head. Jenine didn't want his money, or his professional help. She wanted him, and all that implied.

"You'll get no argument out of me on that one," Robbie quipped.

"Damn it, damn it, damn it," Nat blasted himself.

"Do you drive her to school?"

"No."

"Then start," Robbie ordered. She walked around Nat to the curtained window, expanding across the back wall of the den. She pulled the cord as she spoke. "And pick her up in the evenings until I tell you otherwise. I'm going to pay a call to the sheriff's office to see if we've had or have any foreign visitors in town. Yuk," she said, looking outside at the cold and cloudy sky. "Do you believe this weather? This morning, I would have sworn spring had come early this year. And now, look at it."

Robbie was much too casual. It was time to put his excitement aside and concentrate on what could be a deadly situation.

"Do you think David would try something?" he asked. He already knew the answer to that, he told himself.

Robbie's blue eyes clouded with a hard expression as she stared at him. "How far are you willing to go to keep Natasha from him?" she replied.

"All the way," he said without hesitation.

"Then we can assume he is equally up to the task to get her." She sipped soda—with a fatalistic look on her face.

"I'd rather play it safe than go through the guilts," she said softly.

Bede turned from the window—where he was looking out through the curtain—to stare, as Mubari lumbered into the dingy room of the hotel. Suspicious, he knew Mubari had been gone long enough to eat a thirty-six course meal. But the big man had returned with only a greasy stained bag and a can of soda.

"We are supposed to stay out of sight," he said. "Where have you been?"

Mubari sank into the red chair near the door, popped the top on the can and guzzled down half the contents of the can.

"I said, where have you been," Bede said harsher than before.

Pulling a hamburger out the bag, Mubari snapped, "Out." He folded the paper around the hamburger and took a big bite. "I'm restless. When I get restless, I get hungry. We come all this way to do nothing but sit on our hands like two old women," Mubari grumbled, with a mouthful. "What is the old hyena up to?"

Bede didn't buy Mubari's explanation, but he agreed in sentiment and let the matter pass. "It is not for us to question the minister," he replied, though he wondered as well what Minister Cissoko was planning. He closed the curtain securely and glanced about the room with distaste. The telephone—on the table sandwiched between the two beds—rang.

Chapter Eleven

It was after six when Jenine pulled up in the driveway behind Nat's car. The evening skies were dark, and the air current promised to get colder as the night grew.

So much for the promise of spring, she thought, getting out of the car. With passing interest, she noticed the black van parked on the other side of the street in front of her house as she raced to the front door, hurrying to get out of the cold. She was greeted by the warmth and the silence in the house.

With her back pressed against the door and her eyes closed, she sighed at length her satisfaction at being home. Though tired after a long, hectic day, she felt energized by a sense of accomplishment over the amount of work she had gotten done. Before leaving school, she conducted a light rehearsal with the jazz band, then completed her lesson plans for the week. Knowing her time was short, she had other plans for her evening, she thought, pushing herself off the door.

"Nat? Natasha? Where are you?" she called out, heading to the den. She set her briefcase on the floor next to the couch, then shrugged out of her coat.

Enticed by the aromas from the kitchen, she walked to the adjoining room. Bypassing the fresh green bunch of broccoli left on the cutting board near the sink, she lifted the lids of the dishes on the stove: one pot contained rice, while salmon patties in a thick, red stew of tomatoes and rosemary was in the skillet.

"Hm," she muttered, licking her lips before replacing the lid to saunter around the island. Mail was stacked on a corner.

Perusing the senders' addresses on the front of the envelopes, she decided they were mostly "file-thirteen material." The last was a large brown envelope, its back facing front. She flipped it over and saw the name Nathaniel Padell on a wide, white label. The return address sent all of her inner warning-systems off at once; her whole body tightened, and then she took a breath. Lightning bolts of worry flashed in her eyes as they flew over the face of the envelope she was gripping with trembling hands.

Special delivery; it had come today from Washington, D.C. Her heart skipped a beat in her chest. The danger she had only sensed from afar was closing in quickly, she mused, as the envelope slid from her grasp.

Infused with anxiety, Jenine spun around and dashed down the hall. Reaching the small entryway by the front door, she was halted by the approach of an unfamiliar man, carrying a clip pad. Nat, who towered over him, was right behind.

Looking past the man, she said, "Nat?" There were many questions in her tone.

"Hi babe," he said in a chipper tone.

Watching his approach, she thought he looked too well-controlled—as if to conceal uneasiness. Before she could conduct further inspection, he was bending to kiss her on the cheek. Draping an arm around her shoulder protectively, he said, "I didn't hear you come in."

Staring at the stranger, she replied, "I just got in.

Nat . . . ?" looking back and forth at him and at the red-headed, freckle-faced man smiling at her like he knew something she didn't.

"Honey, this is Oscar Moore from the security company," Nat said.

"Mrs. Padell," Oscar said, extending his hand to her. "It's nice to meet you."

Too stunned to speak, Jenine stared open-mouthed at Nat, her ears ringing with the married title. Functioning on rote instinct, she accepted the fat hand extended to her and shook it lightly.

Answering the questions blurring her gaze, Nat said, "Honey, I decided to have an alarm installed and burglar bars put on the windows." In a tone with the care of defusing a bomb, he continued, "Now, I know we didn't discuss this, but I didn't want us to get bogged down in conversation and no action."

"It's really best to have it done," Oscar said.

With a jerk of her head, Jenine looked up at him. An innocent co-conspirator, she thought, then turned a peeved gaze on Nat. It softened as she noticed a certain tension lurking in the depths of his eyes, although he tried to hide it with a smile. Oscar was still speaking.

"Even though Highland Heights is probably the safest place in the country, you can never be too careful."

"Oscar is going to get his men over here tomorrow morning," Nat said.

"Do you have any questions, Mrs. Padell?" Oscar asked Jenine.

Plenty, Jenine said to herself, but not for you. With a polite smile, she replied, "No. I'm sure you and Nat covered everything."

"Well," Oscar said, "I'll be off. My men and I will be here bright and early in the morning."

"That's fine," Nat replied, rubbing his hands together

excitedly. "Honey, why don't you get ready for dinner, while I show Oscar out."

With a saccharine smile on her face, Jenine replied, "Sure. Honey." Ire joined her anxiety as she marched down the hall to her bedroom. Nat was pulling another version of Horus, the avenging son of Osiris and Isis as if she were a whimpering simpleton. Even though the superhero image brought amusement to her lips, it was not enough to calm her strained nerves about the letter from Washington. When would Nat learn they were in this together? she asked herself silently.

"I'll get ready all right," she said, determination flashing in her eyes, "but not for dinner."

Reaching the room, she pulled out the bottom drawer of the dresser, too hard, and it sagged heavily in her grasp. Biting off a curse, she shoved the drawer back into its slot, then began picking through the assortment of sweat pants and tops.

None matched her mood—red. Her favorites, the gray ones, were dirty, she recalled, muttering a disgusted sigh. She didn't wash the laundry yesterday. Remembering what she had done instead, a warm blush stole across her features and a dull ache of desire rose in her groin.

With a self-derisive moan over the wayward thoughts, threatening to take the sting out of her pique with Nat, she hurried to her feet and was about to leave the room when from the corner of her eye, she spotted the gift box on the bed. Music staffs in a rainbow of colors danced across shining white wrapping paper, with a circle of small pink ribbons centered on top.

The usual questions surfaced in her head. With interest and excitement very much a part of her, Jenine inched to the bed for a closer look. She stole a glance over her shoulder at the doorway. No Nat and no shadows; it was safe to pry.

She carefully dug in the swirl of ribbons, searching for a card, a hint of ownership, but there was none. An inquisitive frown clouded her expression. She began to suspect the gift was a bribe from Nat, who knew she would be upset at his high-handedness.

Installing an alarm in her home, she thought, her eyes glazed with annoyance. The nerve of him! Well, she could not be bought, she thought sassily to herself, arms folded across her bosom. Yet, she couldn't stop staring at the box, feeling a warm glow flow through her.

"Go on. Open it."

Spinning to face Nat leaning against the door, Jenine couldn't dull the sparkle in her gaze as it roamed the length of him. Her exasperation evaporated. She was assailed by her warm thoughts of him. She was a hot-blooded woman, she thought, rationalizing her reaction. It was useless trying to deny her feelings for him.

Cutting a suspicious smile at him, she asked, "A bribe?" nodding in the direction of the bed.

"A gift," he replied in a conciliatory, mesmeric voice. "I'll get dinner on the table. Don't be long."

Even after he vanished, Jenine did not tear into the box, though she was teeming with curiosity over the contents. With forced leisure, she first removed the bow, then peeled the tape from the paper before shaking open the box. The bottom fell and the contents spilled onto the bed. An immensely pleased sigh escaped her throat.

Fingering the ebony collar of the scarlet satin lounging shirt, she held it against her body and rubbed the smooth, cool fabric along the side of her face. A bubble bath was in order, she decided. Dinner could wait.

On the other side of the house, the mellow strings of a jazz guitarist filled the three-room area. Nat was in the kitchen finishing preparations for a dinner Jenine would never forget. Even if she could never forgive him for the many sins he had committed. It was a thought that had become a constant since Robbie disclosed Jenine's feelings for him.

With an apron tied around his waist, he was standing at the counter, chopping broccoli. The news had been uplifting considering the other matter. His joy had been short-lived as reality came crashing down on him like an avalanche, and he felt trapped in the mixed blessings of his situation.

He imagined his late wife's father right behind him, intent on destroying him, while Jenine was in front of him with promising predilections. The weight of the dilemma reflected in his eyes, a pained look as though he had been wounded.

He wanted desperately to believe the situation would be righted, that David would miraculously disappear and he would be free to pursue a life with Jenine. But all too often in the past, his heart and libido crossed signals with reason, the way he knew the world to be.

Pushing his solemn thoughts aside, Nat opened the refrigerator and pulled out a bag of carrots. He dumped them on the board next to the broccoli and began slicing several at a time.

He used to cook for Netta and himself frequently. Many times he had thanked his mother for insisting that all her children learn to cook when they were young. While he enjoyed cooking, living with Netta had made it a matter of necessity because her cooking was bad for one's digestion, he chuckled reminiscently.

With the laughter in his throat fading, Nat slowly submerged himself into the past. Although he tended to focus on the bad, there had been some good times in that short-lived marriage. He liked being married, being part of a family of his own. What he hadn't liked was David's interference and the fact that the mere mention of his name often resulted in an argument.

When David found out Netta was pregnant, he had tried to talk her into getting an abortion. But it was too late: she had already passed the first trimester. Even so, Nat still wasn't secure leaving her alone, he recalled with a bitter frown. He had turned down out-of-town gigs to be around just to make sure she wouldn't cave in to her father's manipulation. Though he knew then that was no way for two people claiming to love each other to act, he was committed to the relationship because of the baby.

He had been the one who spent time poring over books in search of the right name for their baby. It was something Netta had been reluctant to do, claiming they had plenty of time.

Scooping the broccoli and carrots up in his hands to drop them into the steamer, Nat couldn't help thinking that would not have been the case if Jenine was pregnant. She had taken to Natasha as though she'd birthed her herself.

Turning to the skillet, where the contents were bubbling under the low heat, he stirred the stewing salmon. It seemed he had involved himself with another woman whose culinary skills were lacking, he chuckled. Aw, but she made up for it in other ways, he thought smilingly, replacing the lid. Jenine was so unlike Netta in many other ways, it was irrelevant.

While rinsing the knife under a stream of water in the sink, a picture of Jenine pregnant with his child flashed in his mind. The knife slipped, scraping the flesh of his thumb with its sharp blade, drawing blood. Nat barely felt the pain; all his senses were occupied with the visual image.

With wild palpitations beating in his chest, he recalled

he had used no protection with Jenine. He threw back his head and released a guttural moan that mirrored the disgust in his expression.

Jolted by the stinging sensation in his thumb, he held his hand under running water. He began to consider his blessings a curse to others, namely Jenine. How could she love a self-centered bastard like him? he asked of himself. He had really made a mess of things, he thought, blowing out his cheeks.

Beyond his love and an insatiable appetite for her, he was in no position to offer her much more than sex, he thought, recalling the letter. Now, he had put her in double jeopardy.

The music stopped. The din of silence roared in Nat's ear like a refrain of catastrophes.

By the time dinner was complete and all set to be served, Jenine came spinning and dipping like a runway model into the kitchen.

"I love it," she exclaimed.

Immeasurably impressed, Nat stared. He felt every sobering thought in his head disappear, his gaze roaming over her face and figure. Her eyes were clear and bright, cheeks flushed. The red nightshirt heightened her glowing brown porcelain skin; its long tails fell just below her knees, and the slits at the sides disclosed the fine shape of her legs and slender thighs. He fought the urge to take her here and now on the kitchen floor.

"I'm glad you like it," he replied with a seductive gleam in his eyes.

Jenine liked what she saw in his gaze, returning his look with one of her own. With tingling delight coursing through her, she felt herself flowing into his arms, and then she was there, wrapped in a silken cocoon of euphoria.

"Thank you," she said, smiling up at him, arms around his waist.

"I'm glad you liked it," he replied. Feeling both humbled and honored, it was all he could think to say.

"And it feels so good next to my skin," Jenine moaned. Pleased, she buried her head in the middle of his chest where she placed a kiss against the knit sweater. "Thank you, again. But this still doesn't let you off the hook," she said, poking him in the chest.

"All right," he said with laughter in his voice. "But dinner first." Swatting her behind affectionately, "Make yourself useful."

"Ouch," she exclaimed playfully, rubbing her bottom. Noticing the bandage on his thumb, she took his hand to examine it. "What happened to your hand?" she asked.

"I was just being careless," he replied.

Jenine wondered at the musing look in his eyes, but began setting the table with her finest china. Nat attended to the food. After topping their glasses with wine, he seated Jenine at the table.

"How was school today?" he asked.

"Oh, no," she replied, spooning rice onto her plate. "You first." She passed him the rice dish, then reached for the salmon dish. "I saw the letter."

"It'll keep until later," he said in a final tone.

Jenine pushed her hair back, the better to glare at him. With exasperation in her tone, she said with a scolding look, "Nat."

Reaching for her hand across the table, he replied, "Don't worry. Everything's going to be fine. I'll protect you."

Instantly, her eyes flared up, but she cooled it, and pulled her hand from his gentle grasp. Though somewhat offended, the besotted woman in her couldn't take offense at the way he was looking at her, as if she were the most precious thing in his life.

"I don't need protection, I need information," she said in a soft, truculent voice, lowering her gaze to her food. She speared a chunk of salmon and popped it in her mouth.

Tense seconds passed in silence. Dinner was on the verge of ruin. Finally, Nat spoke.

"All right," he said grudgingly. Pushing back from the table, he got up to get the letter from the counter then returned to his seat. He passed the envelope to Jenine, then began piling food on his plate. But he had already lost his appetite.

Staring at the scowl on his face, Jenine pulled the document out of the envelope. She observed Nat pick up his fork, then drop it to the plate with a clink and rest his elbows on the table, his gaze intent, unreadable. Lowering her gaze, she read the document: The essence stated that Mr. Nathaniel Padell, parent and legal guardian of minor, Natasha Padell, was petitioned to appear before Judge Haywood Wycliff in Austin, Texas, March 30, for a hearing involving visitation rights of said minor's paternal grandfather, Mr. David Cissoko.

Absently, setting the letter on the table to stare incredulously at Nat, she asked, "Can he do this?"

"He already has," he replied bitterly. He slouched back in the chair, his hands in his lap under the table. "He's done something else, too. Something that violates even his own religion," Nat mused aloud. He felt his anger rising anew and held himself under tight control.

"Nat?" Jenine prodded with concern.

"I never thought about it before," Nat said as if he'd just gotten a new idea as he sat up straight in the chair.

Confused, Jenine asked, "Thought about what?"

"Netta. She refused to make any kind of preparations before Natasha was born. Now, I'm beginning to suspect she knew all along she would never live to see her child. David has taken it a step further," he said in a faraway tone. "Netta's grave was robbed. Now Natasha can only kneel before an empty grave site." He looked at Jenine with a determined and focused gaze. "I'm keeping the headstone in place. Natasha never has to know the truth."

Dropping the letter to the table, Jenine rushed to Nat. She wrapped her arms around him and held him against her bosom. Blinking back her tears, she nodded, saying, "Of course. It's not important. All Natasha needs to know is that her mother loved her dearly."

Nat trapped Jenine's hand next to his chest, stroking it gently. "I've really gotten you into a fine mess, haven't I?"

Jenine patted him on the shoulder before returning to her seat. "That's not important right now either," she said bravely. "Since David knows where you are, what should we do now? Have you talked to Robbie? How did he find you anyway?" she asked with irritation.

He smiled at her indulgently. "Robbie believes he just put a tail on me, but I think he followed the drumbeat. And yes to your other questions," he said, propping his elbows on the table. "And now, we exercise extreme caution."

"The burglar bars and the alarm," she said matter-of-factly.

"That, and I drop you off at school in the mornings and pick you up in the evenings," he said. "And you, will go nowhere alone, do you hear me?" His gaze widened to deliver the addendum.

"And what about you?" she replied. Feeling an invidious strength stewing in him, she knew he wasn't about to accept this threat from David as calmly as he appeared.

Ignoring the question, Nat took a bite of food. It was tasteless in his mouth.

"You're planning something, aren't you?" Jenine said insistently. Receiving an impatient look and silence, she reached over the table to take his face by the chin and hold it up. Staring directly into his eyes, she said, "Tell me."

"What am I going to do with you?" he said smoothly, and smiled benignly, as if dealing with a temperamental child. He took her hand in his, kissed it, then placed it on the table near her.

"You're going to tell me the truth, Nathaniel Padell," she persisted, two deep lines of uneasiness between her eyes.

A comfortable countenance settled over his features, his eyes gentled. Reclaiming her hand, he held it against his lips, his gaze never leaving her face. With Robbie's revelation on his mind, he couldn't stop the thought that if anything happened to her because of him, he would never be considered a human being ever again, for he would take immense pleasure in killing David Cissoko or anyone who touched a hair on her head.

Jenine watched his eyes harden maliciously as he stared deeply into some private place. She worried that David Cissoko would, if he already hadn't, push Nat past his limits of reason and morality.

"Nat?" she called softly.

As he looked up into her face, she noticed his dark expression give way to desire. A part of her reveled in his open admiration of her, but the other feared for what he might do.

"Do you know how to use a gun?" he asked.

Jenine's hands became icy still on his face before she snatched them from his light possession as she sprang from her seat. She pivoted sharply, then stomped off to the den.

Tossing his napkins on the table, Nat replied, "I thought not."

"Of all the stupid, idiotic things you've ever come up with. This beats all!"

Nat followed her explosively, then stopped abruptly, his hand froze in the air with the point he was going to make. Filled with a need to release the violent anger he'd held in check, he couldn't speak. He had never been good at running from challenges—as was demonstrated by the numerous errors he'd made, he thought. He couldn't stand what running away was doing to his self-esteem.

Jenine noted the remorseful and uptight look shadowing his features. She wanted to hold him in her arms and make his troubles disappear.

Dropping to the couch, she instructed with her hands, "Come here."

Nat obeyed her silky command and allowed her to position him on the floor between her legs. She began massaging his temples, then buried her fingers in his thick, curly hair to rub his scalp.

A deep groan, like a healing sound, came from the back of his throat when her hands traveled down to his neck and shoulders. She enjoyed the feel of his pearly black skin and taut muscles, yielding to the pleasuring pressure of her ministering hands.

"Now, promise me, we will practice extreme caution together," she said with emphasis. "And, that you will not do anything other than what Robbie instructed. Okay?"

"Yes," he said in a dazed voice, succumbing to her strong, gentle touches, webbing more than comfort with the kneading motions of her nimble fingers. The rose scent of those little beads she used in her bath mingled with her own ambrosial essence and assailed his senses to create a different kind of tension in his body. He would have promised her anything as he captured her hands in his to plant a titillating kiss in each palm.

A shiver of excitement tingled inside her, and Jenine closed her eyes, savoring the sensation his lips engraved on the inner surface of her hands. She went willingly when he pulled her down to the floor to straddle his thighs. A sensuous flame burned in his olive-brown eyes, scorching her with intent, and a quiet shudder shot through her.

"You love me." Not quite a question, almost a demand. "Say it," he commanded, his hands beneath the fabric at her hips. "I want to hear it."

"Yes," she replied in a tremulous whisper. Loving him with her gaze, "I love you."

His mouth covered hers hungrily, devouring its softness, his hands tugging at the buttons on the shirt.

Like a dying man given a reprieve, Nat loved her with his hands, his mouth, his soul. Jenine was transported to a glorious place where the Cissokos of the world did not exist. Reality was only a tender touch away.

The next day, Jenine was in her office at school. Tapping the stack of music and notes on her desk, she scanned the room, a finger in her mouth. The first rehearsal for the talent show was soon to start. Fifth- and sixth-period classes had been canceled just for the occasion.

"Knock, knock," Bruce said as he stepped into the room. He was carrying a large black music folder.

"Hi, Bruce," she said absently.

Noticing her expression, he guessed, "What did you lose?"

"I can't find my purse."

"Where did you last have it?" he asked.

"I always leave it in my bottom drawer," she replied.

"Check again, maybe you overlooked it," he suggested.

"I've already checked several times," she replied.

Just then, a student walked into the room as if unsure of himself. "Ms. Jones?" he asked, staring at Jenine hopefully.

Excited and relieved, Jenine said, "My purse! You found it." Crossing to meet the student halfway to take her purse from his hand, "Thank you."

"Somebody turned it in to the office."

"Who?" Jenine asked, her eyes darkening suspiciously. "Where did they find it?"

"You must have left it in the cafeteria," the student replied, to which Jenine muttered a sound of disbelief as her brow rose a fraction.

Bruce said, "Check and see if everything's there."

Jenine set the purse on the desk to search it before declaring, "Nothing's missing," in a bemused tone, wondering if she had really mislaid her purse. She had been somewhat preoccupied, constantly looking over her shoulders and closely scrutinizing the faces of those who were unfamiliar to her. She knew she wouldn't feel truly safe enough to relax her guard until Nat picked her up this evening.

The student turned to leave, then did an about-face. "Oh, Mr. North told me to remind you to plug in the phone."

"Thank you," Jenine said politely behind a funny expression on her face.

"What was that look for?" Bruce asked.

"John has been after me about the phone," she said with dismissal, but pulled it out the drawer and plugged it into the wall, nevertheless. "Now, I'm ready."

"Before we go, I need to get that music from you, so I can make copies for the group, and,"—pulling two sheets of paper from the folder—'here's the line-up for this weekend. And the numbers for the talent show. Gloria asked me to drop them off."

Jenine set the talent-show program on the desk, taking a keen interest in the band's set of numbers. "No rehearsal tonight?" she asked, her fingers moving as though she were playing the music on the score she was holding.

"We'll probably still be in rehearsal for the talent show," he replied. "Remember who we're working with," he said with jest.

Lowering the score to the desk, "I forgot just that quick."

"I wonder what's been on your mind," Bruce said slyly.

"Obviously not rehearsing," she replied blushing. She knew the entire school was aware of her romance. Her joy was real, and it showed.

"Yeah, I can tell. You've been floating around here on a cloud ever since you came back. There's been a perpetual glow on your face, kid. I hate to admit it, but he's a far better man for you than thou," he said dramatically, clutching at his heart.

"You're certainly full of it today," she replied with mirth in her voice. She thought she had a done a good job of hiding her uneasiness about the pending altercation with David Cissoko, as well as the sadness that literally made her heart sink whenever she remembered Nat's imminent departure. She wished for a speedy resolution of either event, so that she could restore some semblance of normalcy in her life. Reminding herself of both dreadful outcomes, she hoped, would prepare her to deal with the actual eventualities.

Sitting on the corner of the desk, Bruce quipped, "Spring is in the air."

"You have over a month to go before you can start blaming your craziness on the weather."

"It's an early spring," he shrugged, before turning serious. "You know, you really do look radiant. You love him very much," he said matter-of-factly.

"Yes," she said softly, after a slight pause, remembering the time when such an admission would have been hotly denied. She smiled a fond smile, her voice taking on a faraway tone. "I do love him. I guess I always have and always will." The latter was said more to herself, with a musing that it was all to be for naught.

"Is something wrong?"

"Wrong? No, nothing's wrong," she replied, shaking her head, thinking back to this morning, wondering where Nat was right now. She had been set to play hooky from school today, and her head was full of plans for the three of them.

Nat was pulling a bulky sweater over his head when she had run into the master suite, eager to share her news with him. She kissed Natasha, who was playing with the toy key ring in her baby bed, before announcing, "I'm not going to school today," and crawling to the middle of the bed.

The impetuous idea had come to her while putting on her makeup. They were going to go shopping, have lunch at the Cavern Inn, then if Natasha was still up to it, take a tour of one of the old caverns in the area. Excited and anticipating the fun they were going to have, she hadn't thought anything of the stillness that came over Nat in the process of putting on his sweater.

"Are you feeling okay?" he asked, getting his boots out of the closet.

"Yeah, I'm fine," she replied. "I just decided to take the day off. I'm sure John won't mind." High-spirited with her plans, she prattled on. "Bruce can cover for me."

"That may not be a good idea." He sat on the side of the bed, his back to her, to tug a boot over his socked foot. "If you don't show up at school, somebody's going to get suspicious. I really think it's best that you go in."

Jenine didn't believe her ears and sat frozen, a puzzled line across her forehead before she inched her way to his side. With her hand on his shoulder, she turned him to face her.

Prepared for her curiosity, his innocent tone was natural as he asked, "What?"

"Suppose you tell me," she replied in a hand-on-her-hips tone of voice.

Holding her chin—"I'm sorry to spoil your plans"—he kissed her on the lips—"I'll make it up to you, I promise." Then he resumed putting on the other boot.

Jenine stared at his back with a wounded look. Nat was blocking her out again, playing the superhero to the damsel in distress. He had yet to accept her fully as the woman she had become, which meant he didn't trust her as an adult, keeping her locked in his image of the innocent young girl.

"Oh, stop it, Nat," she said, with extreme annoyance in her voice, folding her arms across her bosom.

"I don't know what you're talking about!" he professed guilelessly.

"Seems we've had this conversation before," she said with crestfallen finality, moving away from him.

"Now, don't be like that," he said, pulling her back to his side. "I love you. Please believe that. And I would like nothing better than to spend the day with you." His arms snaked around his waist, holding her to him though she squirmed to be free. "Just trust me. This is something I have to do."

He stared at her intently, and the double meaning of his gaze was very obvious. He wanted her as much as she wanted him and was regretting the matter that claimed priority over what she had wanted to do.

She searched his face, lines of worry creasing her forehead. "It's Cissoko, isn't it?" she guessed. When his head bobbed in resignation, she knew from his bleak, tight-lipped expression that nothing she could say or do would stop him from his purpose. "I'm going with you." The determined decree rolled off her tongue faster than even she could digest.

He released her abruptly and went to the closet to pull out his jacket.

"If you're not going to school today, then you girls can stay home together," he said in a conversational tone as though she hadn't spoken at all.

Stepping out of bed, shaking her head forcibly from side to side, she said, "Uh-uh."

He turned to face her, a warning cloud settled on his features. "I don't want to argue with you about this, Jenine."

"We're not going to argue, Nathaniel," she said, side-stepping him to get her coat out of the closet.

"You don't understand," he said imploringly. "This is something I have to do. And it was Robbie's suggestion that we keep up with our routine."

That won him the argument. She relented, though she hadn't felt right about it.

"Jenine? Jenine, where are you?"

She heard her name being called from a foggy distance and looked at Bruce, dazed, before an embarrassed blush spread across her face. "I'm sorry. I guess I was day-dreaming again."

"Are you sure everything's okay?"

Laughing at the thought, she replied, "I'm sure, Bruce.

Everything is fine," she said, adding silently, not counting a block of stupid, male pride.

"Okay, good," he replied, eager to move on to other matters. "I've picked out the song for our group." Jenine frowned at him curiously. "Remember, the talent show? Just because you're the coordinator doesn't let you off the hook from making a fool of yourself like everybody else."

Jenine laughed. "Okay, I'm all here now. What are we doing?"

"A Quincy Jones number from the *Back on the Block* album," he replied.

"Title track?" she asked excitedly.

"No," he replied. "I thought the song Chaka Khan sang was appropriate. Of course, you'll sing the lead." Jenine bunched her face in a frown. " 'One Man Woman,' " he grinned at her.

It was early afternoon, and Nat was tired and hungry. His search for the man he presumed Cissoko had sent to find him had turned up nothing.

Bolstered by the knowledge that Highland Heights wasn't a big town with many places for a newcomer to stay, he had started with the little motels on the outskirts and worked his way back to the center. Surely someone would have noticed a big man with a foreign accent.

It wasn't the best idea, he now thought, but he had to do something, as he seated himself at a back table in Scotty's. The diner was empty; the lunch hour had passed over two hours ago, so he had the place to himself. Scotty had taken his usual order and was in the back preparing a double-meat cheeseburger and a large order of fries while Nat sipped lukewarm coffee.

Where else is there to go? he asked himself, beginning to wish he'd let Jenine come along. Maybe she would have had some suggestions. He'd never forget that sad, solemn face she'd worn all the way to school. And it hurt him to his heart to leave her, but this was something he had to do alone. He had gone through a similar case of the guilts when he left Natasha at the daycare.

"Women," he said out loud with a bittersweet chuckle. He was missing both of his right now. He got up to find the men's room. When he returned shortly, another customer had taken a seat at the counter.

"Nathaniel Padell, I presume," the stranger said to him, stepping off the high stool at the counter to approach Nat.

With his body on alert for any aggressive movement, Nat looked at the big man in the blue checkered shirt, well-worn jeans and scuffed black boots. He was holding a cowboy hat in his hand.

"And who are you?"

"Name's Talbert Murray," he said, holding his hand out to Nat. "But you can call me Tal. I'm the sheriff of Highland Heights. Robbie asked me to be on the lookout for you."

"Have a seat, Tal," Nat offered.

After Talbert slid across the red bench, Nat sat opposite him.

"Why did Robbie ask you to be on the lookout for me?"

"She thinks you might do something foolish. Her words, not mine," he said, holding up his hand in mock defense of an attack.

"Apparently she's told you why I'm here." Nat pushed the cold coffee to the edge of the table.

"Jenine Jones," Talbert replied, training his brown-eyed stare on Nat as though reading his thoughts. "Least, that's what Robbie told me."

"And you don't believe her?" Nat asked with only mild concern.

"Oh, I wouldn't say that," Talbert said with a chuckle. "I just happen to believe it's more to it than that. Robbie's an attorney, so my information is strictly limited to a need-to-know basis. She's an ethical woman."

"Sounds like she has a fan club," Nat replied with a knowing half-grin.

"Yeah," Talbert said, drawling out the one syllable. "And so does Miss Jones," he said, an odd mingling of warning and amusement in his eyes.

"You don't have any cause to worry about Miss Jones," Nat replied, returning Tal's look.

"Good," Talbert declared as though the matter was settled in his mind. "Mind if I smoke?" he asked, pulling a pack of cigarettes and matches from his coat pocket.

"Help yourself."

"Thanks. Robbie won't let me light up around her. Says she doesn't want to watch me while I kill myself," he said, lighting a non-filtered cigarette. He took a long drag off the nicotine stick, savoring its pungent taste. "Look, Nat, I don't know what's going on, but if I can expect trouble, I want to know about it. Now, we're both reasonably intelligent men, and sometimes women don't understand what that means. But, if you and I work together on this thing, the reason, besides Miss Jones, that you're here, I'm sure we can find a peaceful solution where nobody gets hurt. And the women don't even have to know about it. Get my drift?"

Nat wasn't sure how he felt about Sheriff Talbert Murray until he heard Robbie's name in a personal context. But even that wasn't enough to ensure him that Talbert could be trusted. "Is Robbie your woman?"

Talbert let loose a wail of a laugh. "Boy, you sure know how to get to the bottom line. Pardon the 'boy,' nothing personal, I assure you. But to answer your question, yeah."

Nat had his answer. He wiped his hands clean on the napkin, then reached across the table to shake Tal's hand. "I assure you, I didn't take it personally, Talbert."

Scotty, a short, stocky man, came out with Nat's order, which he set on the table before him. "Can I get you something else?" At Nat's nod, he turned to Talbert. "Yours will be out in a minute, Tal."

"Sure thing, Scotty," Talbert said. To Nat, "Go on, don't wait for me. You must have worked up a pretty big appetite by now after driving around Highland Heights."

Chapter Twelve

"I feel like a prisoner in my own home," Jenine said, running her fingers through her hair. She was sitting across the table from Robbie in the conference room at school. "It's those damn bars around the house," she said in a disgruntled tone of voice. "They've been up for three days, and I'haven't gotten used to them. I don't know if I'll ever get used to them."

"It's only for a short time," Robbie replied.

Getting up to walk around the table, Jenine said on a moan, "I know. And don't lecture me about having needed the security anyway, and that it's for my own good."

She had heard enough of the lecture from Nat to last her a lifetime. Precaution had become a dirty word. And Nat had insisted on exercising the safety measures to the letter—day in and day out, the same routine, switching a button off to leave the house, then back on, again locking themselves in for the night.

Holding in a little laugh, Robbie said in as serious a compassionate tone as she could muster, "I won't."

"Oh Robbie," Jenine exclaimed, dropping back in her chair, "I'll be so glad when this is over and I can have my boring, uneventful life back," thinking Nat may not have been present at all of late.

He had become so obsessed with safety that it was affecting their love life. The past couple of nights when she awaked and reached for Nat, the spot next to her was usually cold and empty, for he was up prowling around the house, rechecking the alarm system. There had been times when she was certain she was going to throw a tantrum. Not to mention what happened to her sanity when she saw burglar bars every time she looked out a window.

"With or without Nat and Natasha?" Robbie asked.

Sheepishly, Jenine replied, "You already know the answer to that. I guess you could say I want my cake with ice cream," a bittersweet look on her face.

"That's 'have your cake and eat it, too,' " Robbie corrected.

"Whatever," Jenine shrugged. "Anyway, you knew it before I did."

"No, you knew it before you decided to accept it."

"Did you ever think about becoming a psychiatrist instead of a lawyer?" Jenine quipped fondly, and both women laughed.

With a commiserating smile on her face, Robbie replied, "Been a rough day, huh?"

"You don't know the half of it. Ever since Nat had that alarm system installed, it's done nothing but go off with no provocation. Sheriff Murray calls me every day to make sure I'm okay. Can you imagine that? I barely know the man! Then, this morning, Ms. Barnes at the daycare called me when she couldn't reach Nat because Natasha refused to settle down and hadn't stopped crying since we dropped her off. I had to get one of the secretaries to sit in on my class while I ran over there and put her to sleep. Then, I got back to learn that today's rehearsal had been rescheduled for six-thirty this evening, which meant classes were back on, but Ms. Jones wasn't as prepared as she should have been." She released a long, tired sigh, then put her head on her arms, folded on the table.

"Why don't you leave early and take off tomorrow?"

"Because Nat is adamant that we follow routine, for one." She raised her head to look at Robbie. "Your orders, I understand."

"I don't . . . ," Robbie started in reply, then cut herself off. "Well, I'll rescind that order under the circumstances. You could use the rest."

"Well, you know the saying—no rest for the weary. The talent show is day after tomorrow," Jenine said, "and then, we start at the club this weekend for an unlimited engagement."

"Is there anything I can do?"

"You've already done it," Jenine replied with a kind smile for Robbie. "Just listening to me vent my frustration is enough."

"Then, I'm glad I was of some help," Robbie said, slipping into her coat. "Ethel told me to remind you about the party after the talent show."

"Is this a command performance?"

"You know Ethel," Robbie said in reply. Imitating the social educator's lilting voice, "And bring that young man I've been hearing so much about."

Long after Robbie left and Jenine had returned to her office, she was sitting on a corner of the piano bench woolgathering. Her mind never seemed free of Nat or the familiar lifestyle he had blessed her with, she thought with melancholy threatening to consume her.

"You got it bad and that ain't good," she told herself, before thinking ahead to the day when he would be gone from her life. That, too, was like a warning refrain, always in the back of her mind, even when she tried ignoring it.

His leaving was as certain as death. And that's how she would feel, if she didn't put a stop to the loving and the longing she had for him and the awakened maternal sensibilities she had for his daughter.

With a hand pressed to her abdomen, she imagined it swollen with child, giving birth to a long-limbed, brown baby with playful, olive-brown eyes. A manchild, she decided in her thoughts, her eyes brightening with an adoring mother's visage.

Unexpectedly, reality returned to crush her fantasy, and a grave look came over her features. Jenine chastised herself while pushing to her feet to walk about the room. She would never know that feeling and was only making matters worse dreaming about it, she told herself.

Someone rapped sharply on the door, and she looked up to see the door open and Nat filling the space. Wordlessly, though his roving gaze spoke volumes, he stepped inside the room and closed the door at his back. She felt locked in a time warp, her first view of Nat. Her whole being seemed to be filled with waiting, then the sign came, and she raced into his outstretched arms.

Nat lifted her off the floor and held her to him, his lips brushing hers, a tantalizing invitation for more. Her response was shameless, instant and total. When he released her mouth, she remembered where they were, but didn't care.

He smiled at her with something deeper than mere masculine interest, though he couldn't deny that that too had been a part of her appeal. But right now, he felt that he had never known such longing for someone, never knew he could miss her, the curve of her mouth, the kindness that lurked behind those large eyes, the gentle touch of her hands.

"God, I've missed you the past couple of days," he said.

She shivered imperceptibly at the husky tone of his voice, his bright eyes gobbling her with a loving hungry look. Though they had been physically together, there was an invisible wall between them. They had both been preoccupied with safety precautions, to the exclusion of their own emotional protection.

"Can you leave?" he asked.

Bobbing her head up and down, Jenine replied, "Yeah, but we have the talent-show rehearsal at six-thirty."

"Oh, I'm sure we can manage that," he replied.

"Then let's get out of here before John or Ethel shows up with more work for me to do."

"I'll never get over just how big Texas is," he said with forced awe. Or how easy Texans had made his task.

He watched the blush spread across Ethel Cobb's face, pleased with himself. She was seated beside him in the luxurious back seat of the limousine her husband sent to pick him up from their private airstrip.

"Then that means you've had a good trip," she replied.

"So far," he replied.

"Well, I promise you won't be let down here in Highland Heights. We even have some advantages over our bigger, sister cities. Just wait until you see our Academies. The schools are our pride and joy. I can say without false boasting, we can compete with any school in the country."

"Oh, I'm sure," he replied, smiling his most charming smile.

Such hospitality he'd never expected. The Cobb's private plane had flown him to Highland Heights from Austin where his "dear friends," the Hutchinsons arranged his successful meeting with the judge. And everything was accomplished while he was fulfilling his obligations to his country, he thought, amazed.

The limo rolled to a stop, and the chauffeur jumped out to open the door for its passengers. The honored guest climbed out first, then extended a hand back inside to help Ethel from the car.

Pulling the folds of his long wool gray coat closer to protect himself from the chill, he swept his gaze over the school, whose front door was a few steps away. A big, tall man came out of the double doors.

"Mr. Sawyer," Mrs. Cobb said when he neared.

"Hello again, Mrs. Cobb," John said.

"Mr. John Sawyer, meet one of our distinguished guests, Mr. David Cissoko. Mr. Cissoko, our principal, Mr. John Sawyer."

"How do you do, Mr. Sawyer?" David replied, shaking the younger man's hand.

"Fine, thank you," John replied. "Why don't we get out of the cold, then we can begin our tour of the campus."

They've all played right into his hands. Even Nat himself, David thought as he walked inside the warm building. Now, he would hardly have to lift a finger to exact his goal. Wasn't life grand?

Though Nat refused to tell her where they were going, he promised her an experience she would never forget. And she believed him the moment they strolled into the dining room of The Pecos, the most elegant restaurant the city had to offer, located right in the Sheraton Heights Hotel, where he informed her they had a room upstairs.

The decor, cuisine and service were all designed for people who knew how to enjoy dining, not merely eating, and were willing to pay for the luxury of being lavished with attention and care.

She and Nat shared a table for two in a back corner of the large room. A mural that looked as if the artist had carved the mountains and desert out of the Texas sky, covered the walls of the restaurant. Healthy, cone-bearing plants and miniature pines were strategically placed between and among the tables with high-back chairs, covered with a blue and white velvet fabric, giving the few diners present an atmosphere of seclusion from each other and the rest of the world. Matching table linen and a small, barrel cactus with thick, fleshy stems of gold between two small candles, graced every table.

Dinner was a scrumptious but messy meal of barbecue ribs. As they ate, Nat noticed Jenine looked more relaxed than she had been in days. Even her appetite returned; she was now polishing off dessert.

He hadn't been blinded by the evidence of strain, just slow in responding because of his preoccupation. He felt ashamed of making her an innocent victim of his situation. The sacrifices she made in response to the demands he placed on her were higher than anyone should expect of another person.

Certainly, it was no way to treat the person you loved, regardless of the reason, he told himself. This treat away from school and Natasha was his way of making it up to her, though he felt it wasn't enough, and in spite of the inner voice that told him it wasn't necessary.

Jenine looked up to catch Nat feasting on her with his eyes, and the tasty raspberry and pistachio chocolate cake stuck in her throat. The dessert was nowhere near as appetizing as the man sitting across the table from her. She chewed slowly, her eyes riveted on the rich outlines of his shoulders, straining against the blue suede coat jacket he wore over a light gray shirt, open at the neck.

"If you don't stop looking at me like that, I'm going to have you for dessert," he growled softly in a smooth velvet tone, his stomach twisting with a hard knot of need.

She threw him a kiss and laughed with the joy his presence had given her.

"I missed that one," he said, "throw me another one."

The waiter appeared discreetly at Nat's side of the table and inquired in a low voice, "Is everything to your satisfaction, sir?"

"Perfect."

"Would you care for something else, ma'am?" He looked at Jenine.

"No, thank you," she replied.

With a slight tilt of his head, the waiter disappeared as unobtrusively as he had come.

"Nat, this is wonderful. I can't believe it's three-thirty in the afternoon, and we're alone together."

"Shhh," he said softly in a warning for her to forget reality.

She forked another bite of the cake and remained content to enjoy this very real fantasy Nat created for her. She watched him take a sip of the cognac he'd ordered and purse his lips in satisfaction. The pleasure he derived from such a simple gesture caused a tiny moan of hot desire to escape her lips.

Thoughts of the future seeped into her brain. Jenine envisioned her life without Nat. She knew it would be more devastatingly lonely than it had been before he reentered her existence. Certainly, that time would come, she told herself. And even though she believed him when he said he loved her, she knew that contrary to popular belief, love didn't conquer all. There were definite bounds. She couldn't imagine Nat being satisfied living in Highland Heights, nor did she dare hope that when he left, she would be an integral part of that departure. Not wanting to spoil any parts of her lovely afternoon, she redirected her thoughts to the cake and took another bite.

"I called my mother today," Nat announced lazily.

Jenine looked up in surprise, asking, "What did she say? What did you tell her?"

He chuckled lightly, as he set his glass on the table, twirling it between his hands. "I hardly got a chance to tell her anything." Jenine smiled knowingly. "She did most of the talking."

"When are you ordered to make an appearance before the queen?" she asked, teasing in her tone.

"Not just me, mind you, Miss Smarty. You, Natasha and I are expected no later than Easter. If she doesn't hear from us by then, we can look over our shoulders for the Texas National Guard to be at our heels."

The date he named caused a tingling in the pit of her stomach. "You sure you won't have a bite?" she asked, holding out a fork full of cake to him.

"I'm gonna get mine later," he said before swallowing the remainder of his drink. He savored the taste on his lips, smiling wickedly at Jenine as he did so.

Coaxing the cake down her throat without choking, Jenine asked in as natural a tone as possible, "Did you get around to telling her why you're here?"

"Yeah, I told her," he said, sighing heavily. "And I don't have to tell you she gave me an earful."

His mother's lecturing tone was still ringing in his ear, telling him that had he married Jenine a long time ago, he could be off some place making music instead of traipsing across the country on the run from a crazy African." He chuckled absently before he spoke again.

"Anyway, she had just gotten back from her trip, and so as far as she knows, nobody has tried to get in touch with her. Which surprises me a little."

"Oh? Why should Cissoko get in touch with her? He

hasn't actually been an innocent in this whole mess," she retorted, growing angry at the man who had created the problem in the first place.

"Who knows?" he shrugged. "I don't put much past him."

"When was the last time you talked to Robbie?" Jenine asked, with anxiety in her voice.

"Calm down. Natasha is fine. This is playtime for us, remember? And I want your undivided attention on me," he said, reaching across the table to take her hand.

"I've had enough," she said breathlessly. "Of the cake, I mean."

Nat made love to Jenine with his eyes, the entire elevator ride up to their room. By the time he carried her to the bed of their two-room suite, her body was screaming for his touch.

Jenine helped him remove his slacks—she was as eager as he to experience his possession. Even eternity would not be enough to satisfy her craving for him. She caught him off-balance, surprising him with her strength as she pushed him to the bed and straddled his body.

"Am I in trouble now?" he teased, his gaze grand with abiding for what was to come.

"Yes, you are," she promised, holding him to her dearly before lowering her head to claim his mouth in a searing kiss.

The unexpected afternoon tryst from the rigors of reality ended all too soon for either of their liking, but duty called. After leaving the hotel, they picked up Natasha from the daycare center and returned home for Jenine to get ready for rehearsal. She had just enough time for a quick shower.

Casually dressed in an oversized turtleneck sweater and

baggy pants and boots, she was in her music study, stuffing sheets of music from the desk into her briefcase. She had called Gloria to pick her up, so Nat wouldn't have to take Natasha back out into the cold.

"Jenine. Where are you?"

His voice hinted at exasperation as he bellowed from someplace down the hall, and Jenine smiled impishly. She could consider him worrisome if she didn't enjoy his attention so much.

The more she tried making it easier for them to survive after the imminent departure, the more Nat endeared himself to her in one way or the other. She felt as if she was fighting a losing battle. Maybe even the whole war.

"Jenine!"

Nat then poked his head through the door and stood for a fraction of a second, giving her ample time to risk a quick, impish glance at him, before he entered the room.

"Why didn't you answer?" he chided gently, grabbing her around the waist from behind and growled playfully in her neck. He could no more stop touching her than stop breathing.

"I knew you'd find me, eventually," she said, enormously pleased and delighted by his nearness.

With his head bent, nibbling behind her ear, he asked, "What time will you be back?" His tone revealed more than mere curiosity to know her return.

"Depends," she replied coyly. "You know how rehearsals go."

"I want you to take my car," he said.

Assuming the worst, Jenine stiffened in his embrace. "Why?" she asked in a tone geared for trouble.

"Because I don't trust yours, that's why," he retorted with humor in his voice. "Besides, the weather's too bad for you to try and drive on those worn-out things you call snow tires. I'd rest a lot easier if I knew you weren't stuck on the road someplace."

Breathing easier, she replied, "What if I wreck your car, or it gets stolen?" She angled her head to see his expression, certain it would be quite telling. "I'd spend the rest of my life replacing something I can't eat."

"The damn car is replaceable, woman," he replied gruffly. "You're not."

Staring down into Jenine's stubborn face, her eyes shooting piqued darts at him, Nat sighed in exasperation. There was just no placating her, he thought. She could be as unmovable and obstinate as any of the little mountains surrounding Highland Heights. It was most annoying.

"The truth is," he said with forced patience, "I don't want you or Natasha out of my sight if I can help it. I would rather you didn't go to this rehearsal at all."

Staring up into his face, Jenine saw the living nightmare in his expression. Their wonderful sojourn from reality this afternoon was officially ended, she thought. She could easily hate a man she had never met. His threat to Natasha governed their every action, every second of the day.

"I've already phoned Gloria to pick me up," she confessed, giving him a wobbly smile.

"You are the most infuriating woman I've ever known," he said, pulling her into his embrace.

"Then maybe you shouldn't bother with me," she said cheekily, slipping from his relaxed grasp.

His long arm snaked out, halting her retreat as he jerked her against him. She inhaled sharply at the contact, and flattened her hands against the wall of his chest.

"Maybe I shouldn't," he said silkily, his voice an octave lower than usual. His gaze roamed her face seductively, then dropped to her soft, sweet mouth. "But it's too late.

And hindsight is not my strong suit," he added just before placing slow breezy kisses about her face.

He kissed her nose, then her eyes, and finally, his mouth found hers. Thoughts went spinning around her head until they were no more under his persuasive mouth. Jenine wound her arms around his waist, hugging him closer to her, and returned his surprisingly gentle kiss. It was a kiss to dance to—slow, velvet warm, lulling—a slow-drag, sending currents of desire through her. With a natural wantonness, she pressed her body lightly into his, and he increased the depth of the kiss. A deep, hoarse sound squeezed passed his mouth ravaging hers as he forced her lips to part with his thrusting tongue and swallowed her melodious groan.

The doorbell sounded.

Reluctantly, they pulled apart. Jenine gulped, then pressed her cheek against his heart, which was hammering as erratically as hers.

"Tell Gloria she has lousy timing," he said, releasing a long, audible sigh.

She chuckled. "You tell her," she joked, gazing up at him, an amorous shine lingering in her eyes.

The bell rang again.

"I better go," she said backing from the place where she felt most secure and wanted.

"Finish getting your things together, I'll get the door," he said resignedly, then kissed her on the mouth and left the room.

Jenine turned and flattened her palms atop the desk and closed her eyes, trying to curb her body's craving for his hands, his mouth, his touch. She drew a deep breath and reminded herself that Gloria was waiting.

Nat and Gloria were standing in the foyer when she approached, slipping into her overcoat. She observed

Gloria's greedy-eyed stare at Nat, who seemed uncomfortable under the obvious scrutiny.

Jenine announced her presence with a harrumph, and Gloria jumped, stains of scarlet dotting her cheeks.

"Ready?" Gloria asked nervously.

"I'm ready, if you are," Jenine replied brusquely.

"Jenine?" Nat asked in bewilderment.

He closed the distance between them, staring intently into her face. He didn't dare let her walk out of this house harboring notions that her friend posed a threat, or that he was even mildly attracted.

Jenine grinned mischievously and broke out laughing. "Gotcha," she said.

Nat pulled her into his arms and joined her in laughter. Standing side by side, they faced Gloria, sheepish grins marked their expressions.

"What's going on, you two?" she asked suspiciously.

"Nothing, Gloria," Jenine replied, remnants of laughter in her voice.

"Have you been putting me on?" Gloria asked, amused.

"I couldn't resist," Jenine explained. "You should have seen your face."

"You just wait, Jenine, I'm gonna pay you back for that one."

"I know, and I'll suffer gladly. Now, let's get out of here so we won't be late. I don't want to be there all night."

"Okay. Nat, it was a pleasure seeing you again," Gloria said, her hand held out to Nat.

"The same here, Gloria. You two be careful," he said to Jenine.

Jenine pecked him on the mouth, and he glared at her. Then she found herself locked in his embrace and his lips on hers, ravishing her mouth. And just as quickly, she was released.

Gloria had the good grace to avert her gaze, but was grinning widely.

"I'll pick you up myself," he whispered in a tone that brooked no arguments. Jenine merely nodded her head, still reeling from his kiss. "Oh, Gloria," he said, snapping his fingers as if just remembering to deliver a message.

Gloria looked at him expectantly. "Yes, Nat?"

"Your timing is lousy," he said, disdain in his tone, then a grin colored his features.

Gloria gushed, and it was Jenine's turn to color in embarrassment. She pushed Gloria out of the front door hastily with Nat's laughter trailing behind them.

Nat watched the windshield wipers swing back and forth across the window. Powder white snowflakes were swiped away only to be replaced by more.

He was waiting for Jenine to appear from the side exit of the school building. The engine was idling softly; the car warm and toasty, unlike his feelings.

Since she left the house with Gloria, he had been experiencing an eerie feeling that only intensified as the hours passed. It neither frightened nor calmed him, creating a sensation of one knowing the end was at hand, yet grateful for its arrival.

He had to assume David or his man knew where Jenine lived, but hoped it was not the case for Robbie, who would keep Natasha at her place. Until . . . , he thought, with a strangely calm look on his face.

It might not be a bad idea to have Jenine stay at Robbie's, too. Oh, he would have a fight on his hands then, he thought, as a smile brightened his visage.

"Jenine," he whispered, his mouth curving into an unconscious smile. His woman.

She had been so happy this afternoon, he remembered,

with a kind of sadness overtaking his features. He wished he could give her another occasion at the hotel. But it was a hideaway, a sort of safe house he believed would come in handy later on. He didn't risk disclosing it, if he hadn't already, he thought reflectively, a tight expression replacing his smile.

He thought of the man who had made him an imposition and Jenine an innocent victim. But before his thoughts progressed further, she was getting in the car, babbling excitedly before closing the door.

"Nat, some of the teachers are going to Bennie's. It's a coffee-and-sandwich shop." She sat quietly, holding her breath while watching Nat consider the implied request.

Nat indicated with a nod a familiarity of the place. He guessed where the disclosure was leading. "Honey, I don't think it's a good idea," he said with regret in his tone.

Jenine swallowed the disappointment in her throat. It was probably just as well. With quiet dignity, she nodded her head and strapped herself in the seat belt.

A silent curse rang in Nat's head as he stared at Jenine. Though she tried not to let on her disappointment, animation left her face. She was being a brave little trouper, sacrificing her desires for his—again, he thought, with a sourness in the pit of his stomach.

"All right, for a little while," he said, shifting the car to reverse.

"Are you sure?" A small light lit in her eyes.

"I'm sure," he replied.

She leaned toward him and pressed her lips against his before he took possession of her mouth. She quivered at the sweet tenderness of his kiss and moaned, feeling deprived when he broke it off.

"Sure I can't entice you to go home?" he whispered against her mouth.

His suggestive tone excited her more, despite knowing

he was teasing. "That may not be a bad idea," she replied with a grin.

"Later," he said.

"Deal," she replied, then returned to her side of the car. She rested her head against the back of the seat and sighed with her happiness. She thought she'd better savor every moment of it.

"Rough rehearsal?" he asked, pulling off the lot behind several other cars.

"Not really," she replied. "It's just been a long day."

"Longer than a day," he replied cryptically. He felt her gaze on him. "I know this hasn't been easy on you."

"It hasn't been easy on any of us," she amended.

"Yeah, well, you've had the most to lose," he said.

Jenine didn't comment, thinking he was right. She was the big loser here. When the matter of Natasha's custody was resolved, they would vanish from her life and she would have nothing but her memories. Refusing to let her spirits drop, she changed the conversation. "Where's Natasha?"

"I dropped her off at Robbie's," he replied. "I think I'm going to have to buy her a Nintendo."

"Nat," Jenine scolded with laughter in her voice. "She's only a baby. She's not ready for that."

"I know, but she likes watching the animation," he replied. "You ought to see her when Karyn starts it up."

"Hm," Jenine replied suspiciously. "I do believe it is you and not Natasha who enjoys this game so much."

Jenine fell silent, watchful of Nat, who was judiciously studying the roads and seemingly every car coming toward them and behind them as if looking for disaster. She closed her eyes and tried not to think—about anything, except enjoying another moment to add to her memory collection.

Upon arriving, she introduced Nat to her co-workers,

who converged on Bennie's with the boisterous merrymaking of a group of rowdy teenagers. The place was warm, cozy and inviting with its sock-hop atmosphere, and plastic red-and-white checkered tablecloths and scuffed white-tiled floors. A jukebox was constantly fed with choices representing the twenty-year span of age differences in the selectors. Beer, sandwiches and jokes passed around the table as the workers enjoyed each other's company.

Another fun occasion was over much too soon, though exhaustion was already setting in. Jenine felt a pleasant lethargy as she waved her last, "See you tomorrow," across the parking lot while allowing Nat to help her into the car.

"It's after midnight," Nat said, driving off the parking lot. "Do we risk waking Robbie to get Natasha?"

"We probably should call first," Jenine replied on a yawn.

"Fine time to tell me," he gently chided. "Want to go back to the cafe and call her from there?"

"No, not really," she mumbled.

"I get the picture. Come on over here," he said, pulling her close to his side. "I'll wake you when we get to Robbie's."

After driving for several miles, Nat noticed steady twin beams of headlights in the rear-view mirror. He tried to remember if they had been there when he and Jenine left the cafe.

He slowed down to see if the car behind him would pass. It didn't. Instead, the driver adjusted his speed to follow at the slow pace Nat had set. Nat speeded up. The car behind stayed with him.

"Jenine." He called her name as not to frighten her, though his pulse was racing at top notch speed. "Jenine, wake up. I think we have company."

She lifted her head, mumbling sleepily, "What?"

"We're being followed."

She turned her head with a jerk to look out the back window. Two beams of light blinded her vision and she turned back toward Nat, a terrible tenseness in her body. "Are you sure?" she asked in a small frightened voice.

"Not one hundred percent, but pretty sure. Are you in your seatbelt?" He felt her nod affirmative. "All right, hold on," he cautioned as his foot gassed the pedal, and the fast, luxury car lived up to its reputation for a quick pickup.

Nat chided himself for having made no plans for this scenario. He had assumed the confrontation would match the previous one. Now, he was simply reacting. Again, he thought angrily.

He led the driver in the car behind them on what would have been a scenic tour of a residential area of Highland Heights had the ride been slower and the night, day. But in the dark, he had to concentrate on the unfamiliar streets he whizzed through.

"Nat, this is getting us nowhere," Jenine cried, holding onto the dashboard as the car weaved through a curving street.

She looked out the window and saw that the other car had trouble making the course, its back tires sliding out of control. The car behind them righted, and continued to follow.

"I know. Got any suggestions?"

"We can't go to Robbie's," she said, with fear in her voice. "That's where Natasha is, and that's who they want. They probably already know where I live."

"I got a better idea."

"What?"

"Hang on," he said, and the car darted off in the direction of downtown.

"The police station?" Jenine asked a few minutes later when Nat turned off the engine in front of the building.

"There they go," Nat said, looking out the window to see the car drive by and out of sight. Jenine sagged against him, and he cradled her in his arms. "Come on, let's go inside," he said, kissing the top of her head.

Chapter Thirteen

Jenine felt a sense of déjà vu, lying in bed on her back, eyes wide open. It was dark except for the thin stream of light spilling in from the hallway. She and Nat had returned from the police station hours ago, long enough for her body to have caved in to the exhaustion of the day. But sleep wouldn't come.

Just like before, she thought, rolling onto her stomach in the empty spot where only Nat's scent remained. He was up, performing his usual late-night patrol of the house. Sleep wouldn't come until he returned.

A cold knot formed in her stomach. If she needed him to get to sleep now, what would she do when he was gone from her life forever? she asked herself. She sat up to beat the pillow that held his manly fragrance, before pushing it away.

Her heart was pounding furiously in her chest; she feared she hadn't been as prepared for the inevitable as she'd originally believed. She forced herself to breathe calmly, and slowly, forced reason to her thoughts.

Nat had been hers only for a short while. And she had always known his stay was temporary. Even he had made no promises otherwise.

She had learned to live without Nat once and managed

quite well. She could do it again. Would have to, she thought, curling her body into a tight knot.

Jenine tried directing her thoughts on anything—the band, the upcoming talent show, her music—except Nat. But there was no getting away from the evidence of him in her life, for her thoughts circled to wonder how Natasha was getting along with Robbie and Karyn.

Had the incident which took them to the police not occurred, Natasha would be home with them tonight. With a smile turning up the corners of her lips, she recalled their usual morning ritual. She was going to miss that.

She almost wished Nat had not come back into her life. Then she wouldn't be having this conversation with herself right now. Chances are she would be asleep, dreaming, or at least thinking about the things that happened at school today. All of which seemed insignificant compared to the latest escapade of the evening.

How did David Cissoko find Nat in the first place?

She never bought Nat's explanation about a drumbeat. Since he seemed satisfied with it, she kept her counsel. Robbie, she knew, had been very careful in handling the case, even going to another city to hire a private investigator. Certainly that person was skillful enough not to let on who hired him. She guessed she would never know the answer.

Calling a silent end to her ruminations, Jenine rolled over to lie on her stomach, pulling Nat's pillow under her head.

Nat stood in the dimly lit hallway, staring into the dark room where his drums were assembled. Adrenaline was still running high inside his body as he replayed the chase in his mind.

He hadn't expected it to come to that, remembering the long-distance call he'd placed weeks ago. He had grown weary of the waiting. While fearful they would never stop running, he knew it was only a matter of time before he and Natasha were found. The call was to eliminate the element of surprise. David managed to do that nevertheless.

Shaking his head, Nat laughed derisively for his naiveté, believing David was as anxious as he to be done with this matter that would see no court. "Man-to-man," the African had said, he recalled.

Apparently, his former in-law liked the hunt more than the actual confrontation. He had to interpret that as David's assurance of his conquest. Just as he felt equally confident David would lose.

He recalled his late wife's father had wanted him to come to Washington and bring Natasha as a show of good faith. Tugging at his mustache, with a twisted smile on his mouth, Nat laughed sardonically. David must have thought him a fool.

Granted, a lot of his reactions to the situation were born of pride—"stupid macho pride" as Jenine had put it so often—but he wasn't about to risk losing Natasha. He realized a long time ago that his daughter was safe here with people who put her welfare above their own—with Jenine who treated her better than possibly her own mother would have.

He could make and accept that admission now without qualm. Natasha knew Jenine as her mother; it was Jenine he knew as his woman. She had been and still was his true love since first sight.

"A threat to one was a threat to both," he muttered in the darkness.

Purposeful strides took him to the master bedroom.

Standing in the doorway, he looked in on Jenine, a still form in the bed.

Sensing his presence, Jenine squeezed her eyes shut. It didn't make sense, she chastised herself. One minute she was longing for him, and the next, wishing he would give her more space to figure out what to do about the longing.

She knew when he was near the bed. She felt compelled to acknowledge him, in spite of and because of her confusion.

The bedside light clicked on. The truth came out in a soft yellow glow.

The second her gaze met his she was lost, held mesmerized anew by his eyes, smoldering with promises she knew he could keep. The bed sank with his weight, and she looked at him with wistful and tender eyes.

What was it about this man that drew her to her doom, she wondered shortly before her hand, seemingly with a will of its own, performed the act of an inherent need within her. She loved the smooth flesh covering his features—the firm jaw relaxing in her palm, mouth opening invitingly beneath her fingers, nostrils of his broad nose flaring and breathing hot air, stirring the hairs of his mustache. A thumb smoothed the thin hairs of his long eyebrows.

Nat took her hand in both of his and pressed it against his mouth. He stared into her brown eyes, saw love written in their depths. A magnificent shudder ran the length of him.

As if in a single movement, he was up, taking off the T-shirt and running pant's he'd slipped on to scout out the house. Soon, he was standing completely disrobed.

Jenine watched him watching her, poised as if awaiting an invitation or issuing a challenge. She neither knew, nor

cared which; she was a helpless to deny the growing
hunger within her. She lost contact with his eyes only
during the second it took to pull the gown over her head,
and lie picture-perfect in a seductive pose. Her invitation,
or challenge.

A hint of a smile and a slightly cocked brow flitted
across his face. He leaned, just slightly to feather-touch
the bottom of a foot, then the other before that same
ethereal contact skimmed her body, causing tiny moans,
pleasure-whimpers, to slip past her lips. The hand
stopped between her thighs; its pressure increased, rubbing over the hidden treasure beyond the wiry hairs.

Nat looked for her reaction and was not disappointed.
Her almond-shaped eyes were nearly closed and gasping
pants of air went in and out of the small opening between
her lips.

She had given so much.

It was the last thought he had before his head replaced
his hand.

Jenine was standing in the dressing room before the
full-length door mirror. She simply sizzled with love; not
even the new sculptured look given her by the student
makeup artist could hide how she felt as she appraised
herself in the mirror, laughter laughing back at her.

The senior had gone all out on her costume for the
Talent Show. Her hair had been slicked back, then
combed to the front of her head and streaked with red
paint. She had had to call a halt to the green contact
lenses the student had wanted her to wear, but agreed to
the heavy use of eyeliner, making her eyes look longer and
slanted. Yellow shadow glittered her lids, and her cheeks
were blushed with a peachy red. Two shades of color had

been applied to her lips, after they had been lined with a dark brown eyeliner pencil.

The outfit was a black sleeveless leather jacket with intricate designs of silver buckles and zippers at the shoulders and front pockets, over a matching miniskirt. The black leather boots with a silver toe and ankle belt were her own, and completed her costume.

A knock on the door interrupted Jenine's self-perusal. "Who's there?" she asked, remembering she had been given strict instructions by the student stage manager to remain in her room until she was called.

"It's Clifton, open up."

Jenine burst out laughing the moment Clifton entered, sporting a ripped white undershirt and prewashed jeans hugging his thin, slender hips. His dark brown hair was also styled in a punkish look, and streaked yellow and purple.

"I don't think you're in a position to laugh," he said gruffly with amusement in his voice, "you look as ridiculous as I do. Those little monsters wanted to shave my beard and mustache. Said it wasn't the all-American, clean look they were striving for," he added with a harrumph in his tone.

"I wonder what they did to Ms. Spaulding," Jenine said curiously, trying to picture the voice teacher, a big woman, in short, tight leather.

"I'm sure I don't want to know," Clifton quipped, fingering the yellow streak in his hair. "By the way, you have nice legs. I don't think I've seen this much of them before."

"Thank you," she replied with a curtsy. "Have a good look at them now because you won't see this much of me again, in a very long time."

"I wonder what that fellow of yours will say when he sees you."

"Oh, he'll love it."

"I wish I shared his sense of humor," Clifton said dryly.

An abrupt rap on the door was followed by a young man, wearing a headset and carrying a notepad. "Here you are," he directed to Clifton. "I thought I told you to stay put, Mr. Segaro."

"Sorry."

"Well, you're on in one minute," the young stage manager said. "Get in place, please."

"Yes, sir," Clifton said, following a giggling Jenine out of the room, trailed by the student.

The foursome—Clifton, Jenine, Bruce and Angela Spaulding—were standing on the side of the stage peeping out into the audience from behind the curtain. Members of the audience were literally rolling down the isles with laughter at the three male teachers on stage, dressed in tutus, performing a dying swan to Tchaikovsky's *Swan Lake*.

"Get in place," the stage manager ordered.

Bruce, who wore a gaudy necklace in place of a shirt over leather pants and boots, and Angela, looking stuffed in the tight fitting jean jumpsuit, along with Clifton and Jenine, all took their places on the moveable platform upstage.

They were given the cue, and Miss Spaulding started the computerized drum introduction to the song as the curtains were ripped open. The band began to play, and Jenine, gripping the microphone off the stand, burst out performing, "One Man Woman."

The audience of students and parents roared; seeing their no-nonsense teachers in wild getups was a sight to behold. Then the audience calmed in amazement; students in particular were impressed as they watched. Mr. Segara, the string teacher, known for his dislike of electronic instruments, was plucking the electric guitar better than any rock star. Ms. Spaulding, the classical-music teacher on synthesizer and keyboard playing funk, though her movements were slightly offbeat. Mr. Richards, the band teacher who was always immaculately dressed, shirtless. And Ms. Jones, an avid listener and spokeswoman of jazz, naked by her standards, shoulders and hips rocking to the funky beat of the music as she played the audience.

Jenine really didn't want to go to the party at the Cobbs' after the Talent Show. She knew she'd be teased unmercifully for her Chaka Khan performance and was too tired to grin and bear it all night. Nat had already given her an earful about her performance and taste in costumes.

"You don't dress like that for me at home," he teased in her ear.

They were standing at the front door of the Cobbs' mansion. Cars lined the driveway and street, and party sounds came drifting through the door.

"Oh, I'm sure I can find something a little more appropriate to wear for you," she replied, grinning coyly at him.

"You witch," he growled, pulling her into his arms to kiss her on the mouth, hard and passionate.

"Ooops," Ethel Cobb exclaimed when she opened the door. Nat and Jenine broke apart guiltily. "Come in," invited the lady of the house, elegantly dressed in a gold-sequined floor-length caftan. "We were just talking about you," she said to Jenine.

"Oh, no," Jenine groaned.

She and Nat stepped into the gaily lit foyer. Beyond were even more guests, women dressed in various colors and designs of evening wear, and men, mostly in black suits or appropriate dark colors. People filled the mansion rooms to over-capacity, sipping drinks supplied by waiters weaving through the crowds. Live music drifted from a back room and competed to be heard above the din of the numerous conversations going on.

"Come on. I won't have you hiding or sneaking off together," Ethel admonished mildly, passing their coats to the maid, who was standing nearby. "Jenine, you were absolutely great on the Talent Show. I was immensely pleased by the job you did. Young man, I hope you appreciate this woman who's so obviously committed to a monogamous relationship," the matron-educator winked at Nat.

Jenine blushed embarrassingly before she spoke. "Mrs. Cobb, I'd like you to meet Nathaniel Padell. Nat, this is Mrs. Cobb, the founder of Highland Heights Academy."

"Nice to meet you, Mrs. Cobb," Nat said, extending a hand. "I think you have the best school in the country," he complimented her sincerely.

"Well, with teachers like Jenine, it's easy, Nat," Ethel replied. "May I call you Nat?"

"Yes, ma'am."

"Oh please, call me Ethel. Jenine, why don't you take Nat in and introduce him around? I'm sure I'll see you before you leave. And no sneaking out."

"She never invited me to call her Ethel," Jenine whispered in Nat's ear, leading the way through the crowd.

The ribbing turned out not to be as bad as Jenine had feared. Surprisingly, she was enjoying herself. So was Nat. Bruce had coaxed him into joining the impromptu combo set up in the spacious family room.

Just across the way, Jenine ran into John, standing near the food-laden table set up in the dining room.

"You aren't planning to leave us and take a band on the road, are you?" John asked jokingly.

"You're not going to get rid of me that easily," she replied, eyeing the several food choices on the table.

"Certainly you've thought about it," he continued to probe.

Jenine looked up at him in a sidelong glance with mild amusement, trying to read into his thoughts. She couldn't discern if he was as serious as his tone indicated. Popping a cheese ball into her mouth, she said, "John, I've never known you to skirt around an issue."

Laughing, John replied, "You got me." He took a sip of his drink before he spoke again, his tone serious. "The truth is, you're good, Ms. Jones. I'm sure I've told you that before. You might say, I need some more assurance that you're not going to leave us to seek fame and fortune elsewhere."

Jenine blushed under high praise. She said quietly, "Thank you for the compliment."

"But?" he prompted.

"Ms. Jones."

Jenine and John turned to see Michael Cobb, a ruddy-faced, butterball of a man approaching.

"Excuse me." Michael said, taking Jenine's hand in his. "There are some people who have been asking to meet you, my dear." To John, "I'm sure you won't mind if I borrow her for a few minutes. It's in the line of duty."

Jenine allowed Michael Cobb to guide her to the living room where two men were conversing near the wall-length fireplace.

"Miss Jones, this is Mr. Lawrence Jacobs."

Jenine shook hands with the taller of the two men, who looked to be in his early forties, and smiled as she acknowledged, "Mr. Jacobs."

"And this is Mr. David Cissoko," Michael said with a note of importance in his tone.

In a short time, no longer than a breath, Jenine's facial

muscles slackened and the polite smile of greeting she had worn jelled into utter astonishment. Face-to-face with the man who had played God with her life—responsible for bringing Nat into her sedentary world, then taking him away again—she felt numb, as if her feelings were paralyzed. In that instant, she realized she and Nat only had a fairy-tale romance that was too fragile for the real world.

"Mr. Cissoko is the Minister of Culture and Education of Nubacush, East Africa," Michael continued. "He's interested in setting up a student-exchange program between our students and those from his country," he added, dollar figures flashing in his eyes.

Jenine didn't know how long the startled, wary look remained on her face, but her cheeks and mouth felt stiff under the pleasant mask she now wore.

"David, this is Jenine Jones," Michael said. "She is one of our most favorite teachers. You saw why tonight," he added with a smile.

Staring at David Cissoko, Jenine corrected the mental pictures she'd created of him to that of the handsome brown-skinned man with straight black hair who stood before her, his hand extended. She tore her gaze from his engaging smile—a smile that didn't reach his piercing eyes that were assessing her as keenly as she was assessing him—and she forced herself to perform the mandatory show of politeness expected of her.

"Mr. Cissoko," she said, her hand enclosed limply in his. She didn't know how she managed her voice, for panic like she'd never known before welled in her throat.

"Minister Cissoko has been in a town a few days," Michael said to Jenine, cueing her to speak, "and so far, I think we've managed to impress him."

Jenine knew she was supposed to be talking about the school, but the topic paled under her fear, her pulse skittering for safety within her body. She merely stared, tongue-tied and obsessed by one thought: Find Nat, her brain screamed.

"Ms. Jones heads up our music department. Our kids have really prospered under her leadership. They recently returned from an international jazz-band competition where our kids took second place. I don't have to tell you, we're really proud of them," Michael boasted. "But of course, all of the praise goes to Ms. Jones. We demand a lot from our teachers, particularly those in the arts. As you saw for yourselves tonight, they have to perform on stage as well as in the classroom. And all for peanuts."

The sound of hollow laughter echoed in Jenine's head, and finally, reached her brain. Feeling her wits renewing themselves, she knew she mustn't give Nat's enemy the satisfaction of seeing just how truly ruffled she was. Though her stomach felt like a volcano in eruption and her palms were damp with perspiration, she joined the discussion.

She fielded questions about the school's philosophy from Mr. Jacobs. Responding likewise to David's inquiries about academic standards and teacher qualifications, she sensed he was merely going through the motions, pretending interest. As she was. Finally, unable to withstand the oblique conversation any longer, when David opened his mouth to ask another question, Jenine excused herself.

"There are several other teachers present," she said. "I'm sure one of them will be eager to answer all the questions you have about the Academy. Mr. Jacobs," she nodded, then took her leave.

Heading toward the den, she bumped into Robbie and Sheriff Talbert Murray, whose arms were wrapped intimately around Robbie's waist. She arched an inquiring brow, then smiled at the answering look she got from Robbie, but was too intent on finding Nat to comment.

She was about to rush pass them when Talbert caught her by the arm.

"I'm gonna have to give you a ticket for speeding in a pedestrian zone, Ms. Jones," he teased with laughter in his voice.

"Yeah," Robbie chimed, "where are you going in such a hurry?" She eyed Jenine speculatively, noting her frowned forehead and fear lurking in her gaze. She removed herself from Talbert's embrace and asked, "What's wrong? Has Karyn called?"

"No," Jenine replied after clearing her throat. She didn't want to needlessly have Robbie thinking the worst, though she had herself wondered if Cissoko's man had been to Robbie's home. "He's here."

"Who's here?" Robbie asked.

"Cissoko. Natasha's grandfather. I need to get Nat."

"Here? Where?" Robbie replied anxiously, looking around trying to spot him.

"Here at the Cobbs', in this house," Jenine whispered harshly.

"That arrogant son-of-a," Robbie started, before closing her mouth shut. She drew from a power within herself and masked her emotions under her usually calm and unruffled composure. Talbert touched her on the shoulders lightly, and she turned to look up at him and smiled, letting him know that she could handle the situation.

"I'm going to get Nat and we're getting out of here," Jenine announced.

Robbie nodded her understanding with a half-smile, and Jenine rushed through the crowd, her anxiety growing with every step. Nearly tripping in her hurry, she found Nat deeply involved in playing, but couldn't think of a polite way to get his attention. So she walked over and whispered in his ear, "I need to see you urgently."

The annoyance Nat felt at being interrupted faded

when he looked up to see who had tapped him on the shoulder. He stared with a curious frown at Jenine, and saw fear burning intensely in her gaze. He dropped the drumsticks as discreetly as possible, earning a puzzled look from Bruce.

Nat followed Jenine to a corner on the other side of the room near the bookcases lined against the wall. "Honey, what is it?" he asked, his hands on her shoulders.

"David Cissoko is here," she replied calmly, in complete contrast to her racing heart.

"You mean here at the party?" he asked incredulously.

She nodded her head, drawing in a deep breath, then replied, "In the living room, talking to Mr. Cobb. We need to hurry and get Natasha."

"In a minute," he said in a voice turned as cold as frozen ice, his expression set in stone. He dropped his hands to his side and told her absently, "Go call Karyn and see if everything's okay. I'll meet you at the car."

"What are you going to do?" she asked, more frightened at the expression on his face. "Nat?"

Shaking off her light possession of his hand, Nat commanded harshly, "Go do what I say," then walked off towards the living room.

He saw Mrs. Cobb. She was like a butterfly, spreading her attention to each and every one of her guests, seeing to their wants. Then he spotted him. Robbie and Talbert had joined the conversation with David Cissoko, Mr. Cobb and another man he hadn't met.

Nat made his way across the room casually, speaking to those who stopped him until he reached his destination. He felt Robbie's eyes on him, sizing him up questioningly, but his gaze was locked on David.

"Hello, David," he said without preamble.

"Hello, Nathaniel," David said expectantly. "It's good

to see you again," he added as though the two had parted amicably.

"Is it?" Nat asked, his brow raised sardonically, a twisted smile on his lips.

"Yes," David returned, his polite, knowing smile in place.

Nat merely nodded at the look David gave him. His eyes blinked in recognition of the challenge.

"Nat?" Robbie said, looking back and forth between the two adversaries. "What's going on here?"

"I'll tell you about it later," Nat said absently, still not taking his eyes off David.

The two men quietly appraised each other, secretive expressions alight in their eyes. The hostility between Nat and David was tangible, causing the others around them to become uncomfortable.

"Can I get anyone a drink?" Mr. Cobb blurted out to break the tensed silence.

"Nat," Jenine said with a tentativeness in her tone, eyes bright with anxiety. She feared he or David would take their obvious dislike for each other to the next level.

"It's okay, baby," Nat replied with a broad smile on his mouth. As he took her hand and raised it to his mouth affectionately, he never took his eyes off David. "Everything's going to be all right."

Chapter Fourteen

"I called him," Nat said in a toneless voice. "I called David several weeks ago."

Robbie froze in the middle of her pace, as did Talbert, a cup of coffee poised at his lips. Jenine wavered, trying to comprehend what she had just heard. Three pairs of shocked gazes flew to Nat, then shifted to each other.

Resuming her pace, Robbie said, "I see," in a small voice. "So, that explains a lot," she said aloud to herself.

Still in a state of stunned silence, Jenine stared at Nat's steady profile. His elegant lean form was postured in practiced reposed, with hands folded over his midsection and long legs stretched past the coffee table, ankles crossed. A breath trembled in her chest as she was struck by a fate she didn't want to believe. Twice betrayed by the same man, she thought.

Consciously, Jenine sidled next to an armrest on the couch, opposite and as far away from Nat as possible. He wouldn't look at her, and that was just as telling as his admission, she thought. She now knew just how eager he had been to get away from Highland Heights. She took it personally.

Robbie erupted. "Of all the stupid, arrogant, egotistical, male macho pride bullshit!"

"Robbie!" Jenine shouted with chiding. "That's enough," she said in a low, composed voice, thinking she knew all she needed to know.

She guessed she had already accepted the truth, accounting for the surprising calm that had come over her. It was Natasha whom they had to consider now. Nothing else mattered.

"It's already done," she said resigned. "Why don't we just assess the damage and figure the next step."

"You're right, of course," Robbie said on a breathy sigh. "I'm sorry." She ambled momentarily before sitting on the edge of a stool. "It just makes me so mad when a client goes behind my back after I have expressly advised him to let me handle everything," pounding a fist in her hand. Shrugging her shoulders, "But, I guess I should have seen it coming," she said in a broken whisper.

Jenine felt disturbing quakes in her serenity, thinking she too, should have seen it coming. Even more so than Robbie, she possessed a fifteen-year-old advance warning.

Robbie rubbed the tight muscles forming in the back of her neck, then dropped her hands to her sides. "I don't know what more I can do."

"Can't Nat continue with legal proceedings against David?" Jenine asked. She wondered how she could continue so objectively when she wanted to be alone with her thoughts, her shame and her agony? But resolved to carry on for Natasha's sake, she clung to pride to conceal her inner turmoil. "Just because David doesn't want to go to court, doesn't mean Nat has to follow suit."

"Nat has already followed suit," Robbie retorted. She looked at Jenine with commiseration and apology. "Neither apparently wants to settle this in court," she said, gesturing fruitlessly with her hands.

Jenine quickly deciphered the alternative to which Robbie alluded. It would be manly. Macho, she thought, her lips pressed together in a thin line of displeasure. Probably illegal and unquestionably dangerous.

With tears glistening in her pain-filled brown eyes, Jenine looked from Robbie and Talbert to Nat. "What about Natasha?" she demanded. Grabbing Nat by the arm, "What about Natasha? "Are you forgetting her?" she asked with possessive desperation in a thick and unsteady voice.

"Hey, look, this is the way David wants it," Nat replied, his voice cold, exact and final. Jerking from her grasp, he sprang to his feet. He ran a tired hand across his head; a pained tolerance marred his expression. He was tired of being chastised by women who had no concept of what it meant to be a man, and equally tired of questioning his own judgments.

"You can't expect a man who thinks he's above the law to act within the boundaries of the law," Nat said with emphasis, body poised as if braced for an attack.

He looked into two pairs of eyes returning his stern gaze. Neither belonged to Jenine; each showed its own distinct look of concern. He relaxed his stance somewhat. But he felt her eyes boring into him, and his emotions split agonizingly into separate directions. He didn't like hurting her, yet he was compelled to follow the course he thought best.

"I knew that," Nat continued, his voice containing a strong suggestion of self-reproach, "but I wouldn't listen." He shook his head pensively from side to side and spoke as if talking to himself. "I shouldn't have let you talk me into trying to deal with David through the legal system. It just wouldn't have worked."

"Then," Talbert said quietly, staring into the black, cold coffee, "I guess it's in my hands next." He looked up to stare at Nat with hardened eyes.

"Robbie?" Jenine pleaded.

Robbie duplicated her helpless gesture. "I'm sorry," she said in a barely audible tone.

Natasha was in her baby bed, babbling excitedly on the edge of tears when Nat walked into the master bedroom. Jenine had left him to see Robbie and Talbert out.

It was time to let her get it out of her system, he thought, confident he could convince her that he had done the right thing. Their lives would be so much better than before—as soon as David was permanently out of the picture.

"Jenine?" he called, looking about the room.

There was no answer, and he bit off a curse. Maybe it wasn't going to be as easy as he expected. He headed for the guest bedroom Jenine had occupied for a short time. It was a logical place for him to look, all things considered.

Finding the bedroom empty, he retraced his steps to the master suite. "Jenine?"

He heard the commode flush, shortly followed by gargling from the adjoining bathroom. He picked Natasha up and sat on the bed with her, waiting for Jenine to appear.

"Isn't it past your bedtime?" he asked playfully of Natasha, who had already begun to busy herself by crawling toward the lamp table next to the bed. "Come back here," he commanded, pulling her by the feet to the center of the bed.

Jenine walked purposefully into the bedroom to see the two Padells playing on the bed. Natasha's ecstatic giggles filled the air as Nat blew bubbles on her stomach in play. A cold shiver spread over her. She felt as though the family they had been was fast slipping from her grasp. Nat had created a desirable situation, then taken it away from her, she thought with a sour-faced expression.

"There's Jenine," Nat said to Natasha, pointing a finger in Jenine's direction.

Jenine suppressed her black mood under the appearance of indifference. Even that emotion melted, however, when Natasha crawled to the foot of the bed where she was standing, and lifted her arms. She instinctively granted the infant's wish.

"Aren't you ready to go to sleep yet?" she asked, rubbing noses with Natasha.

Natasha displayed her pleasure with giggles and by wrapping her arms around Jenine's neck. She was sorely going to miss this, she thought, summoning every ounce of strength within her not to cry, hugging the baby close to her.

Nat felt a glorious happiness rise in his heart as he observed the exchange of guileless affection between the two most important females in his life. It was such a fulfilling sensation, it scared him. Silently, he vowed to ensure that neither Jenine nor Natasha lost the other.

He watched their play wordlessly, his gaze particularly keen on Jenine. The smile on his face was heartfelt throughout him, and his pupils dilated with the rise of excitement below his waist. He stared unabashed at the caramel-dipped complexioned woman who was his lover, his friend. He wished his child would hurry and fall asleep.

"Je-nine," he coaxed in his most sensual bedroom voice.

In a natural movement, Jenine turned her back to him. She perched on the edge of the bed to play patty-cake with Natasha.

"Jenine?" he said concerned, scooting down the bed near her and Natasha. When she still refused to acknowledge him, he turned her face by the chin to look at him.

With irritation marring her expression, Jenine swatted

his hand away. She was determined to keep her mouth shut, for there was nothing left to say. She continued to ignore him by playing with Natasha.

"Oh, I get it." He spoke with a half-grin on his face, but anger underlined that tone. "You're still mad at me." Seconds passed, and she still refused to acknowledge him. "All right," he sighed, forcing patience to himself. He'd sit back and let her get it out of her system. He folded his hands under his arms and waited.

And waited . . . for her anger to dissipate and forgiveness to come, confident she would come to her senses and realize he had done the right thing. He waited to cap the night in sweet passion. It might be one of the few they had left before the ultimate and final fight with David, he thought. He was ready for whatever form it took.

Nat watched and waited as Jenine changed Natasha's diaper, sprinkling a liberal dose of powder. Suppressing his growing impatience, he said nothing as Jenine changed Natasha into a sleeping gown. His eyes began to narrow into slits of annoyance when she left the room with the baby in her arms, then returned with a bottle. His impatience got the better of him when Jenine sat on the side of the bed and tried to feed Natasha, who seemed to think they were playing a game as she merely toyed with the nipple.

Baffled, "Jenine, will you talk to me?" he implored finally.

Jenine responded to the note of pleading in his face. Such a handsome face, she thought, deeply sighing before she spoke. "What's there to say, Nat?"

He stammered before the words righted themselves in his mind. "I thought you were on my side. I thought you understood."

"Oh, I understand, Nat," Jenine replied. Her voice was quiet, tranquil, stubborn, matching her demeanor. She had no intentions of getting into an argument or shouting match with Nat. Deciding Natasha wasn't hungry, she set the bottle on the baby table, then set the baby free to crawl about the bed.

"I did what I thought was best for Natasha," Nat replied with emphasis.

"No, Nat," she said, shaking her head from side to side. "You did what Nat wanted most to do," her accusing voice stabbed the air. "Natasha was perfectly content here."

"Natasha is in no position to know what she wants," he replied in a tense, clipped voice.

"My point exactly," Jenine replied, barely concealing the insolence in her voice.

The long deep look they exchanged infuriated Nat. "You don't understand because you don't want to understand," he murmured satirically, on his way out the room. Reaching the door, he pulled up, whirled about to face her. "You're still mad at me about leaving, aren't you? That's what this is about," he said with assurance. "Something that happened fifteen years ago." At her pinched-faced stare, he both asked and stated, "Isn't it," his confidence wavering.

"Is that what you think?" she said with a sarcastic tsk. "That I'm carrying a fifteen-year-old grudge? If that's what you think, you've got a lot of growing up to do, Nat."

"Don't you see I did what was best at the time," he said against her denial, committed to his assessment of the situation. "Come on Jenine. Think," he implored exasperated. "You know I had to leave back then."

"Nat, if that's what you want to believe, fine," she said, pleased at how nonchalant she sounded. "Everything always has to evolve around you, what you want, what you believe. It all boils down to your greedy ego."

"That's not true," he denied.

"Yeah, you were the only one who wanted to conquer the world with your music," she said in her facile tongue.

"We both wanted it," he asserted excitedly. "But we couldn't have done it together," he said, an edge of desperation in his voice. "I was ready to leave. You weren't. That's not an indictment, or an ugly mark against your personality. That's the simple truth."

"You wouldn't know truth if it played taps," she retorted.

Ignoring her insult, Nat reasoned on. "The farthest you'd ever been from home was with your high-school band. The supervision was almost as tight as when you stayed at home with your mother. I'm surprised she let you go that far," he said snorting.

"Face it, Nat," she said in a weary voice, "we've always been at cross purposes."

"No," he said, "we were never at cross purposes. Only different stages in our lives. But never crossed. If I would have stayed, you know what would have happened. Most likely neither of us would have left. We would have had heaven knows how many kids by now. Working . . . No, probably teaching in some inner-city school, trying to make ends meet, feeling hopelessly trapped."

"Is that how I've made you feel . . . hopelessly trapped?" she asked, masking her hurt in an empty gaze and tone. "Then put that out of your mind. My door is as open for your departure as it was to your arrival."

"There you go again, putting words in my mouth. That's not what I meant at all. I'm only saying that's how it would have been had I not left. You knew I wanted you. It was hard keeping my hands off you." With his voice gentling, he said, "You were so sweet, and getting finer by the day and everything. On top of that, you understood music. Even better than I did."

In spite of herself, Jenine was pleased by the compliment. But it didn't change anything between them, she thought. She recognized the truth in his crystal ball assertion, but it had nothing to do with the present. He had simply grown tired of her and was ready to leave. Contacting David only speeded up the process. That's all she wanted him to admit.

"If I had stayed, I would have destroyed the both of us," he said. "Whether you want to admit it or not, you know it's the truth. Like right now. The truth is, everything I've done has been based on what I thought was right . . . for Natasha, for you, for me. Can't you see that?"

"Things get too complicated for you, and off you go without concern for the person most affected by your decision," she said. "The truth is, you ran fifteen years ago and you haven't stopped running."

"Oh, forget it," he said. "I'm through trying to talk to you. I don't know what you want from me!" throwing up his hands.

"How about a little honesty?" Jenine replied, holding Natasha at her side. Pinning him with her cold brown eyes, she said, "You got tired of waiting for David to find you, so you called him."

"That's right," Nat bit off like a curse. "It would have taken him forever to find us in this little old town."

"In which case, you were safe until you got to court," she reasoned in a cold, yet soft voice. "But you couldn't wait."

"Don't you see it would have done no good?" he shouted defensively. "I don't even believe David intended going to court in the first place. While I would have been bogged down in the legal system, he would have stolen Natasha and been halfway to Africa. Once she was there, no court in the world could have helped me get her back. They may be good after the fact, but it's a risk I wasn't willing to take. David's hand had to be forced. It's the only chance I had of getting him off our backs. And this was the only way I could think of to do it."

"Why didn't you consult me? Or Robbie?" she asked, wondering why she was bothering to fight when she knew it was useless. Nat was ready to return to the bright lights and glamour of his previous lifestyle and had been anxious to do so from the beginning. Why couldn't she just let it rest, she thought. The sooner she got it over with, the sooner the hurt would go away, and she would heal.

"Because you would have tried to talk me out of it," he said.

He noticed the imperceptible nod of Jenine's head in agreement. But he felt little comfort in their agreement on this small matter.

"I've only been reacting to other people's decisions since this started," he said, his anger dissipating. "It was time to initiate a plan of my own."

Still, Jenine thought as she sighed, Nat couldn't be honest with her or himself. His rationale seemed worn, thin and hollow, typical macho shallowness. It was a pitiful situation. Here she was trying to let him go and he was fighting it, probably out of some sense of gratitude to her.

"You still can't admit the truth, can you?" she replied, shaking her head as if baffled.

"You keep hollering about the truth," he said with frustration in his tone. "I've given you the truth and you still persist in trying to make me look like the bad guy. Well, I'm through defending my actions to you. And let me remind you of one thing, Miss Jones. Natasha is my child, not yours. And I don't want my child," he said significantly, his olive brown eyes dazzling with fury, "growing up to be a coward who hides behind a career in a small town where the most exciting thing that happens is a talent show put on by teachers!"

Unnerved by the attack, Jenine felt her head spinning. She sputtered, so furious, so full of hurting she could hardly speak. Even Natasha quieted at the silence that reigned in the room.

Deciding it was another case of everything having been said, Jenine quietly got to her feet with Natasha on her hip. She put the baby in Nat's arms, then walked out the room with all the dignity she could muster.

Jenine walked into the guest bedroom, dressed in her robe, a towel wrapped around her head. She had just gotten out of the shower, where she had hoped to wash away the grime of regret and hurt under its hot sprays.

It helped little. She felt drained from the argument with Nat; her eyes were still puffy from the tears she'd shed.

The house was unusually quiet, but she was too absorbed by her own musing—the angry, hurting words they had hurled at each other—to notice.

She had to make herself presentable. There was a show to do in a couple of hours, and the band was counting on her being in fine, performing shape, she told herself, looking through the rack of clothes in the closet.

She remembered that the outfit she'd intended to wear was in the other closet and she cursed silently. She pulled the robe around her tightly to leave the room, but indecision rendered her frozen.

The doorbell rang. She would give Nat enough time to answer the door, then go to the room, she decided. She wasn't ready to withstand another confrontation with him. The repeated chime of the doorbell goaded her into unplanned action. As she hurried to the front door, she couldn't help but peek into the master room. It bore the telltale signs of a disappearance, and her heart slammed against her ribs, her eyes widened with painful astonishment.

Natasha's baby bag and carrier were missing, as were other little items like the box powder, diapers and baby wipes. She hurried down the hall to the room Nat had commandeered for drumming. Apparently, he hadn't had time to pack them. Though it meant he would return, she reasoned to herself, the presence of them was of no consolation. Their stay was as transient as their owner.

The doorbell rang again, and she meandered to answer it.

"I was beginning to think no one was home," Robbie said.

Jenine swallowed the tear stuck in her throat before she spoke. "Not counting me, no one is. Nat took Natasha and left."

Bruce squeezed Jenine affectionately to him, then released her, a bittersweet grin on his face.

"What was that for?" she asked before backing out of his light grasp.

They were in the dressing room Bruce had talked the club's manager into providing for Jenine. The walls in the closet-sized space had recently been painted white, and the turpentine smell was suffocating. A dressing table, with makeup lights around the mirror, and a backless stool were against the wall across the room.

"I know you're hurting," Bruce said.

Jenine stilled at the vanity table where she was sitting and stared at her hollow-eyed reflection in the mirror. After Robbie left from her short visit—she had only come to apologize to Jenine and Nat for losing her temper last night—Jenine discovered a note tacked to the phone in the kitchen. "We both need some space. I'll pick you up for school Monday morning as usual." It was signed simply "Nat." No love or any other parting salutation.

"Jenine," Bruce said, placing a hand on her shoulder.

Her reflection smiled a half-smile at him. "I thought I had hidden it pretty well." She began busying herself, freshening her makeup.

"You did," he said, "from the others. The audience sure couldn't tell by the way you played. But I've been around you longer." Dragging a chair next to where she sat, "Want to talk about it? We got a few minutes."

She dropped the eyeliner pencil and faced him with a somber expression. "No, I don't think so."

"Want to beg out of the Sunday-night show?"

Jenine laughed. "If I said yes, you'd die right there in that chair." Bruce chuckled with a shamefaced expression. "You'd better go and let me change for the next set."

He nodded, feeling a sense of helplessness that showed in his eyes. He stood and opened his mouth to argue, but changed his mind. "Okay. Eight minutes, Ms. Jones," he said, then left.

Preparing to take the stage for the last set, the group, minus Bruce, was assembled at the steps of the stage. Bruce approached them, waving a piece of paper in his hand.

"We got a request for some blues."

"That's over my head, I'm afraid," Clifton said.

"Jenine?" Bruce said, eyeing her with a puppy-dog look. "Solo?"

Her shoulders drooped in bitter humor, and she agreed with a barely audible, "What the hell," throwing up her hands.

* * *

The stage was dark except for the spotlight shining on the face of the lone pianist at the black baby-grand piano. An uncanny hush settled over the audience when Jenine began to play, expressing her hurt in bluesy chords. Black notes of sorrow, profound and absolute, hit the air and left their misery lingering. She played from the heart; a heart that had been open to love, and betrayed.

The song composed itself; Jenine was merely the instrument by which the pain was exposed. And when she finished, a stillness remained in the air before the room suddenly erupted in applause. The group came out on stage, clapping as fiercely as those in the audience. Bruce led Jenine downstage to take a bow; the audience was on its feet in acclamation.

Jenine felt like a fraud.

Chapter Fifteen

The first set was over. Jenine was sitting in her dressing room, catching her wind for the second show that would start in a few minutes.

She needed the break more than ever. She had a slight headache and a revolution was raging in her stomach. She managed to turn in a solid performance, but she was drained by the effort.

Now, she knew how it felt to have a broken heart, she thought, the back of her head pressed against the wall, eyes closed. What she had been going through—sleepless nights and unable to keep food down—were just side effects of losing in love.

Once she got Nat out of her system, she would feel better, she told herself. But until he was gone from the city and his paternity assured by whatever means he and David decided upon, she could expect to be sick with worry on top of everything else.

Nathaniel Padell was such a proud man, she thought, sighing heavily. Activity was not simply what he did, but an inherent part of his nature. She truly understood his inability to sit idly by, letting his future be determined externally. It must have been killing him on the inside all the time he had remained silent, privately mulling over the decision to call David. She couldn't blame him for wanting to take matters into his own hands, even though she abhorred the deceitful way he went about it.

Although she couldn't say for certain how she would have reacted in his situation, she suspected she would have disagreed, simply because of the danger to Natasha's future. The result could still blow up in his face, and the chance of losing his daughter was greater than had he let the court decide, she thought, her expression compassionate, troubled, still.

A knock on the door interrupted her thoughts, and she asked lethargically because it was all the energy she could muster, "Yes?"

"Are you decent?" Bruce asked from the other side of the door.

"Give me a second," she replied, pulling herself up to adjust the white, floor-length terry robe she was wearing. "Come in."

"Here are the crackers and soda you requested," he said upon entering, carrying a can of Coke and packs of saltines.

"Thanks a million," she said, tearing into the food substances, hopeful they would help settle her stomach.

"There's another matter that I hate to disturb you with, heaven knows you need the break." Hesitantly, he said, "Look, I know it's not any of my business . . ."

Jenine cut him off with a warning glance. Bruce had been hovering about her as if expecting her to collapse at any moment, she thought, mildly irritated. He behaved a lot like Nat, treating her as if she were some hothouse flower who needed a protector. The only thing that saved him from her full wrath was knowing he was trying to help. She followed the cracker with a sip of the Coke.

With a resigned sigh, Bruce said, "There's a man out here who insists on seeing you."

"You know I don't see anybody between shows," she said, biting into another cracker.

"I know that," he said. "This African dude . . . ," he started again.

Alarmed, Jenine choked, spitting soda all over the place. She knew instantly to whom Bruce referred: David Cissoko. In all probability, he was the only African in town.

"Hey, slow down," he admonished, patting her on the back. "All right now?"

With her mind fluttering in anxiety, Jenine replied, "Yeah, I'm fine." Absently, she set the can on the vanity table, her thoughts were running in a galloping race with her pulse.

"Anyway, this guy," he said. "I think he was at the Cobbs' party the other night. He's insisting on seeing you. Do you want to be bothered, or shall I have the management toss him out on his you-know-what?"

"I don't want to see him." Jenine voiced her first inclination, though she couldn't help wondering why David Cissoko wanted to see her.

"The manager told him, I told him, but the guy is persistent. He started making a scene, so Tommy brought him backstage. But I can just as well have Tommy kick him out, if that's what you want," Bruce said, with relish for the violent idea.

With a pensive shimmer in the shadow of her eyes, Jenine sat on the small cot and searched her mind for a plausible explanation to why David Cissoko had sought her out. Nervously, she began to finger the lapels of the robe, wondering whether or not to accept the visit and what it meant. Curiosity prevailed.

"Okay, I'll see him," she said.

Noticing her disquiet, Bruce asked, "Are you sure? You don't look too convinced."

"No, no, I'll be fine," she replied vaguely. Aware of Bruce's cautious countenance, she said, "Really, it's okay. If you want, you can stand at the door and listen."

He tilted his brow, looked at her with uncertainty and surprised her with his nearly hostile tone, "Does this have anything to do with Nat?"

Jenine arched a brow in amused contempt.

"Okay," he said, his hands held up in mock surrender. "I'm minding my own business."

"Give me two minutes to change, then send him in."

Seconds later, she stood, steadied her heartbeat with her hands, then opened the door.

"Come in."

David Cissoko walked in, a humble, apologetic smile on his handsome face. Jenine doubted he was a man of delicate scruples.

"Miss Jones, I am so happy you consented to see me. Your man told me you normally don't do this, and I really appreciate your breaking the rules."

"What do you want?" she asked. Her tone was aggressive and without thought or care for niceties.

"Can we sit?" He indicated the cot with his hand.

"No, we can't."

"I see," he said, bobbing his head knowingly.

"Do you, Mr. Cissoko?" she asked.

"I suspect my son-in-law has told you some very bad things about me. And," he elongated the word, "I suppose in a way, I would do the same thing if I were in his shoes," he said in an indulgent voice.

Jenine folded her arms across her chest and glared at him impatiently. "Get to the point."

"I see you are not going to make it easy for me."

"Why should I?"

"Do you always make up your mind without knowing all the facts?"

The mild rebuke teased Jenine's conscience, but only for a second. She had to counsel herself to be careful around this man, for David Cissoko was a highly skilled diplomat. "What facts might those be, Mr. Cissoko?"

Folding his hands in back of him, David Cissoko donned the expression of a troubled and pained man.

"I realize I have handled this all wrong," he said somberly. "Nathaniel is a very proud man, as I am," he added with a half-smile, "and he doesn't respond well to my hot temper. But, I promise you, Miss Jones, I mean no harm to him nor to my grandbaby. I just want to be able to spend some time with her. Am I wrong for wanting that, I ask you?"

Jenine was given no chance to reply, even if she had an answer to the innocently put query.

"I have instructed my attorney to drop the matter as a show of good faith," he continued. "I am hopeful that Nathaniel and I can work this out between us, without the interference of some stranger."

"What does that have to do with me?" Jenine asked, her expression a hostile frown.

"It saddens me greatly that I will be unable to spend time with my daughter's child," he said.

The reply was unexpected and chilled Jenine to the bone as she realized the implication. "What exactly are you asking me to do?" she asked with squinted eyes as she peered at him as if trying to read past his guileless expression.

"I understand you have been taking very good care of my grandbaby," he replied, rubbing his hands together as if about to feast on a tasty meal. "But, of course, the Cobbs assure me you're excellent with children. You see, I shall have to return to my home for a few months," he said, then fell silent, leaving her to guess the remainder of his thought.

"And?" Jenine prodded, trying not to give herself away.

"I'm asking that you intercede on a grandfather's behalf and let me get one glimpse of Natasha," he replied in one smooth breath.

"I don't believe you," Jenine said with profound incredulity, backing away from him. She spun around, giving him her back, a hand buried in her hair. She simply could not believe he had the gall to make such a request of her.

"I mean no harm to my granddaughter as I'm sure Nathaniel has implied," he said with parenthesis. "I have no other children, Miss Jones. Annette was my only child. Is it so wrong of me to want to be a part of my grandchild's life? She is after all my own flesh and blood. What have I done that is so sinister? Tell me," he said almost desperately.

Jenine turned facing him. Bad guys seldom looked the part, she thought, examining the tall, distinguished-looking man critically. She searched his face, his demeanor, anything for a look or gesture that would betray him, proving he was not what he appeared to be. But there was nothing sinister about his smile, no guile in his manner. His eyes, the same dark shade of brown as Natasha's, were gentle and kind-looking. Neither a smirk nor insolent expression crossed his handsome face.

In spite of everything she knew, or rather, had been told about David—the transgressions against law and God he allegedly committed, she couldn't reconcile the fiend in her dreams—who'd been very real—with this man, this kindly grandfather. The picture didn't fit.

Could Nat, in his usual macho zeal compounded by fatherhood, have been mistaken? she wondered, with mixed feelings surging through her.

"Are you saying," she asked carefully, "that Nat never

had grounds to fear the possibility of your kidnapping Natasha and taking her out of the country?"

He laughed and clasped his hands together. "That couldn't be further from the truth," he denied eloquently. "Is that what Nat believes? That I want to take his child from him? Do I seem like such a heartless man to you, Miss Jones? I have had a child taken from me, but there is nothing I can do to bring her back. But believe me when I say that I would not dare impose such a hardship on a parent. I love my grandbaby as much as Nathaniel does."

"Then why didn't you visit Natasha when you had the chance?"

"He would not permit it," he replied simply. "He refused, and quite adamantly I might add."

"You would have me believe that Nat concocted a bizarre story just to keep you from visiting Natasha?"

"Yes, I would. I would have you believe it because it is the truth, Miss Jones," he said in a quiet, emphatic voice. He took a card from his inside coat pocket and held it out to her.

There was a knock on the door, and Bruce announced, "Jenine, five minutes."

"Okay," she shouted back.

Picking up before the interruption, David said, "I'm not asking you to make a decision right now. Here," passing her a card, "I can be reached at the number on the back. I believe you recognize it as the Cobbs' home number. Think it over. Please."

"My accepting this card does not constitute a promise to do anything except think about what you've told me," Jenine replied firmly.

"I understand. Anything that you do will be extremely appreciated. Again, thank you for your time."

Jenine stared at the door long after David had left. She flipped the card over and over in her hand. Though she now had both sides of the story, she was hard pressed to believe David Cissoko's view. Part of the reason, she knew, had to do with her feelings about Nat. But David was so persuasive, and regardless of her wariness about him, she had to consider a possibility that was a source of conflict within her: whether Nat, in his own admitted dislike of his father-in-law, had convinced himself David posed a threat to Natasha when there may have been no danger at all.

Another knock on the door sent her scurrying to dress for the second set.

After the show, Bruce drove Jenine home. She was silent and thoughtful the entire ride. The card David had given her was in her purse; that which he asked her to consider was on her mind.

She debated whether to call Nat to inform him about the visit. She had a pretty good idea of where he and his daughter were staying. But just the thought of calling him caused a nervous flutter in her stomach.

By the time Bruce pulled up in her driveway, she'd decided. The break between her and Nat had been made, and it was best to keep it that way. She would notify Robbie first thing in the morning of her meeting with David Cissoko and leave the final decision in her capable hands as Nat's attorney.

"Need a ride in the morning?" Bruce asked before Jenine got out of the car.

"No thanks," she replied.

"Is Nat picking you up?"

"Bruce," Jenine said with admonishment in a tired, rhythmic voice.

"Okay, okay. Just checking."

"Thanks," she smiled at him fondly, then hurried from the car to get inside from the cold.

Even after locking up and turning on the alarm, she stood staring at the door for what seemed like hours. She thought of the empty bedroom awaiting her and couldn't seem to make herself move, as though her entire being rebelled against going any further into the house. Finally, she did; her feet felt encased in lead shoes.

She stopped at the open door on her right as if summoned. Though she already knew what she would find, she turned on the lights. Nat had confiscated the unused bedroom for his drums, the only evidence that remained of his presence. They were everywhere—like Nat used to be in her home—and of every imaginable size and shape.

She smelled the lingering scent of his fragrance, felt his presence in a tangible form. She could even envision his long, magnificent body settled behind the drum set, a stick held perfectly in each hand.

A fear she had never known attacked her being, and Jenine thought how foolish she had been to think herself prepared to handle his departure from her life. Her imagination of the hurt was nothing like this, her eyes watering with tears and a sad, staccato beat pounding in her heart.

Propping herself against the doorframe, she belittled her hurt, reminding herself that Nat was accustomed to the bright lights of big cities, the adulation of crowds, and women far more worldly than she. Those things were an everyday experience for him. How could she have let herself hope for a moment he would be satisfied living in Highland Heights, or that she was a powerful enough attraction to keep him here?

A sob broke through the tenuous hold she had over herself, seizing her body with tumultuous tears. She slid to the floor, clutching her middle. There were no answers to her tearful pondering: Why did it hurt so much? and, When would it end?

Finally, the crying ceased, leaving intermittent sniffles. She wiped her face with the back of her hand and drew a heavy-hearted breath.

She had only had Nat for a little while, she reasoned. And had always known he would be a temporary diversion, not a permanent fixture in her life. Delusions of the power of love had made her wish for more, and now she was paying the price for losing sight of reality. Yet, she was glad she had known the thing that people the world over sought to have as a meaningful part of their lives.

Slowly, Jenine got to her feet and turned to leave. But she couldn't, not just yet—the feeling was like her love for Nat. There was no way to unlove him. Walking away was not going to be easy.

Sauntering to the drum set, she fingered each piece. Lastly, she flicked the cymbal with her finger; its tenor pitch pinged, then joined the silence ringing throughout the house.

This was not her instrument, she thought. And Nat was not her man. Soon, the room would contain no evidence of having been used. And likewise, her life would contain no signs of having been loved. An inner voice contradicted her, but she ignored it.

Turning off the light, Jenine quickly left the room for her own. Her instrument beckoned, and she sat before the piano.

She must remember who her friends were, she told herself, placing her hands on the slender, short ivory sticks. The song came to her; the one that had come with Nat, that was to be played for no one but Nat. She began to play, to sing the sweet, sad song for the last time.

Only, she couldn't. Her fingers refused.

Jenine clamped her hands over her mouth to stifle the

cry trying to claw its way out of her, then closed the piano and pushed herself up to her feet. She ambled about the room.

He was the most exasperating man she'd ever met. Yet, she believed if he rang that doorbell right now, she would be in his arms begging him for another chance. Where was her pride now? she wondered, hugging herself.

"At least, I have my music," she whispered sadly.

Convincing herself she felt a little better than she had when she arrived, Jenine glanced at the room a final time. Just as she was about the darken the light, the doorbell rang, and with it, her heart lurched excitedly. Nat had returned!

"We can't find hide nor hair of a stranger in town," Talbert said, shaking his head.

He was standing at the serving tray in the hotel suite, pouring coffee, while Nat was staring out into the cold, bright morning.

"Whoever you saw in that blue Lincoln must have driven straight to the next town. But, don't worry, everybody's still on alert."

"I wish I could have gotten the license-plate numbers," Nat said. He ran a hand across his head as he turned facing the sheriff.

With a shrug, Talbert replied, "It's probably a rental. And there are not that many Lincolns in this part of the country," he added, tilting his cup in a salute. "How's Miss Jones this morning?"

Nat fell momentarily silent. He should have known Talbert would ask about Jenine.

"Fine," he replied finally, "I guess." Feeling Talbert's eyes boring a hole in his back, he turned, facing the town's sheriff. "I'm sure Robbie has told you by now we decided to give each other a little space. Well," he shrugged guilt-ily, "I decided. Natasha and I have been here at the hotel since then Saturday."

"I see," Talbert said quietly, lowering the cup to the coffee table.

"Well, I'm glad you do, cause I damn sure don't," Nat replied with frustration in his voice and regret coloring his countenance.

"Son," Talbert said in a fatherly tone, "the man who can figure out the female mind could make a mint selling that information to the rest of us dummies."

"I couldn't make her understand," he said, more to himself than to Talbert, who nodded with understanding. "There was a time when she agreed with whatever I said or suggested," running his fingers through his hair.

As long as he lived, he would never forget Jenine's sad, hurtful eyes, brown liquid pools of dejection, or the horri-ble things he'd said that caused it. He had seen that look before—when he'd refused his mother's offer to help. "You're too proud for your own good, Nathaniel," he heard his mother's gentle scolding echoing in his head.

After burying Netta, she accompanied him and Nata-sha back to New York and helped them settle in until Ms. Cramer could free her schedule to start earlier than ini-tially planned. It had taken two weeks; his mother stayed one, taking care of her "baby boy" and newest grand-baby. She would have stayed longer had he not been hell-bent on proving that he was capable of being a suc-cessful, single parent.

Oh, how soon we forget, he thought to himself with chiding.

"Times change," Talbert said with rumination.

"Yeah. And how," Nat retorted. "I love her, you know," he said softly.

Regardless of the cause that had brought him to Highland Heights, he had to admit, he had never been more comfortable in his life since he left home. Not that he hadn't met any really nice, decent people in his business, but with the exception of about three or four, he didn't have any close friends outside the business. He had missed that feeling of being able to share little-known parts of himself without having that information used to manipulate him for something. He had gotten that here—with Jenine.

"And that goes double for Natasha. She took to Jenine instantly, like she knew she was safe and loved, and all that," he said, filled with the memories of his daughter and Jenine together.

"Miss Jones has a reputation for being good with children," Talbert said.

"Well, she knew I was going to pick her up this morning, but she left anyway," Nat said with irritation in his voice and expression. "Now, does that make sense? With everything that's going on, you'd think she would at least stick to our plans. But, nooo, Miss Independent couldn't wait to strike out on her own."

"Well, you know how these women are," Talbert said. "They get it in their heads sometimes that you're taking advantage of them, or doing something to mask your real reasons when there's nothing more to it than what you said it was."

Dumbfounded, Nat said, "What?"

"Yeah, it confuses me, too," Talbert replied laughingly.

Talking with his hands, Nat said, "No, I mean about the part where they put another interpretation on something, and it's all wrong."

"Oh, that," Talbert said. "I don't know if I can repeat it," he laughed. "It's way beyond me."

"Yeah," Nat said absently, his expression thoughtful.

"Where's Natasha now?"

Nat looked at him with a blank stare, his mind elsewhere. "Oh, she finally cried herself to sleep. She's mad at me, too." Throwing up his hands up in defeat, he said, "I can't seem to win."

Talbert heard the strain in Nat's voice. He ignored it. "Don't worry, everything is gonna turn out fine," he said, staring at Nat's somber expression with commiseration. "Just give her time."

"Right," Nat said skeptically.

With deep concern and worry on her face, Robbie paced the carpeted floor in her den. She wondered what was keeping Talbert, whom she had called a few minutes ago.

Replaying the conversation she'd had with Ethel Cobb a few short minutes ago, she took a sip of her cold coffee, then leaned against the bar. Ethel had exclaimed she needed to speak with her about a school-related matter. But it hadn't been the only thing on the founder's mind.

The two women were sitting in Robbie's kitchen, drinking coffee. She had followed Ethel's roundabout conversation with growing impatience and finally demanded, "Ethel, will you get to the point?"

Ethel stiffened at the sharpness in her tone, she recalled, and she had felt chagrined. Ethel had been a good friend to her, helping to get her law practice started in Highland Heights ten years ago. She owed Ethel a little more than impatience.

"I'm sorry, Ethel," Robbie said contritely. "I didn't get much sleep last night." She knew Ethel would automatically assume Talbert was the reason for her late night and she would be forgiven.

"I had always hoped you two would get together,"

Ethel said. "He's such a nice man. I wish you'd give him a chance."

Robbie smiled and nodded in agreement, but she wasn't about to let Ethel get started on another tangent. "Now, what has you all fired up and anxious this early?" she said, forcing an easy manner to her voice.

Ethel fiddled with the handle on the cup before replying hesitantly, "It's Jenine Jones." Robbie was instantly on the alert. "Well, it's not Jenine really, but the mother of one of her students. Mrs. Stevens. You remember her, don't you?"

Robbie relaxed. She had been apprised of Mrs. Stevens's threat to file a suit against the school before Jenine put her son out of the music program.

"Ethel," she said patiently, "I think you know better than I do that Jenine considered this matter carefully before she acted on it."

"The woman is threatening to sue the school," Ethel retorted in a huff. "What I think doesn't count! I've worked too long and hard to jeopardize the reputation of the school."

"You're blowing this out of proportion," Robbie countered, rising to refill her cup. "Mr. North was in complete agreement with Jenine, and so was the counselor," she added, getting a can of cream from the refrigerator. She poured a drop of the thick white liquid into her coffee and returned to the table.

"I know, but Jenine hasn't been acting like herself lately," Ethel said puzzled.

Sipping her coffee, Robbie eyed Ethel speculatively over the rim of the cup, wondering what the real reason was behind Ethel's comment. "Look Ethel, why don't you just tell me what's really troubling you," she coaxed.

Ethel set the cup hard on the table. "Mr. North thinks we might lose Jenine." Crossing her arms on the table,

"It's that man living with her," with disgust in her voice. Robbie laughed. "It's not funny. She's one of our best teachers. I picked her myself."

"So that gives you the right to try to run her life?" Robbie replied with a slightly raised brow of reproach.

Flustered, Ethel spoke with her hands, "No, but she owes the school more respect than to up and leave," snapping her fingers, "just like that."

"Who said she was leaving?"

"No one, but the signs are there," Ethel replied. "Like this morning when I went to the school to talk to her about this Stevens matter, she wasn't there."

Robbie smiled in her cup, thinking that at least Jenine and Nat had made up and were using their time wisely.

"And she didn't even call," Ethel said in a huff.

Robbie stiffened, her brow wrinkled, as she slowly set her cup on the table. "She didn't call to say she wouldn't be in?" she asked for clarification.

"No," Ethel replied miffed. "That's the kind of behavior I'm talking about. That's not like the Jenine Jones I hired."

No, it wasn't like Jenine at all, Robbie thought. "Excuse me a second, Ethel," she said, getting up to walk to the phone on the wall near the sink counter. She quickly dialed Jenine's number. A frown darkened her expression when she received no answer. Dialing a second number, she replied, "This is Robbie Franks. Is the sheriff in?"

The doorbell rang, snapping Robbie back to the present. She raced to the front of the house and opened the door.

"I came as soon as I got the message," Talbert said, stepping inside. "What's up?"

"Have you talked to Nat this morning?" she asked.

"Yeah. I went by the hotel early this morning," Talbert replied. "I was just leaving . . ."

Robbie cut him off, asking anxiously, "Was Jenine with him?"

"Nope," he said. "He hasn't seen her since he left her place the other night. He was supposed to pick her up for school this morning, but she must have decided not to wait for him."

"Jenine didn't go to school today," Robbie said, her hand at her throat. "She didn't call in either."

Chapter Sixteen

Jenine awakened from a frightening dream, tears streaming down her face. Slowly, she sat up and took in her surroundings. Except for the glow of a small light on the other side of the glass partition, it was dark, giving the illusion of a quiet peace.

Filled with remembering, she huddled herself in a protective knot on the narrow bed and pulled the rough knapsack covering close to her.

If only she had been careful, Jenine chided herself tearfully, her thoughts skipping back to how she had come to be a prisoner. She had been thinking about Nat, ready to cast her pride aside and accept him on any terms if only he would walk through the door. When the doorbell rang, ecstatic relief and forgiveness permeated her entire being. Believing her prayers had been answered, she didn't give a second thought to the careless way she had flung open the door.

Instead of Nat, her captors were standing there with strange expressions on their faces. They were even more surprised than she, not expecting the quarry to fall so easily into their hands, she thought with hindsight. The pair reminded her of the comic-book characters Mutt and Jeff. But there was nothing comical about this odd couple.

The polite one was tall and straight, lithe and supple in build. He had high strong bones and large inquisitive eyes. The other was a fat, placid stereotype of a bartender with the beady eyes of a hawk and protruding potbelly that prevented him from buttoning the wool sports coat he wore at all times.

While neither had physically threatened her, it was implied in their ominous presence. They had simply requested that she "Come along quietly," empowered by the fact that Jenine couldn't resist them if she had tried.

They had driven around the city, seemingly aimlessly at the time. She now knew it had been simply to assure themselves they were not being followed before they brought her here.

Here, was one of several hangars a few yards from the landing strip for those fortunate enough to own their own planes, like the Cobbs. Commercial flights never used the place; commoners like herself who wanted to travel by air had to drive to the airports in Lubbock or Amarillo.

She wondered whether Nat had discovered this place when he was driving around the city looking for signs of David's presence. Even if he had, she thought with pessimism darkening her heart, there was no guarantee he would remember it or think to look for her here. No one used this place except the Cobbs and their wealthy friends, meaning David Cissoko had access to it, as well.

The only beam of hope Jenine allowed herself was knowing Nat would look for her. Though he had a tendency to go off half-cocked, his sense of duty and responsibility to those he cared about was strong. And she loved all those qualities about him, she thought, a breath trembling in her chest. He may not want her, but he wouldn't abandon her, she told herself.

How could she have doubted Nat even for a second, she asked herself, feeling like a traitor. Recalling her quandary about David's sincere paternal performance, she was assailed by a bitter rush of remembrance: If it looks too good to be true, then it isn't—she recited the adage whose wisdom she had ignored.

She didn't have to be wide awake to guess she was safe until David Cissoko got what he wanted—her in exchange for Natasha. She never would have guessed that he'd planned to use her as bait. Although she didn't want to think about it, she pondered the lengths he would go in order to have his demand met.

How long had she been here? she wondered, looking around the room for a clock. How much longer would she be held prisoner? What if Nat couldn't find her before David Cissoko got his wish?

Giving in to hopelessness and despair of ever being rescued, Jenine stuffed as much of her hand as possible in her mouth to silence the mourning cry within her. She had wanted Nat more than life. And in a way, it looked as if she was going to get what she wished for. How's that for irony? she thought.

Her stomach churned with her crazy emotions, fear topping the list. She felt it rising up her throat and bolted for the door. She bumped into one of her captors; it was the big one. Shouting in a language she could not understand, he grabbed her roughly by the arm and jerked her back and forth like a rag doll. She threw up all over him.

Natasha's baby talk livened the tense atmosphere in the living room of the hotel suite. Robbie and Talbert were sitting on the sofa watching Nat, who had a cold, hard-pinched expression on his face. Gone was his usual fluidity as he shoved diapers and bottles carelessly into the diaper bag.

"He has her," Nat blazed tightly. He wanted to scream

the rage and remorse that had been building up inside him since Talbert and Robbie told him about Jenine's disappearance only moments ago.

"The Cobbs swear David Cissoko hasn't been out of their sight," Talbert repeated patiently, running a frustrated hand across his head.

"I don't give a damn what they said," Nat yelled, throwing the bag on the floor. "He has her and you know it," staring at Talbert with a fierce look.

Talbert lowered his gaze to the cowboy hat in his hand, absently twisting the brim of the big black hat.

"A crime has been committed, so where's the law?" Nat demanded harshly.

"Nat," Robbie said patiently, "Talbert is doing everything possible to find Jenine."

"Everything possible is not enough," he snapped.

"Da-da," Natasha babbled, holding out her arms for Nat.

Taking Natasha, he held her tenderly against his chest. Though the hands patting his face were tiny and smoother than silk, he imagined them Jenine's hands, loving and gentle on his flesh. It was Jenine's scent he smelled instead of the baby powder that had been sprinkled on Natasha.

He smiled at his daughter with none of the fury he felt, and bathed her with loving eyes that stung with unshed tears. In trying to protect one, he had endangered the other, he thought, feeling caught in a web of his own weaving. After kissing Natasha on the cheek, he returned her to Robbie.

Looking vacant and spent, Nat ran a hand across his face and over his head. Dropping his hands to his sides and his brows drawn together in an agonized expression, he said, "Look, I'm sorry." He threw his hands up in a helpless gesture. "I know it's not your fault."

"It's not anybody's fault," Robbie corrected.

Nat chuckled insolently. "Thanks," he said in a quiet, despondent tone, "but we all know who the culprits are." He expired a quick, heavy breath, then turned with a quick snap of his shoulders and strode from the room with purpose in his long-legged gait.

Stroking Talbert's back with her free hand, Robbie said, "It's not your fault."

"I know that," Talbert replied. "But there's a man here who's hurting," nodding in the direction of the adjoining room where Nat had gone. "I feel like my hands are tied behind my back. I can't even bring this Cissoko fellow in for questioning." Slapping the hat on his knee, he added, "Hell, I can't even talk to him!"

"Even if you could, you wouldn't get any more out of him than you did at the Cobbs," Robbie said. "We just have to find Jenine. With her statement, then the law can begin to do its job."

"Tell that to Nat," Talbert said mumbling, head bowed looking at his boots. He pushed himself up from the couch to stand in front of the window. The tensing of his jaw showed his deep frustration. He glanced absently out the window, then faced Robbie.

"You know we have to consider the worst," he said in a measured tone. He saw the tremor touch Robbie's mouth and bunched the hat in his hands. "If David has kidnapped Ms. Jones as a ransom for Natasha, he's can't afford to have a witness."

With her lips trembling, Robbie whimpered, then covered her mouth with her hand. Clearing her throat, she said, "But surely, he wouldn't risk a, a, . . ." Her voice faltered, then died out.

Supplying the idea Robbie couldn't voice, Talbert said, "A murder charge." He chortled snidely. "If a man is willing to go so far as to risk a felony charge for kidnapping, you can assume he'll go all the way. We already know from the investigator that he has no scruples. Stealing from his own people . . . ," he snorted his disdain. "Well, I just wanted you to know it's a possibility," he said as if it was a foregone conclusion.

Nat returned, zipping up his leather coat. There was a stalking intent in his walk and decision was firm on his face. Wordlessly, he guided Natasha's arms in the pink wool coat, buttoned it up, then tied a knit cap under her chin.

"Where are you going?" Robbie asked anxiously.

"Jenine's," Nat replied. "David will call me there," he said with prosaic confidence.

Robbie and Talbert exchanged glances, then Talbert nodded solemnly in agreement.

"I'll put a tap on the phone," Talbert said.

Nat took Natasha in one arm, picked up her bag with the other and adjusted it across his shoulder. Striding to the door, he stopped to look at Robbie and Talbert, his gaze sweeping them with a long, silent scrutiny.

On the ride to Jenine's, Nat felt all the emotions and thoughts when he had first driven into town in search of a haven. The only difference, he mused, was that it was daylight now, and though it was cold, the sun was shining brightly in the high blue sky.

His thoughts returned to that night when he was sick to his stomach, thinking himself a coward. He had almost turned around and left while standing at her front door, a finger suspended inches from the doorbell. It was against his nature to share his troubles, but Natasha's safety was more important than his pride.

Or so he had reasoned that night, he thought bitterly. He remembered sweating with his indecision in spite of the brisk wind blowing its cold breeze around him. He was sweating now.

He recalled his accusation to Jenine that she was bitter, holding his departure fifteen years ago against him. It had been in his initial thoughts upon arriving in town, wondering whether she would refuse him entry into her home. But she hadn't, he thought with a bittersweet smile, before his face collapsed into a set of wrinkling, thinking maybe she should have.

Instead, he rang the doorbell and Jenine appeared. All thoughts about pride, conflicting emotions and momentarily, even Natasha were forgotten. He had been content to simply correct the mental picture he had drawn of Jenine based on his outdated memory.

His intentions regarding Jenine had always been misguided, he thought. Like before, he hadn't intended anything more than friendship. This time, he had only wanted a safe place to hide for a little while. Instead, he had fallen in love with Jenine all over again. If, he had ever stopped loving her in the first place.

Jenine exaggerated her weakened state, allowing the taller of her two captors to help her back into the small office just off the main hangar. Having just emptied her already empty stomach for the second time this morning, she felt fatigue oozing from every pore.

As she lay on the cot and pulled the rough knapsack over her, she noticed he was still standing over her. He glanced at his partner who had come to the doorway. She understood the look of concern in his gaze as he spoke in what she assumed was an African language, then the heavyset man lumbered off.

The big man returned shortly with a can of Coke and two slices of bread in a styrofoam container. He gave them to her tall captive, who then passed the offerings on before leaving Jenine to do as she pleased.

She watched him confer with his chubby companion through the glass partition that was part of the fourth wall, dividing her cell from the more spacious hangar, housing a small plane. She glanced at the phone on the beat-up desk, then looked up to stare into the watchful gaze of the fat man.

Feeling as if he had read her thoughts, Jenine quickly lowered her eyes to the bread. Thinking her back was literally and figuratively pressed against the wall, she broke off pieces of the hard, white bread and washed each bite down with Coke.

She was imagining the worst-case scenario, and the stale bread stuck in her throat. A sip of soda followed to help wash it down. Regardless of how unpleasant the vision of her demise loomed in her mind, she knew she couldn't discount the possibility that David Cissoko would have her killed if Nat didn't comply with his demand for Natasha.

With certainty the strongest positive emotion in her, Jenine realized she would have to rely on her own wits to free herself. Nat would never agree to such an exchange. It was a trade even she couldn't sanction.

Nat was sitting on a hard steel folding chair, a long, narrow bass drum trapped between his legs. Like a motor-driven mechanism, his hands beat the smooth, yellowed parchment stretched over the ends of the conga, creating multiple images and sounds reflecting his troubled soul.

His body was drenched in perspiration. He should have been exhausted from the continuous pounding, but the violence bubbling within him fueled his body with an unending source of energy.

He had to find Jenine. But to do that, he had to put her out of his mind, close the door on his memories of her and think with the mind of an African warrior-general like David Cissoko.

He had come back to the scene of his crime, he thought. Her scent was not just all over the place, but in him; her sweet innocent smell mixed with the stench of his flagrant guilt. If it weren't for him, she would be safe, doing what she loved, teaching music to young people eager for her knowledge. He should have never left her alone and defenseless.

His thoughts returned to what Talbert had said about a woman's interpretation. Assuming Talbert knew what he was talking about, then Jenine handed him walking papers because she thought it was what he wanted. And if that were the case, then he was to blame because he had created this lover's gaffe with his selfish and pride-driven actions. If he had only shared more of himself, he thought.

He had to put an end to the self-punishment, in order to atone for his mistakes, Nat reminded himself. Shutting his eyes tight, he directed his thoughts to the task before him. Every inch of his long-fingered hands touched the drum, creating a kind of kinetic art with sound.

He pounded the drums until his hands hurt and painful aches shot up his arms like hot-tipped arrows. The rhythm slowed, the sound softened, then all ceased, leaving only his breathing in the din of silence. He wiped the sweat from his forehead with the balls of his hands. The water in his eyes was tears; he left them alone and dried his palms against his jeans.

Setting the drum on the floor next to the chair, Nat stood to stretch his long frame. He strolled to the back of the room to open the curtains, letting sunshine into the room. With his legs spread apart and hands on his hips, he rolled his head on his neck.

Not a muscle popped; he was loose and relaxed, focused on his prime subject. What would David do now? he asked himself. What would he do if he were in David's shoes?

In a sudden blaze of insight, Nat realized it wasn't a warrior or an African mind he had to contend with, but a possessive, jealous father who was obsessed with acquiring an object, not just a granddaughter, to dominate. Spitting out a savage curse, he pushed himself away from the window. Jenine was in the clutches of a madman who would do anything to punish Nat for taking his daughter from him.

Running his fingers through his hair, Nat felt control slipping away as fear threatened to overtake him. He drew in a deep breath, pulled back his shoulders and lifted his granite-molded jaw.

He hadn't wanted to accept that David's capabilities extended to murder, he now knew. Nor had he seriously entertained the idea that David would dare attempt murder in this country where his family's name was virtually unknown and unfeared. But then on the other hand, he thought, maybe there was more to the hands-off posture the police had taken when he reported an attempted kidnapping by a foreign diplomat.

The loud shrill of the phone jarred Nat out of his reverie. He raced from the room to snatch up the phone on the table in the master bedroom.

"Hello."

There was no mistaking the voice of the educated African on the other end. Nat's dark face twisted to a vicious expression; fury glittered like burning coals in his eyes. The more he listened, the tighter he gripped the slender receiver and the more incensed he became. His mouth dipped into an even deeper frown. Bastard! he thought, but kept his counsel. He couldn't afford to let his emotions run unchecked now.

"Yes," Nat replied dryly.

Slowly, he hung up the phone. His chest expanded and contracted in rhythm of the forced steady control of his breathing. His gaze fell to Jenine's dress bag and makeup kit on the bed, as the call replayed in his mind.

"Nathaniel. This is David. I have Miss Jones, as you've no doubt guessed by now. She's safe and will remain so as long as you do as I say. You know what I want. A daughter for a daughter. I'm offering you an equal exchange. You will bring my granddaughter to me. I shall call you with instructions at the same time tomorrow. If you disobey, Miss Jones will suffer for your stupidity. Do we understand each other, Nathaniel?"

Nat looked at clock. It was twelve-thirty. He had twenty-four hours in which to find Jenine.

First, he had to figure out what to do with Natasha. He didn't dare take her to Robbie's. For all he knew, David had men waiting there just in case an opportunity presented itself.

On the other hand, a man driving around with a baby would be noticed, so he couldn't take Natasha with him either. He would have to come up with something else, somewhere safe with someone David couldn't be familiar with, or was least likely to look.

He had never disobeyed a court order in all of his twenty-five years of law enforcement, Talbert thought, mulling over the official document inside his jacket pocket. He was standing at Jenine's front door, wearing a reproving countenance for what he had to do.

There had been a few times in his career when he was tempted to charge into a courtroom and shoot the judge.

Those had usually involved cases where known criminals had been thrust back on an innocent public faster than he could put his pants on. Once, there had been a child-abuse case he'd had the misfortune to work on, and since then, nothing else came close to making him question the wisdom of the law.

Until now, he thought. He pressed the doorbell.

Nat stirred slowly as the ringing intrusion filtered through his consciousness. He raised his head to look at the clock; it was 9:24. He calculated he had dozed off about forty minutes ago. He had only come home to shower and change before he planned to head back out again.

A little less than three hours to find Jenine and return home before David called, he thought, running his fingers through his hair.

Swinging his feet to the floor, he zipped his rumpled jeans and stepped into his tennis shoes. The buzzer went off again before he got to the door.

"Talbert? What are you doing here so early in the morning?"

"Nat," Talbert said tiredly, pulling off his hat as he stepped inside. "I'm afraid I got some bad news for you." He closed the door. "You're not going to like this at all."

Looking at the white envelope Talbert was extending to him, Nat asked, "What's this?"

Shoving the envelope in Nat's hand, Talbert replied, "Go on, open it up."

Taut with attention, Nat read the name outside the envelope, then pulled out the official document. Glutto-nously feeding on the printed words, he staggered with disbelief, his expression contorting with full-fledged fury.

"What the hell is this supposed to mean? Tell me,

Talbert," he demanded angrily, shaking the paper in the sheriff's face. "Tell me this does not mean, what I think it means." Nat wished he could play it off as some kind of cruel joke, but his mind had already accepted the truth. "That bastard," he said, thinking David was taking no chances on leaving empty-handed.

"I know how you feel, Nat, but I . . ."

Nat cut him off, shouting, "No you don't know how I feel, damn it," crumbling the paper in his hand.

"Nat," Talbert said with consoling intentions in his voice and expression.

"It's funny, isn't it," Nat cut him off, chuckling with a snort. "A foreigner can come into this country and have his rights protected better than someone born here. Ain't that a blip!" He stormed off to the kitchen.

Nat was putting coffee on when Talbert joined him. The older man dropped his black cowboy hat on the countertop of the island.

Pulling two coffee mugs from a top cabinet, Nat asked, "What's the plan?"

"I'm to deliver Natasha to her grandfather," Talbert replied.

"You're to deliver her where, Talbert?" Nat asked forcefully, setting the cups down with a thud on the counter top.

"I can't tell you that, Nat," Talbert replied, shaking his head. "I'm sorry."

"I see," Nat said with a nod of his head.

"I can't run the risk of having you going off half-cocked and people getting hurt," Talbert explained with exasperation lining his voice.

"What about my hurt, Talbert, huh? What about Natasha and Jenine? You know something smells, but you're going to keep walking into the stink anyway?"

"Nat, I know . . . ," Talbert said before cutting off the

unsatisfactory sympathetic refrain. "Robbie is working as we speak to get a restraining order. But until or unless she's successful, I'm bound by law."

Nat cut Talbert a savage look with a roll of his eyes.

"Don't make me the heavy here, Nat," he sighed. "Robbie tried to call you, but no one answered the phone. Where have you been?"

"Out," Nat snapped, getting spoons from a drawer and the sugar bowl, while silently counting off the passing of time in his head.

He needed more information, though he knew Talbert had been as forthcoming as he was going to be. The sheriff had guessed right about him making an attempt to stop David by any means necessary. What Talbert didn't know, however, was that even he couldn't stop him. Coaching patience to himself, Nat faced the sheriff, a can of cream in his hands.

"Who is this judge?" he asked.

"A close friend of the Cobbs'. Somehow or other, your in-law convinced them to help him get temporary custody of Natasha. And, as I understand it from a conversation Robbie had with Mrs. Cobb, she was already convinced that you had committed some horrendous crime based on the innuendoes Cissoko had already fed her. This was just a simple solution as far as the Cobbs were concerned. All they had to do was pick up the phone and call their very good friend Judge Norton."

Following a roaring din of silence, Talbert, in a soft voice, said, "You don't know how much it pains me to ask you to please get Natasha ready."

Nat emitted a chuckle, before all-out laughter erupted from him. He thought for once he had a step on David. "She's not here," he said through the laughter. "I knew better than to trust that bastard a second time."

"A second time?" Talbert asked.

"Yeah," Nat said, with a sardonic chuckle.

"What do you mean?"

"David called me yesterday," Nat replied. "Apparently you didn't get the phone tapped," a slightly raised brow at Talbert.

"I did," Talbert said defensively. "There were no calls in or out of the place, and you were nowhere to be found."

"Well," Nat said, "he was to the point. If I wanted no harm to come to Jenine, I would await further instructions on the exchange."

Wordlessly, Talbert looked down at his balled fist on the counter, his thick brows tilting inward on his square, serious face. He merely toyed with the spoon.

"How does a man get out of Highland Heights in a hurry, Talbert?" Nat asked, cutting a sidelong glance at the sheriff as he poured coffee in each cup.

He watched Talbert's lip twitch. For a second, he thought Talbert would abandon his law-abiding conscience. But the sheriff remained silent, and Nat had to squash the notion to beat the information out of him. Instead, he reminded himself to use his head.

"That means there's an airport somewhere," he guessed.

Talbert drank a sip of coffee before he responded. "The nearest airport is over a hundred miles away," he said in a nonchalant tone of voice.

"Uh-huh," Nat replied thoughtfully. He continued to dig. "Michael Cobb strikes me as an impatient kind of man. And thorough," as though an afterthought. "A long drive wouldn't suit him," he speculated aloud.

Talbert held fast to his secrets. "Where is she, Nat?" he asked, setting the cup on the counter. "Where's Natasha?"

With an innocent countenance, Nat replied in an even

tone, "I can't tell you that, Talbert." Angling his body as if turning away, "But I will tell you this."

"Wha . . . ?" was all Talbert got out, the "t" never passed his lips, replaced by a guttural groan as Nat delivered a front snap-kick to his groin. The sheriff doubled over debilitated, holding himself as the pain streaked up to his stomach. A well-placed elbow to the base of his neck finished him off.

"The law stinks," Nat replied softly, looking down at Talbert's still body spread across the floor. "Sorry, Tal," he said, stepping over the sheriff's unconscious form sprawled on the floor.

Jenine looked through the glass partition and saw neither of her captors. Slowly, she got up and inched her way to the door. She had planned that if one stopped her exit, she would feign a need to go to the bathroom. They had become accustomed to her many trips to the toilet and didn't seemed suspicious about them. She was halfway across the room when the phone rang.

The leaner of her captors strolled into the room to find her sitting meekly on the cot, hands folded in her lap. He answered the phone, seeming to barely pay her any attention. The conversation was brief, and spoken, as usual, in a language she didn't understand. He hung up the phone, then looked at Jenine with something like regret in his eyes before leaving, calling out to his partner.

Jenine guessed that the caller was David. The look in her captor's eyes didn't bode well for her, she thought. Thinking her time had run out, panic ran rampant within her, dangerously increasing her heartbeat.

She had to get control of herself. Think! Jenine coached silently, her hand at her throat, her brown eyes glassy marbles of terror. She scanned her surroundings—paint was chipped in certain spots of the dull gray walls, but there were no openings, no escape routes in the small square room. Her only way out was also the way in. And it was guarded.

Jenine rebelled against her sinking spirit, deliberately hitting the back of her head against the wall, as if to knock out the despair clawing at her insides.

A weapon! If she could find something to use as a weapon, she thought, eagerly searching the room with desperation clouding her eyes. "Damn!" she whispered gruffly. Nothing in the room was moveable except the cot. Quitting was out of the question, she told herself sternly, biting down on her lip.

There had to be a way out. There simply had to be, she thought desperately. Then she remembered the bathroom. It was in the back of the hangar. And it had a window. A tiny one. She would have to have an eel's skin to slip through, but at least it was accessible to her. She knew she looked sick; the last trip to the bathroom had proved that. Fatigue had settled in pockets under her bleary eyes and her clothes were rumpled, adding to her haggard look. She had nothing to lose by trying, she told herself, taking a deep breath of courage.

Clutching her middle, Jenine cried out. A terrible keening moan vibrated from her throat, her expression pained. Seconds later both men came to the door. With her body folded in half, she looked at the taller of the two with pleading in her eyes.

"My stomach. I'm sick," she groaned pitifully, her face contorted in agony. "I need to see a doctor!"

The men exchanged glances; only the taller seemed worried. He said something to his partner in their unfamiliar language. Jenine moaned again, then bit down on her bottom lip as if to prevent another cry from escaping her mouth.

The tall man went to the phone and started dialing a number, before he was stopped by the fat man. Yapping admonishment in his heavy accent, he slammed the receiver back on the hook and glowered at the thin man.

Jenine could tell that the closest she was going to get to medical help was the bathroom, but rebelled against defeat. The bathroom, after all, was her desired destination.

She whimpered with sincerity through her phony pain. It was enough to raise the level of concern expressed in the tall captor's gaze. He came to the cot to help Jenine to her feet. She leaned into his wiry strength, allowing him to guide her out the room in the back of the hangar.

Nat had a clear view of the row of hangars on the other side of the high fence. A small plane had been partially rolled out of the fourth hangar. He assumed it was David's getaway transportation.

He had parked the car under a large tree not far from the narrow, dirt road. A few feet ahead of him, he read the posted sign—Airport Personnel & Private Owners Only—and laughed silently. There was even a stop point booth, as empty as the rest of the place appeared.

He pulled out the gun from inside his jacket, double-checking the clip, then flipped off the safety lock before sticking it back inside his pocket. An intense level of noise roared in his ears; it was his heart. He leaned his head against the headrest and took several deep breaths.

He envisioned Talbert lying on the floor in Jenine's house. He'd hated having to do that. The sheriff and Robbie had offered nothing but kindness and support to him and Natasha.

They had also given him no choice. He tried it their way, relying on the laws created by man. Each time, he had come up short.

Now, it was time for nature's law. While he had yet to think through a plan, he was confident that the opportunity would present itself, and he would take it without hesitation.

After Talbert indirectly told him David's travel plans, it had been simple to deduce that Jenine would be held captive close to the point of exchange. If David intended a trade, which he no longer believed since being served the papers which granted David temporary custody of Natasha.

Getting out of the car, Nat walked up to the fence and pulled at the gate. It wasn't locked, but it was old and made a squeaky noise when he pried it open.

Peering anxiously across the way to see if anyone or anything had been disturbed, he raced across the dirt path to the first hangar and pressed himself against the tin wall. His breathing and heartbeat combined to sound like an amplified metronome ticking at a vivace tempo in his chest.

Inside the gate, he set out to explore the area, moving stealthily to the next hangar. Just then, the door at the fourth opened. With a quick intake of breath, Nat plastered himself against the light metal wall and watched with deathly quiet as a tall man stepped out in the opening. Just as unexpectedly as the door was opened, it was closed and the man disappeared back inside.

Tension scaled mountaintop heights. Nat cleansed his lungs, exhaling a long gush of air. He wiped the telling beads of sweat from his face with the back of his hand.

From the direction he had come, he saw a car approach. As it neared, he noticed the inactive siren on top. Highland Height's finest were either cruising on regular patrol, or on top of the situation. After what seemed like forever, the police car turned around and drove off.

With his heart beating hard, Nat didn't know whether

to be relieved or disappointed. Directing his attention back to the tin shack two doors away, he felt he had never been so scared in his life.

Not for himself, for without Jenine or Natasha, his life meant nothing. Adrenaline kicked in, charging his fear like a rocket engine.

The ugly grey walls in the restroom were a welcome sight. The tall captor was standing on the other side of the door, but Jenine knew he wouldn't barge in on her. He was no doubt confident she had no way out, and the knowledge created a sense of defeat in her as she looked up at the tiny window.

There was no top on the commode, so she climbed upon the seat, steadying herself by placing a hand on the wall. She wiped the frost buildup off the window so she could peer at the woods beyond. If only she could get to them, she thought, unlatching the window.

She shoved. She tugged, but the window didn't budge. It was sealed tight, super-glued to the base. With despair returning, she heard a loud, crashing noise. It was followed by the tongues of her two captors in rapid-fire speech calling out to each other. She lost her footing and slipped off the stool to land in a heap on the floor between the wall and the commode. Hastily, she pulled herself up and opened the door to be knocked back by the heavy African falling into her.

Nat had caught the first man by surprise, slamming the handle of his gun across the back of the man's head. As he straightened to face his second enemy, the gun was knocked out of his hand.

He was at least making a fight of it when he heard Jenine yell. He made the mistake of taking his eyes off his opponent, who charged him like a bull. Both of them went sprawling to the hard cement floor, with Nat at the bottom.

Blocking out Jenine's screaming, Nat concentrated all his efforts on freeing himself from the burden of big-handed, fat fists crashing into his face. Able to wiggle free, he scampered to his feet up like a clumsy gazelle to race around the twin-engine plane in the center of the hangar away from the big African who was pursuing him.

From the corner of his eye, he saw Jenine crawling on the concrete floor to sit against the door and double over. He cried out her name and raced toward her only to run smack-dab into the elephant-size opposition.

The man, though enormous in size, was as agile as a fish in water. In that instant, Nat recognized him as the intruder who had tried to kidnap Natasha. He knew he had to be extremely careful. Not only did the man out-weigh him by a good one hundred pounds, but his enemy was skilled in a self-defense technique that was alien to him.

Mubari was coiled and ready to strike. Confidently, he smiled at Nat with a beer-commercial joviality. He sensed that victory was near.

With a strange, cold excitement filling his whole being, Nat charged headlong into the belly of the beast. He was stopped dead in his tracks, lifted in the air and turned upside down. The beast tossed him aside like a pesky fly, and he landed on the hard cement floor with a bounce, banging his head against the wall.

Grasping and grunting, his enemy laughed trium-phantly as he shook his head to clear his vision of the flashing lights. Before Nat could shake off his daze, he felt himself being raised again, his feet no longer on solid ground. A pair of beefy hands were around his neck, squeezing, shaking him like a rag doll.

Nat squirmed, trying to loosen his captor's grip, to no avail. He managed to see a toothy grin, hear the hyenalike laughter as panic began to rise and consciousness began to wane.

There was no way he could win a fistfight with this brute, he realized, seconds before instincts kicked in. He slammed a foot viciously into the groin of his captor.

It wasn't textbook graceful, but effective. He was released promptly in a straight drop to the floor. Short-winded, Nat rolled under the plane, listening to the whimpers of pain.

Mubari was regaining his wits. Though still holding his testicles, he fought off the effects of the blow nevertheless.

Nat searched his floor-level surroundings anxiously, looking for anything that would even the odds. Near the tail of the plane, he saw a large tool box and crawled for it on all fours. From his floor position, he could see that his enemy had fully recovered and was heading his way.

The opponent lowered himself on all fours, determined to get Nat, even if it meant crawling under the plane. With the adrenaline of fear and all the pent-up anger he'd stored waiting for his confrontation with David Cissoko, Nat swung back his arm, clutching the airplane wrench with both hands, then brought it forth.

The blow grazed the side of Mubari's head, but it was enough to slow him down. Grunting, he lost his balance and dropped to the floor, cushioning his fall with his hands.

Still wound up, Nat reared up again to strike, giving his enemy no chance to recover. The wrench was an extension of his hands and infused with malevolent power. He brought his arms back, his face a mask of rage, and started to swing.

"Nat! No!"

Chapter Seventeen

"Je-nine."

Disoriented, Jenine wet her lips with her tongue to answer, but no sound would come. Her throat was parched dry. She had no idea how long she and Nat had been standing in the entryway. Nor could she remember them coming into the house.

Lifting her exhausted and dazed eyes to Nat, she felt it all coming together for her. She gasped as a host of emotions swirled through her like a tornado. Face to face with the multiple meanings of his rescue, she stared at him with something very fragile in her eyes.

"Come here, baby," Nat said. He felt her stiffen in his embrace, and his guilt heightened. But he wasn't about to let her go. Ever again. "Shh," he comforted, stroking her back.

Her body seemed to know its needs better than she, Jenine thought, sagging into his solid warmth. Then the tears began to fall, and she cried softly in his chest for what could have been and what could never be.

"You're safe now," he said. "Everything's all right."

Up and down and around, he rubbed her back, his large hands protective and comforting, while gently rocking her from side to side, his chin on the top of her head.

Time seemed to slip away from her again before she felt the subtle changes in her body that were far from impersonal. Nat noticed it, too, but thankfully said nothing, did nothing except continue to hold her.

The doorbell rang and they jumped apart like guilty teenagers.

"I guess I'm still a little edgy," Nat said chuckling.

Jenine swallowed hard and nodded wordlessly. Nat opened the door to Robbie, who hugged him briefly before turning her gaze on Jenine.

"I just wanted to assure myself that you were okay," Robbie said, a smile trembling on her lips.

Jenine was surprised to see the water in her eyes and rushed into her friend's arms.

"I was so worried," Robbie said through her tears. "Talbert told me you were okay, but I just had to see for myself," she held Jenine away from her, smiled at her with joyful relief in her tearful gaze.

"I'm fine," Jenine assured her. Except my heart feels like a brittle ball about to crumble into fine pieces, she thought. "It couldn't have worked out better if you'd planned it yourself," she said, forcing a smile to her lips.

Robbie cleared her throat before she spoke. "Okay," she said, wiping her eyes. "Okay." She laughed a real hard, solid laugh, then exhaled a cleansing breath. "Talbert is waiting. I better go." To Nat, "You take good care of her."

"You heard Robbie," Nat said after Robbie was gone. "I think the first order of business is a shower." Jenine nodded her head. "And while you're doing that, I'll find something to eat."

A short time later, Nat walked into the bedroom, carrying a tray of food. He discovered Jenine in bed, fast asleep, the covers pulled up to her chin. He set the tray on the dresser, and carefully sat on the side of the bed as not to disturb her.

He fingered a wisp of her hair, as soft and fine as Natasha's. That he had almost cost Jenine her life would forever haunt him, he thought, though he knew she would never do or say anything to remind him of it. Even now it was a scary feeling, more frightening than the thought of losing his daughter.

They were so different in temperament, he and Jenine, like oil and water, it was amazing she had put up with him and his fierce need to protect her, he thought. She had more guts than he wanted to credit her with, and he had to admit that she was right about one thing: she and Natasha were the smart ones in this family. He had better prepare himself now to lose lots of arguments, he thought with a silent chuckle.

He filled his lungs with air. Gratitude was merely one of the emotions he felt, and minuscule compared to the other. It was beyond him, he thought, the power a four-letter word had to influence over and against one's will. Even when he had been telling himself he had nothing but a refrain of painful history to offer Jenine, he had been unable to govern his emotions. He guessed there was some truth in the telling song—love made you do crazy things.

The room was pitch dark. Jenine stirred, then began to struggle in earnest at the arms pulling at her, trying to pin her down. She screamed, "Nat."

"It's me, Jenine. It's Nat. You're safe. It's all right."

Disoriented, she whimpered. "Nat?"

"Yes, it's me," he said, kissing her tenderly on the forehead. "You're just having a bad dream." He reached out to click on the lamp light. "See?"

Running her fingers through her hair, Jenine respired heavily and nodded. Slowly, her breathing began to return to normal, before she became anxious again.

"Where's Natasha?" she asked frantically.

"In her room sleeping," Nat said.

So he had left her to get Natasha. But he'd come back, she thought with a frown, digesting the knowledge. "David?" she asked. "What about David?"

"Screaming his diplomatic head off in jail," Nat replied with a smile in his voice. "Think you can get back to sleep now?" rubbing her shoulders.

"Oh, that feels good," she moaned.

Nat pulled the gown over her head and instructed, "Lie down on your stomach."

Jenine did as she was told, then felt Nat straddle her back before his hands began to work magic on her shoulders. The just-right pressure of his long fingers soon absorbed the tension from her body, and as well, erased remnants of the haunted sleep from her mind. It gave her something else on which to focus, to feel, to collect and remember.

"Am I too hard?" he asked.

"No," Jenine muttered in reply. She couldn't help the smile that stole into her voice, nor the artless sigh that accompanied her ragged breath.

"Let me know if I'm too rough," he said.

Jenine mumbled an affirmative reply, knowing he would never be too rough. As if time were of no importance, his hands continued down her back, almost caressing in touch.

Keenly attentive to her breathing, Nat watched with pure masculine satisfaction as she tried to appear unaffected when he could almost smell her excitement. He, too, had to be careful, lest he become entangled in his pleasure-giving trap.

Jenine felt his hands slip to her thigh. The touch triggered an age-old yearning, and the air expelled from her lungs in one wild gasp.

"Too hard?" Nat inquired, an innocent lilt in his deep voice.

Jenine, with her lips pressed together, let him know she knew he knew his touch was far from hurtful.

"You'll tell me, won't you?" he asked with lascivious entreaty in his voice.

Jenine promised she would with a mumble.

"How 'bout this?" he asked, kneading the other thigh, equally enticing under his hands. He felt his mouth begin to water.

"Wonderful," she moaned.

Nat ran a finger in the soft flesh behind her knee; he knew it was a sensitive spot, and waited for his reward.

"Nat."

With her tone dipped in need, Jenine elongated his monosyllabic name into two. She was allowed to roll onto her back and she met his flinty gaze head on. His eyes were narrowed seductively while his gaze slid down her brown satin body from her face, to her shoulders, her breasts. The grin on his mouth was wide with a savory look. She felt a familiar shiver of awareness under his hands-on expression.

"Hm?" he replied innocently.

"Pretty proud of yourself, aren't you?" she said with a beguiling smile in her eyes and on her lips. Nat shrugged. She crooked a finger at him and beckoned. He obeyed the look of scorching intent in her eyes, settling his long, lean frame atop her.

"Ma'am?" he said in the tone of a respectful student.

Her senses were already throbbing with the strength and feel and scent of him. She wished she could bottle the lethal combination for her personal safekeeping.

With her hands buried in his hair, she held his face a breath away from hers to touch his lips with hers, light as a brush stroke, and he smiled against her mouth. She tasted the smile on his cool, firm mouth with her tongue, tracing its span from one corner to the other, causing his senses to flutter in response to her breezy touch.

She took his lips in a soft, moist kiss before her tongue swept inside his mouth in search of more treasures. Her hands skimmed over the smooth textures of his back and sides, stretching to stroke his firm buttocks. Everything she wanted and couldn't have was wrapped up in this kiss; the meaning of love was part and parcel of this kiss, and she reveled in the giving as much as the taking.

The provocative blend of sensual stimulation was like an excavator in Nat, extracting a reserve of untapped sensibilities. Instinctively, his weight sank deeper into her soft body, making her fully aware of the hunger she ignited in him. And she delivered, enacting an achingly sweet exploration of his mouth. The pressure of the kiss increased, and their tongues danced together in a silent refrain.

Jenine knew she couldn't keep it up; her body and her willpower were slipping away. Soon, her own desires would blaze out of control.

In simultaneous need for air, they pulled apart, albeit reluctantly. Each drew long, deep breaths, and laughed together for no other reason than that it felt good to do so.

"That was lesson one," she said when her breathing permitted.

"Oh, Miss Jones, you can teach me anytime," he replied.

She felt the thundering of his heart pounding against her breasts and his uneven breathing on her cheek as he held her close. She smiled, opened her mouth to speak when his head disappeared from sight. Instead of words, a small sound of wonder came from her throat: Nat was nibbling at the underside of her bosom where dark-tipped breasts were in stiff attention.

The air vibrated with more than mere sexual desire; the room was steeped in an inner warmth and eternal hope. The sound level was low, and except for tonal contrasts, it was constant with uncontrollable urgency wrought by stimulation and anticipation.

Jenine rejoiced in her feelings—emotional and physical—those desires inherently hers and those elicited from her. The heat from his smooth, hard flesh was intoxicating, and she drew herself closer to him, tasting, kissing, stroking every inch she could reach, with tantalizing possessiveness.

Nat enjoyed his woman greedily, ensuring an ecstatic reaction from her to his every exquisite stimuli. No part of her was neglected: his hands and mouth teased and fondled, sending molten shafts of sensation the full length of her. He kissed and suckled, completely demolishing all inhibitions. And he teased and fondled some more, whispering his love for each part of her body, the ritual unending. Until she was nothing but pure gasping passion, and he felt he would explode with his desires.

Their bodies came together with the reverence of tender love and the passion of seduction. Jenine felt if she'd died in that instant she would not regret her life; Nat, glad to be home.

In a perfect blend of harmony and melody, Jenine and Nat found the rhythm that bound their bodies. Slow and steady arches and thrusts intensified, each possessing the other in tune with their twin lusty, insatiable needs.

"Je-nine . . . !" "Nat . . . !" "Jenine . . . !" "Nat . . . !" Their names became a song on the other's lips. And, "I love you . . . I love you," an impassioned pledge, a commitment.

Jenine screamed with her release, a starburst of ecstasy. Seconds later, the earth fell away and Nat went with her to that place of rapture. He placed a deep tender kiss on her lips, then rolled to his side and pulled her next to him.

Nat felt a commitment to the words.

Jenine wished for more memories to store.

Jenine entered the house through the back door into the kitchen. Taking off her coat, she dropped it with her other possessions on the couch in the family room then meandered to the kitchen. She poured herself a glass of orange juice.

Circling the island, juice in hand, she thought the house seemed even quieter than usual. Nat had told her nothing of his plans before she left for school this morning, and she hadn't inquired, she recalled.

Intentionally, she thought with a shrug, taking a swallow of juice.

Now, she wondered when she would get used to it again. Sauntering to the television, she turned on the set just for its noise value. A newsman was promising details on the excitement in a small Texas town with the expulsion of an African diplomat from the country following a kidnapping attempt.

She'd had enough reminders of her adventure, Jenine thought. She clicked the set off, then dropped on the couch and kicked off her shoes.

Gazing absently at the blank TV screen, she recalled that little teaching had been done today. It was Wednesday, her first day back to school. Her students were balloons of excitement, about to burst with their curiosity about her ordeal.

She had no choice but to satisfy them, carefully editing the ugly parts which had stolen into her sleep for the past two nights. The dream, or better yet, she amended silently, the nightmare always began with Nat acting out in a blind rage.

Just recalling her fear that he was going to kill his heavyset opponent: the iron tool with V-shaped jagged-edged jaws . . . his powerful grip around a powerful weapon, arm arched in the air about to strike . . . pure venom ablaze in his eyes . . . a warrior's cry of vengeance on his lips, Jenine shuddered. The tape continued to roll in her mind.

Suddenly, people seemed to have sprung out from everywhere. Uniformed police officers, with Sheriff Talbert Murray leading the way, burst into the hangar.

She found herself pulled against the solid wall of Nat's chest, his heart pounding crazily against her bosom. He planted kisses all over her face, assuring himself she had not been harmed with frantic touches.

Then Talbert called Nat to a corner and a heated discussion unfolded between them. As if out of nowhere, a right cross from the sheriff connected with Nat's jaw, staggering him. Talbert left him to check on his prisoners. After an ambulance attendant examined the fallen captors, he declared them fit for prison. The two men were handcuffed and put in police cars.

She had given up hope of finding out what the altercation was all about, as Nat had only said, "It's between men." She knew to leave it alone, she thought, sipping her juice, crossing her ankles on the coffee table.

Nat and she were next to last to leave the scene. Talbert followed in his police car after instructing them to return home until he needed them to answer questions at the police station.

Rising to saunter about the room, Jenine didn't want to remember the rest now. She was saving that memory to add to her collection for later when she would really need something to get her through the lonely nights and quiet times like now.

She turned one way, then the other, indecision lining her forehead. She had forgotten what she intended to do. Scanning the room, her gaze rested on the double-framed, color portraits on a single shelf, taken during one of their familial outings. One was of Natasha, dressed in a wide-skirted, blue velvet dress with a pink ribbon belt at her waistline, and white shoes. She was looking up at the camera. Her impish eyes and smiling mouth were so like Nat's it was uncanny, Jenine thought.

In the other expensive silver-lined picture, Jenine was standing alongside Nat, who was seated with Natasha in his arms. She was smiling at herself. Pride and joy shone in her eyes, a wide grin set on her mouth. Her left hand was resting on Nat's right shoulder. He looked equally pleased with himself.

They had been a good-looking family, she thought. The past tense thought made her throat ache with regret. She smiled sadly, thinking that misery loves company, as she remembered David hadn't gotten what he wanted either.

Talbert had been more active than either she or Nat would have guessed. When David must have realized things were not going as he intended, he had tried to leave the Cobbs' home. One of Highland Height's finest, however, was there to prevent such an unscheduled trip. Until this morning, the African diplomat had spent time in the city's jail. According to Robbie, his cries of diplomatic immunity had fallen on deaf ears until agents from the FBI arrived to escort him out of the country.

Everything had been wrapped up in a neat, little package. Except her. Only the bow remained, she thought with a sardonic mutter in the back of her throat.

Wondering what was taking Nat so long before he

finished the job, she folded the twin pictures closed. Laying them flat, face-down on the shelf, Jenine returned to the kitchen to set the empty glass in the sink.

She thought about fixing herself a light snack, but she wasn't hungry. She decided to grab something on her way out later; she had a rehearsal with Bruce's group in a couple of hours. Though reviewing class notes for tomorrow would take up some of her time, she didn't feel like doing that either.

Do it anyway, she told herself, opening her briefcase.

Sitting on a stool at the island, she began reading through the pages of typed notes from a manila folder. Before long, she was staring across the room, daydreaming.

Conceding that her concentration was not what it should be, she gave up on her assignment and returned the folder to her briefcase.

She didn't like this procrastination, she screamed silently with frustration. Why was Nat toying with her? Why didn't he just get it over with? This game of drawing out the inevitable only gave her false hopes and played havoc with her stomach. She ran her fingers through her hair, then dropped her hands to her sides, shoulders drooped in despair.

Stretching her arms over her head, she thought maybe a nice, hot shower and change of clothes would help relieve the disquiet she felt, and she headed for her bedroom.

She stepped into the room, gasped sharply and froze in her tracks. With a hand at her pounding heart, her expression a big question mark, she advanced into the room. Her eyes darted about, picking out the familiar from the new.

Curtains and matching comforter with bold stripes of subdued colors—olive, brown, tan—covered the windows and bed. A large oil painting of an anonymous jazz musician hung over a new headboard of crescent-shape, the same oak color as the dresser. A rocking chair was in the once-empty spot near the window and a dressing table had been set against the wall, opposite the bed.

Jenine wondered what it all meant. She slid open the closet door to discover Nat's clothes hanging next to hers. She backed to the door of the room, then hurried down the hall to the guest room. Natasha's baby bed was set against the wall where the dresser had been, and the white curtains with big colorful balls had been relocated.

While cautioning herself against getting overly excited and coming up with fanciful interpretations, adhering to the advice was humanly impossible. She hurried back to the family room and plopped in a chair, finger stuck in her mouth, visage thoughtful.

None of what she saw meant anything, she told herself, repeating her old arguments. Nat simply decided to extend his stay a few days. After all, he was a little more considerate than the eat-and-run type. He would hang around a little longer just to ensure himself she was in as near a contented condition as when he had found her.

She could bemoan the delay and drive herself crazy, or she could resign herself to make the most of however longer he planned to stay and take whatever he had to offer. It was a short mull, a quick decision.

Jenine went to the phone and dialed. "Bruce, Jenine. I'm not going to make rehearsal tonight. No, nothing's wrong. Bruce," with warning in her voice. "Okay. See you tomorrow."

Replacing the receiver, she began to drum her fingers on the countertop, then stilled her hands and looked at the time. Where was Nat? she asked herself. What was her impulsive lover up to, this time?

An hour later, 5:30, Jenine was practicing in her music

study. Two hours later, 7:30, she fixed a sandwich and forced herself to review her notes for school. Three hours later, 8:30, she showered, dressed for bed, and by 9 o'-clock was watching television.

Nat found Jenine lying on the couch in the family room, the late-night movie playing to a sleeping audience of one. He shrugged out of his overcoat and tossed it on the chair, then sat on the edge of the couch. He debated whether or not to wake her. It was late, past midnight. She needed her sleep.

But he was so full of excitement he didn't know if he could contain himself until tomorrow. If she had gone to rehearsal she would just be getting in about now herself, he argued silently. Why didn't she go to rehearsal, he wondered.

"Jenine." He shook her lightly.

Jenine moaned, then her eyes fluttered open. "Nat," she said, struggling to sit up. "Where have you been?"

"What's the matter?" he asked. "Why didn't you go to rehearsal?"

Rubbing her eyes, she replied, "I must have dozed off."

"I guess so," he replied smilingly. "Are you all right?"

"Yeah. Fine."

"Then come on, let's get you to bed," he said, slipping his arms under her.

"I can walk," she said with mild protest.

"Yeah, I know," he replied, carrying her from the room.

Nat set her in bed and watched her stretch, her body arching invitingly. His gaze roved the brown peaches-and-cream flesh visible in the see-through, yellow silk gown. Bending, he dipped his head to capture a protruding nipple between his lips. Feeling her jolt of desire pass through him, he moaned as one with her. Lifting his head, he said, "I opened a Pandora's box and got Isis."

Jenine stiffened. Her memory came flooding back.

"What's the matter?" he asked, stretching out on the bed beside her.

"Isis was the goddess of fertility in Egyptian mythology," she replied, wetting her lips nervously.

"Yeah, I know," he shrugged. "So?"

Breathing easier, she said with a humorous grin, "You're mixing mythology. Pandora belongs to the Greeks."

He shrugged, replying, "Well, whatever. I'd rather mix another ology," his voice low and purposefully seductive as he nuzzled her neck.

"Well, I'm not fertile," she blurted, hands folded across her stomach.

Nat sat up to stare at her with a puzzled frown. "Jenine, what's the matter?"

She shook her head, replying, "Nothing."

"Yes, it is. Tell me," he implored. "No more secrets, Jenine," he said when she remained stubbornly quiet.

"Where have you been? Where's Natasha?" she asked.

"Can't you ever ask one question at a time?" he replied laughingly.

"Can't you answer a question without asking one?" she retorted.

"All right," he said, folding his arms across his chest. "Natasha is spending the night with Gloria." Jenine raised a brow at him. "Hey, she volunteered," he said. "Anyway, I wanted us to be alone." He looked around the room, and thought how unsatisfactory the surroundings were. "Feel up to going out?"

Her lips set in a bemused twist was her reply.

"I didn't think so," he said. "Well, I've had a busy day."

"I can tell," she replied, eyes darting about the room.

"Like it?" he asked.

"Why did you do it?"

"Well, that's what I wanted to talk about," he replied hesitantly. He cleared his throat. "We need to talk."

There a faint tremor in his voice. It sounded an awful lot like regret, she thought. He was finally going to tell her he was leaving. She watched him get up to hang his suitcoat in the closet before returning to sit on the side of the bed.

"Okay," she nodded agreeably, thinking it was better to get it over with as quickly as possible. She stacked pillows at her back, returned her hands to her lap, and looked at him expectantly. None of the despair she felt showed on her face. His smile, when it came, tilted up the corners of his mouth before reaching his eyes, the olive centers piercing her soul with warmth.

Jenine inhaled raggedly. A nervous smile played at her lips before she reached out to cover his hand with hers in a comforting gesture. She reminded herself of the promise to make this parting easy on them both. She just wished he would hurry and get it over with. She didn't know how much longer she could keep her resolve, or the tears at bay.

Nat swallowed hard, then cleared his throat before he said in a louder than normal voice. "I talked to my agent today."

He had also met his mother in Dallas where he'd flown to make a major purchase, he recalled. He coached himself to calm down and dropped his voice to natural before he spoke again.

"And he reminded me that I've been out of circulation too long and missed a lot of opportunities. I told him to commit me to a project coming up on the West Coast."

He averted his head and swore internally, for that wasn't what he had intended to say. So preoccupied with his bungling performance, he missed the crestfallen expression that befell Jenine's face before she replaced it with an emotionless mask.

"I see," she said. Twiddling her thumbs, she felt the swell of tears in the back of her eyes.

Nat looked at her sharply. There was a suspicious line at the corners of his mouth, then understanding appeared in his eyes.

"Obviously you don't," he retorted softly. "We have a lot to do within the next three weeks, so listen carefully."

His tone had changed to a command, and he had schooled all emotions from his face. The sheen of soon-to-be-shed tears cast a glaze to her eyes, and he felt a moment of chagrin for teasing her.

"The way I figure it," he said matter-of-factly, taking her hand in his, "you have about a week to prepare for our wedding and arrange for a week off from school for the honeymoon." Undaunted by the utterly stunned expression on her face, he continued nonchalantly. "I'll only be able to stay a few days when we get back because it'll be time for me to leave for L.A. But while I'm gone . . ."

That was as far as he got, for Jenine effectively silenced him by throwing herself into his arms to capture his mouth with hers for a kiss that made him weak and light-headed.

Tearing her mouth from his, she looked at him softly, teary-eyed with joy. "I ought to kick you out for that," she said, half laughing, half crying. "But I guess I'll keep you. And it'll serve you right if I make your life as miserable as you've made the last minute of mine."

He laughed—a glorious sound that reverberated throughout the room—and squeezed her lovingly to him. "Oh, there's something else." He opened his hand to reveal a pear-shaped diamond engagement ring, and two matching gold bands. "Highland has a lot of things to offer, but it's rather limited in the fine jewelry department and I didn't have time to wait. I flew to Dallas, then missed my flight back. That's why I'm so late."

With tears falling freely down her face, Jenine stared at the symbols of unity in the palm of his hand, then up at Nat. His gaze matched the hue of love in hers.

"Jenine, will you marry me?" he asked reverently.

Too moved for words, she nodded her head and smiled through her tears. Nat slid the engagement ring on the third finger of her left hand, then raised it to his lips and kissed her hand reverently.

"I love you," he said, wiping the tears from her eyes.

"I love you, too," she whispered softly as she embraced him and kissed his cheek, her arms solid and strong around him.

"Oh, God, Jenine," he moaned, burying his head in her neck. He possessed her lips in a lingering kiss. Releasing her mouth, he said, "You don't know how long I've waited to hear that without a cloud hanging over our heads."

"I've always loved you, Nat, cloud or no cloud," she said. "And I always will. Only you," caressing him with her eyes, her hands trembling as they touched his face, his chest.

"Me, too," he said. "No other woman has ever come close to making me feel the way you do."

She drew his face to hers in a renewed embrace, and there they remained, locked in the cocoon they formed around each other indefinitely.

"There's so much I want to do for you," he said, "share with you," pulling back to gaze into her eyes, brimming to overflowing with love. "There are a few things I'd like to do to you, too," he said in a sensual suggestive tone, for his body was growing hot with unchecked passion. "Maybe even get you fertile."

Jenine laughed in sheer joy and he swallowed her supreme happiness, reclaiming her mouth. His lips were warm and tender on hers. She tasted the future in his kiss and sighed a sweet refrain.

SENSUAL AND HEARTWARMING
ARABESQUE ROMANCES FEATURE
AFRICAN-AMERICAN CHARACTERS!

BEGUILED   (0046, $4.99)
by Eboni Snoe
After Raquel agrees to impersonate a missing heiress for just one night, a daring abduction makes her the captive of seductive Nate Bowman. Across the exotic Caribbean seas to the perilous wilds of Central America . . . and into the savage heart of desire, Nate and Raquel play a dangerous game. But soon the masquerade will be over. And will they then lose the one thing that matters most . . . their love?

WHISPERS OF LOVE   (0055, $4.99)
by Shirley Hailstock
Robyn Richards had to fake her own death, change her identity, and forever forsake her husband Grant, after testifying against a crime syndicate. But, five years later, the daughter born after her disappearance is in need of help only Grant can give. Can Robyn maintain her disguise from the ever present threat of the syndicate—and can she keep herself from falling in love all over again?

HAPPILY EVER AFTER   (0064, $4.99)
In a week's time, Lauren Taylor fell madly in love with famed author Cal Samuels and impulsively agreed to be his wife. But when she abruptly left him, it was for reasons she dared not express. Five years later, Cal is back, and the flames of desire are as hot as ever, but, can they start over again and make it work this time?

Available wherever paperbacks are sold, or order direct from the Publisher. Send cover price plus 50¢ per copy for mailing and handling to Penguin USA, P.O. Box 999, c/o Dept. 17109, Bergenfield, NJ 07621. Residents of New York and Tennessee must include sales tax. DO NOT SEND CASH.